The Dark Side of the City

The Dark Side of the City

by

Howard Giordano

International Standard Book Number 13:
Hardcover 978-1-60452-187-0
Trade Paperback 978-1-60452-188-7
eBook 978-1-60452-189-4

International Standard Book Number 10:
Hardback 1-60452-187-2
Softback 1-60452-188-0
eBook 1-60452-189-9

Library of Congress Control Number: 2022937901

BluewaterPress LLC
2922 Bella Flore Ter
New Smyrna Beach, Florida 32168

http://www.bluewaterpress.com

Dedication

I would like to dedicate this novel to all the men and women of law enforcement everywhere. If there is any segment of our professional population that deserves more admiration and support in today's political climate, it is the uniformed police and undercover detectives. These brave protectors of our liberty put their lives on the line for us every day.

"Never open your mouth, unless you're in the dentist chair."

— Sammy "The Bull" Gravano

Chapter One

Upper East Side, Manhattan - Mon A.M. 4/06

Thirty-five years—Harry Fox was sure of it. He'd calculated the passage of time without hesitation. He was young then and worked for a Madison Avenue ad agency when his heart left his chest and never returned.

A Ralph Lauren polo hung over his pressed chinos, and his rubber-soled deck shoes squeaked on the tiled supermarket floor. Harry had steered his cart of groceries past the frozen food display and approached an empty checkout aisle. That's when he saw her—or so he thought.

She stood outside D'Agostino's large front window with her back pressed to the glass. A man in a midnight black sharkskin suit and a gray Borsalino fedora with the brim snapped down over his eyes had captured her attention. A black limo, parked at the curb with its motor running, added to the scene's curiosity .

Harry stood suspended with indecision. Was it her or was he imagining it, wishing it? When she turned her head to look up Third Avenue, he thought he saw enough of her profile to determine the face belonged to the woman cupid had deposited in the excavations of his soul—three decades ago.

He stared through the window for several seconds, watching the pair, unsure of how to interpret the scene. It appeared her conversation with the black suit had become agitated. Her head shook. No, no, it said. With surprising abruptness, the man took hold of her arm and thrust her toward the parked limo.

The wail of a hook and ladder fire truck filled Harry's ears as it raced north along Third Avenue. Its shrill sound jarred him, as though alerting him to a danger he failed to understand. Harry shoved his cart to one side and broke into long strides through the automated exit door and out onto the street. "Nicole," he shouted. "Nicole, it's Harry." His voice carried a wave of panic .

The limo driver, a burly-looking thug in a blue Members Only waist-high jacket, had leaped out of the car and raced around the back to open the rear door. The big man noticed Harry speeding toward him and stepped into his path. His open hand crashed against the frantic man's chest with the force of a battering ram, sending him to the sidewalk.

"Stay outta this, asshole. It ain't your business," the thug said. He reached to open the limo's rear door while he kept his focus on the prone Harry Fox.

A middle-aged woman exited the supermarket gripping a cloth D'Agostino bag filled with groceries. Harry watched as she looked down at him and up at the thug, then scooted off.

Before the man in the Borsalino could push Nicole onto the rear seat and slide in, her eyes landed on Harry's stare and his stricken expression. She bobbed her head as a signal of recognition.

"Playboy Club . . . Roy Dickerson," she screamed before the car door slammed shut.

Harry heard her. But what did it mean? The Playboy Club in Manhattan no longer existed. It had closed its doors in the mid-eighties.

"Forget about it, pal," the driver snarled as he stood over him. "This never happened, if you know what I mean." A tight smile appeared, and as though to add weight to his warning, he slammed his heavily booted toe into Harry's ribcage. Seconds after Harry recovered his breath and opened his eyes, the limo driver, the Borsalino hat, and the brief love of his life disappeared into the heavy traffic of Third Avenue. But not before Harry noted the limo's license plate number.

* * *

Chelsea Area, Manhattan - Wed. A.M. 4/08

Luke Rizzo looked up when he heard the light tap-tap-tap. It sounded like a fingernail against the door frame. "Come in," he called out. "It's open." Rizzo turned and whispered into the telephone. "I gotta go, sweetheart. I'll talk to you later." He hung up and rose from his chair. The office door crept open.

A tall man in a battered felt hat and a dark blue, pencil-striped suit paused in the doorway, and then shrugged as if he'd remembered something he'd left behind. He turned to leave, but before he could disappear, Rizzo called to him. "Wait a minute. Who you looking for?"

The stranger froze and, holding the door open with one hand, stared back at Rizzo for a time. "You're Luke Rizzo?" he asked in a flat tone.

Rizzo wasn't certain if it was a question or a statement. He chuckled and said, "I was when I came to work this morning." He moved out from behind his desk and approached his visitor. "What's on your mind?"

The man gazed past Rizzo's head, his eyes circling the room like someone needing guidance. "May I come in?"

"For God's sake, you're in. Close the damn door and have a seat." Rizzo gestured to the two chairs on either side of his desk. "Pick one. Then sit down so we can see how I can help you."

The stranger entered, carried his lanky frame across the room, and lowered himself into the chair closest to him. But not before he shot a glance over his shoulder as if worried someone had followed him. "Ah, Mr. Rizzo, I'm sorry . . . I don't mean to be . . . ah . . . this jumpy."

Rizzo returned to his desk, all the while keeping his eyes fixed on the nervous ninny. "Okay, relax. Take a breath. Let's start by telling me who you are. What's your name?" The scent of his aftershave was overpowering.

The man removed his hat, set it on his lap, and stretched his long legs. He leaned back, placed his elbows on the arms of the chair, and then closed his eyes.

He had a handsome face and shiny silver hair, trimmed. Rizzo guessed he was chasing seventy, but the texture of his cheeks, smooth and free of wrinkles, gave him a youthful look. Rizzo could see no lines under his eyes—unusual for someone in his age bracket. Good genes, Rizzo figured.

A white broadcloth shirt under his suit jacket and a rep tie made him appear like someone attending a board of directors' meeting. His bony fingers clutched the armrests with fierceness.

"What's your name?"

He flinched and his eyes popped open upon hearing Rizzo's repeated question. "Oh, I'm sorry. It's Harry Fox. Please forgive me. I'm beside myself with worry. I've experienced nothing like . . ."

The stare returned. Rizzo was afraid he might doze off again. "Like what, Mr. Fox? Are you in trouble?"

Fox jerked his legs back and leaned forward. "Huh, no, no. Um . . . I mean, yes. I guess you could say that."

With patience swiftly eluding him, Rizzo asked in a non-threatening tone, "You wanna tell me about it?"

"Of course." Fox fell silent again, his eyes squeezed. He appeared to be considering how to begin.

"Let's start with a simple question," Rizzo prompted. "How'd you come by knocking on my door? Someone recommend me, or did you find me in the yellow pages under soft touch?"

Fox looked up at Rizzo with a forced grin. "Yes, I should have mentioned it at the start. Sorry. A mutual friend, FBI Agent Jack Fields, suggested I speak with you. He said you were a good private investigator. You could help me find someone— someone I believe is in danger."

"Okay," Rizzo said. "That's good for openers. But before you tell me the story, you want coffee?" He motioned to the Mr. Coffee carafe on the table behind his desk. "It's freshly brewed." Rizzo hesitated. "Or maybe not, if you think it will jack up your anxiety level any more than it is."

Fox's eyes dropped to his lap. When he looked up, he said, "Sorry, I'm okay. A cup would be fine."

Rizzo filled two mugs from the carafe and carried them to the coffee table in front of the sofa. He nodded to Fox to change seats, and the man moved to one end of the sofa. Rizzo turned one of the chairs to face him, watching him blow a few puffs into the mug before taking a sip. A question buzzed in Rizzo's head. What was the man's connection with the FBI?

In the past, Rizzo's off-and-on friendship with Jack Fields had rumbled over a few rocky periods of harsh exchanges and allegations of interference. Their last encounter resulted in taking down a notorious sex-slave operation and putting a serious dent in a Puerto Rican cartel's drug-smuggling fortunes. His business with Fields had ended in all smiles.

"For the record," Rizzo said, "how do you connect with the FBI? Are you involved with government work?"

The man's wide-eyed gaze lasted several seconds before he nodded with an understanding of Rizzo's question.

"Oh, God, no. Agent Fields is a neighbor. He lives on the same floor in my East Side condo . . . Seventy-second and Third. I knew he was a federal agent, so I imposed on him for advice."

"You tell him your problem? The trouble this someone is in?"

"I said I needed to find a person, someone I felt was in danger."

Rizzo's brow rippled. Son-of-a-bitch. Now Fields thinks I'm running a missing person bureau.

"Okay. Who's this person you need to find? How come you don't know where he is? What makes you think he's in danger? Start from the beginning."

"I know this will sound crazy, but it's a woman."

"Isn't it always?"

"I fell in love with her thirty-five years ago, and I haven't laid eyes on her since—until this past Wednesday."

"How long did your relationship last?"

Fox hesitated. "One date."

Rizzo fought back a smile. "And you say she's disappeared?"

"Yes. She was kidnapped."

* * *

Howard Beach, Queens, NY - Thurs. P.M. 4/09

Il Cucina Sicilian was quiet. Pete Barone, seated at a four-top with two older men, glanced around. He couldn't count the number of times he'd dined here. His uncle's favorite restaurant in the Howard Beach section of the borough of Queens was never busy on a weeknight. The residents of this Italian neighborhood were working-class, blue-collar people. On weekends, the locals would arrive to savor authentic Sicilian fare and occupy all twelve tables with crimson red linen tablecloths.

The restaurant's owner referred to the table where Barone and the two dark-suited men sat as *Il Tavolo di Capitan*, the captain's table. Positioned at the back-left corner, it provided the occupants a clear view of the restaurant's front entrance.

A picturesque mural—painted, not papered—covered most of the wall behind them. The scene was of the colorful harbor in *Castellammare del Golfo*, the popular vacation spot on the northwestern coast of Sicily. Fishing boats and pleasure craft, of all sizes, dotted the harbor's shoreline in democratic harmony. Anyone inquiring of the mural's location received the same answer: "That's where Enrico's family is from,"—Enrico being the restaurant's owner and chef. With a nod toward the need for tact, Enrico never mentioned that Joseph Bonanno, the crime boss of an early mob empire in the US, also hailed from there.

Soft mandolin music emanated from hidden speakers, not loud enough to interfere with the *sotto voce* conversation of the three men lingering over the owner's complementary after-dinner *cannolis*, but loud enough to serve as background noise to obscure whatever they were saying. The mob, ever alert to the marvels of electronic surveillance, always made certain whenever and wherever they took a meet, someone was playing a radio, flushing a toilet, turning on a television, or running a bathroom shower.

Pete Barone sipped his espresso, alternating with a taste of Sambuca, and tried to explain how his former working partner in their five sports bars learned about the family's business. The two older men—Carmine D'Angelo, the Gambino family's underboss, and his *capo regio*, Sal Fusco, known as Sal "The Hat" because of his ever-present Borsalino—listened patiently.

"Yeah, he saw you coming out of my office after meeting with me one night. The piece in the *Daily News*—the bullshit they wrote about you—he must have seen it. He recognized you from your photo."

D'Angelo moved the demitasse cup from his mouth and placed it on the saucer in front of him. His deep-set, dark eyes traveled down his wide nose, and a penetrating stare settled on Barone, the youngest of his deceased wife's three nephews. "And you couldn't convince him he was mistaken? I wasn't the one in the photo?"

"I did . . . I mean, I tried. He kept pushing it. It frustrated me and I gave in. I'm friends with the guy a lotta years, since my college days. We were roommates, always tight. We trusted each other."

Barone heard Sal Fusco snicker, but he didn't take his eyes from D'Angelo.

"I told him he had nothing to do with that end of the business. To keep his mouth shut or something would happen he wouldn't like. 'Not to worry,' he said. I believed him."

Fusco pushed back the Borsalino from his forehead. He put his elbows on the table, clasped his hands under his chin, and looked over to Barone. Smirking, he said, "You were wrong, weren't you? He didn't clam up, did he? How would the broad know? She ain't saying, but who else could it be? Am I right?"

D'Angelo interrupted, "*Abasta!* Let me ask you something. Was your partner—before he cashed out of the business—banging her, getting in her pants, like that?"

Barone felt his neck warming. He remembered the several futile attempts he'd made to seduce her. He decided not to disclose his embarrassing lack of success but reveal what his partner kept insisting about the woman.

"I doubt it," Barone said with a hint of authority. "She's gay. That's what Dickerson told me when he hired her. Although," he said, "I thought maybe he was bullshitting me."

"And you kept hittin' on her?" Fusco said. "*Marone! Che cidrule!* She said she told you if you didn't back off, she was gonna open her yap, go to the cops. Pretty fucking stupid, I'd say."

Barone cut his eyes to D'Angelo and back to Fusco. His shoulders rose. With a palms-up gesture, he pushed out his hands toward the *capo*. "I had no idea she knew anything until she mouthed off and threatened me."

"All right, all right," D'Angelo cut in. "What's done is done." He turned to his nephew. "So how do we handle this? Is there something we can do to keep her quiet without getting drastic?"

"Yeah, drop the bitch in the river," Fusco said in a low voice. "What I shoulda done in the first place when I had her in the limo."

D'Angelo ignored Fusco's rant and continued his focus on Barone. "Any ideas?"

Barone leaned back in his chair, did an eye roll, and shook his head like a handicapper watching his sure thing cross the finish line dead last. "I'm damned pissed."

"Hey, so are we," Fusco said. "You think we're sittin' here discussing your fiasco because we enjoy having this good-old-boy time?"

"No, what I mean is I'm pissed we had to lose her, her talents."

Fusco cut in again. "Whatcha talking? Didn't you say you never scored with the broad, she's a lez?"

"No, you *ciuccio*, that's not what I'm talking about."

The *capo's* eyebrows shot up. He glared at Barone and then turned to D'Angelo. "Any other associate member calls me a jackass, he'd be dead. He should know that. Dontcha think?"

"Sorry, Sal," Barone said, making an effort to sound contrite. "What I'm saying is she's the best restaurant manager Time-Out Enterprises ever had. Her business sense was amazing. The customers loved her."

D'Angelo raised his hand, signaling to end the back and forth. "*Sta ta zee*." He leaned across to Fusco and asked, "Where is she now?"

"At one of the fleabag motels, the one on Rockaway Boulevard. The manager is keeping an eye on her."

Carmine D'Angelo sat back and lowered his chin to his chest. His eyes remained open, darting side to side in their sockets as though searching for a landing spot. When the exercise ended, he looked up at Barone.

"Maybe you could coax her back to working for you again? I mean, if she's that valuable to the restaurants. Why not make her an offer she can't refuse, as they say in the movies?"

Barone's eyes widened. "You serious? Bring her back into the business?"

"Why not? You never heard the old saying, 'Keep your friends close and your enemies closer?'"

Barone sat transfixed. He sensed a reaction gliding from surprise to consternation to enlightenment, all within a half-second.

"You know," he said upon digesting the full implications of his uncle's suggestion, "she might go for it. And if she did, she'd be a complicit employee. Part of the game. She'd have no reason to threaten anyone. If she did, she'd be burning her own ass."

D'Angelo turned to Fusco. "You agree, *paesano*?"

Fusco replied with a resigned shrug. He was not pleased with the decision, and it showed.

The dark eyes of the underboss returned to Barone. "I'd suggest you offer the woman a generous deal. Sweeten it like doubling what you were paying her. You no longer have a partner. You can afford it. And *niputi*, keep it in your pants. *Capice*?"

"I will, uncle," Barone said. "No problem."

Fusco inhaled audibly, and then, squeezing his lips and puffing his cheeks, he let out a blast of air. "Ain't we forgettin' the other problem?"

"What's that?" D'Angelo asked.

"The ex-partner . . . this guy Roy Dickerson. He knows. He's the one what told the broad. Wadda we do about him? Let him walk around wherever he's got to? He's like a God-damned defused grenade. Could explode anytime."

"You know where he is?" D'Angelo asked his nephew.

"I think he moved somewhere out-of-state. I'm not sure."

D'Angelo leaned back in his seat, his ten fingers steepled under his chin, his eyes closed. When he opened them, he turned to Fusco and said, "I guess we need to find him, send a message."

Chapter Two

West Side, Manhattan - Thurs. P.M. 4/09

Seth, the server at Joe Allen's, a bistro in the heart of the city's theater district, hovered over them like one of those Visiting Angels contracted to help during the twilight of your life. Flo Rizzo thought he was cute, but Luke Rizzo would have preferred a bit more distance. Each time he'd try to tell her about his new client, Seth, the aspiring thespian, would interrupt: "How you two doin'?" Then it was, "How's the strip steak?" Or "Ready for another Jack Daniels?" The last time it was, "Can I clear away your salad plates?"

"He has the hots for you," Rizzo told his wife.

"Don't be a goose. He knows who we are. We come here often enough. He likes us."

"That's a crock. The guy is aware I'm a heavy tipper."

"Oh, you're so jaded," she said. She lifted the Big Jack and drained it. "Who's this guy, Ray . . . Roy . . . whatever?"

In the past, Rizzo was reluctant to discuss his ongoing cases with Flo. Since this assignment began yesterday, he had developed nothing to set her nerves on edge—worrying. He was comfortable revealing what little he'd learned about it thus far.

"I shouldn't be discussing this case with you, but it's still early. It's Roy Dickerson. Not Ray."

"And who was he to her?"

"He was the promotion manager of *Playboy Magazine* at the time Harry Fox was an advertising account supervisor. His Madison Avenue ad agency handled the Schweppes account."

"Did she work for him?"

"If you let me finish, I'll explain how the three of them connect. God, you're impatient."

Flo smiled. "I'm sorry, sweet pea. Finish."

"They were having a lunch meeting at the Playboy Club on Fifty-ninth Street. They needed to discuss a joint promotion they had in the works. The woman, Nicole Adams, was a Playboy Bunny. She waited on them. Fox went bonkers over her. *Amore a prima vista.*"

"I love it when you talk dirty," she said with a grin.

"That's not dirty, you evil-minded witch. It means love at first sight."

"Sweet pea, I guessed that. This little old southern gal may come from Kentucky, but she's not a rube."

Rizzo pushed the shoestring fries around on his plate and noticed the bistro emptying; those were early diners with theater tickets rushing to make an eight o'clock curtain. Rizzo and Flo, and a few other late diners, would soon have the place to themselves until around ten when the post-theater crowd filled the bar area until the wee hours. This routine was the nature of most of the restaurants on Forty-sixth Street's Restaurant Row.

Flo caught his eye when he looked up from the fries. "And that happened thirty-five years ago?"

"That's what he said. He returned to the club later in the afternoon and hung around outside until she got off work."

Flo's brow rippled and her eyes crawled down her nose. "Isn't that considered stalking?"

"Claims his behavior surprised even him. He'd never done anything like that before. 'I'm a conservative man,' he told me."

"They ever meet up?"

"Yeah. They had dinner the same night, and he fell in love."

"Their only date?"

"So he says."

Seth, the attentive server, reined up at their table after Rizzo flagged him down. "Hey, handsome, another Jack Daniels over ice for the lady and a refill on my iced tea, please."

Seth stared down at Flo for several seconds. His smile could have illuminated Madison Square Garden. The waiter moved off toward the bar, and Rizzo shook his head. "You think this looks similar to Harry Fox's love story, except in reverse? And Seth's Bunny tail doesn't even show."

"Do you suppose, if I killed time outside the restaurant until he's off work, I might get lucky?"

"Sure, if The Vice Squad doesn't pick you up for soliciting before he shows up."

"You're jealous."

"Not hardly. To be honest, I'm proud as hell of you. If a guy half your age can become smitten with you, it goes to prove you're still the sexy, beautiful woman I married."

Handsome Seth returned with her Jack Daniels and Rizzo's iced tea. He stood smiling at Flo for a brief time and finally left. Flo raised the Big Jack and said, "Here's to the best husband in the entire world." She paused and looked into his eyes. "And here's to the wildest lovemaking I will treat him to when we get home."

Rizzo lifted halfway out of his chair. "Waiter, check please," he shouted. Seth looked over, but Rizzo waved him off. "Just kidding," he called.

They sat quietly, enjoying the humor of their exchange, until Flo asked, "So what's the role of this Roy Dickerson? Why did she yell out his name when they forced her into the limo?"

"Fox doesn't know. I need to find Dickerson. See how he fits into the scenario. That's gonna be a challenge. Fox heard Dickerson had left the magazine and moved out of state to start his own business. God knows where he went."

"Was Dickerson romantically involved with her?"

"I doubt it. According to what Dickerson told Fox, Nicole Adams was not straight."

Flo's eyes opened wide. "Really? You mean a Playboy Bunny could be a lesbian?"

"Dickerson was aware of it for a good while. From early on, when she first became a Bunny. He did a photo shoot for the magazine with her and a few other bunnies. And she knew he knew."

"I simply cannot believe she'd be gay."

"Why not? As long as they were good-looking with nice figures. And Nicole was a knockout, according to Fox."

"But—"

"Dickerson said a few of them at the club were of that persuasion."

The amazed expression remained on Flo's face.

"They made good money, and besides, the club's management had a strict rule against Bunnies fooling around with customers."

"So Fox didn't know she was gay?"

"No clue until Dickerson broke the news to him a couple of days later. He was so over-the-moon about her, he wouldn't have sensed it if he had a month to figure it out."

"And yet she went to dinner with him?"

"That's why Nicole panicked. Right after that first night, she realized Fox wasn't interested in a simple friendship."

"Well, yeah."

"She was afraid she'd led him on. Maybe get into trouble with the club's management. It's why she used Dickerson to deliver the bombshell to Fox. The curtain came down after their first dinner."

"Oh, good Lord, that must have devastated him."

"Yeah, it did, but he got past it. The next year, he married a woman he'd already been dating. It lasted three decades until she passed away from breast cancer."

"Poor guy," she said. She reached over to take his hand in hers as if she were commiserating with him and not Harry Fox.

Rizzo gazed at Flo for several seconds, enjoying the softness of her touch. He realized how lucky he was to have married her. He traveled back to those days before they met, when booze and broads controlled his life.

Flo smiled as if she'd been reading his mind, and he continued to relate the tale of the Fox and the Bunny.

"After the funeral, he sold the house in Connecticut, moved to the city, and bought a condo on the Upper East Side—the same building as Jack Fields. Yeah, they're neighbors. My luck, right?"

"You mean the FBI Jack Fields?"

"None other. It's how Fox ended up coming to me for help. Fields gave him my name. The guy wants me to find and rescue the girl from whatever danger she's in."

"Can you?"

"I'll give it a shot. My starting point is to locate this guy, Dickerson. See if he has any info on the woman. Like what's happened to her since Playboy closed the club's doors in 1986."

"What sort of danger is she in?"

"Don't know. Judging from his description of the two bozos who dragged her off the street, it wouldn't surprise me if they were mobbed up."

"Oh, dear. And you still want to take on this challenge?"

"Who then, if not me? The guy needs help. I want to help."

Flo leaned into the table. "At the risk of repeating myself—oh, dear."

"It won't be that bad. A little snooping around, I follow the trail, see where it leads, then ask questions of a few people. That's all it amounts to. You shouldn't worry."

"Until the gangsters start to shoot at you. What will you do then?"

"Never happen."

Flo glared at him. "I need another drink."

* * *

Chelsea Area, Manhattan - Fri. P.M. 4/10

After traversing Madison Square Park, dodging children, and ducking dogs on retractable leashes, Rizzo waited at the traffic light to cross to the southwest corner of Broadway. He still tasted the sautéed onions that had smothered the cheeseburger he'd consumed at lunch. Twelve-thirty was peak lunchtime in Manhattan. A variety of vehicles clogged Chelsea's arteries and crosswalks. Workers of both sexes, all ages, shapes, and sizes, flooded the sidewalks and intersections as they hurried to dine at their chosen locations.

Madison Square Park, a historic intersection in the Chelsea area, is where Broadway and the former Bowery Road, now Fifth Avenue, came together in the early 19th century. After a dozen productive years with the NYPD, and after being forced into retirement with a three-quarter disability pension, Narcotics Detective Luke Rizzo had selected this section of Manhattan to locate his investigation business. Rizzo set up shop in a modest office on the fourth floor of the Flatiron Building. This iconic edifice sat wedged between Broadway and Fifth Avenue, where they converged at Twenty-third Street.

Last year, approaching the date his lease was expiring, the building's managing agent informed him a current tenant, a major publishing company, had contracted to take over the entire building, starting in the next eighteen months. Therefore, the management would not consider renewing or issuing new leases. Rizzo scrambled to find a suitable replacement in the same area. To his great relief, he found space in a five-story, more mundane building on the west side of Fifth Avenue, directly across from the Flatiron. He'd moved in two months ago.

He crossed the wide avenue, fast-stepped his way around a sea of slower walkers and stopped at the corner newsstand to pick up a *New York Post*. His attention landed on the stand's magazine display and the recent issue of *Playboy Magazine*. He paid for the newspaper and magazine, entered the small lobby of his building, and waited for the elevator. When the door opened, he moved to one side to allow two women in their mid-twenties to exit, secretaries from the law firm on the fifth floor. He hid the magazine inside the folded *New York Post* and shot them a friendly smile. "Enjoy your lunch, ladies."

Rizzo rode the elevator to the fourth floor and entered his office. He dropped the newspaper and magazine on the desk. Before sitting, he gazed out the window behind him. The view overlooked Fifth Avenue and across to his prior office space. He frowned. His enjoyment of the sky and morning sun, glinting off windows of higher office buildings to the west, was now a thing of the past. He missed it.

The size of his new office was fifteen percent larger than the old one—a minor concession to his lost view. The extra space inspired the purchase of new furnishings from the Crate and Barrel store: two upholstered side chairs, a bigger sofa, and a coffee table.

His slightly beat-up wood desk, a model from the seventies, faced the door. A Mr. Coffee machine sat on a small metal table to the side of the desk, within reach whenever he required a shot of caffeine to help keep him from drowsing.

The pint-sized SentrySafe, resting on the floor at the back of the supply closet, secured his three firearms: a snub-nosed Cobra .38 Special, an NYPD-issued 9mm Glock 17, and a slightly lighter 365 Sig Sauer 9mm. All things considered, Rizzo was a happy camper in his new digs.

Rizzo opened the magazine to the page listing the corporate officers. He looked down the row of names, not expecting to see Roy Dickerson's, found the general telephone number and dialed. With patience, he went through the Robo-menu until it connected him with the office of the HR Director.

"Human Resources, this is Linda," the voice answered. It had the sound of a vocal smile. "How may I help you?"

"Hi, Linda. My name is Lucas Rizzo. I'm a private investigator. I'm calling to see if you'd be willing to assist me in finding a former employee. The law firm representing the estate of this person's deceased relative has hired me to find the gentleman."

A not surprising introspective pause followed. "How long ago was he employed at the magazine?"

"Well, we're not sure of his departure date. The best information we have is he was there in the '80s and '90s. He was the magazine's promotion manager."

Rizzo heard the second pause more as a function of incredulity. "Look, I know it was a long time ago. He was a young man then. The magazine could have employed him long after. If you go back into the personnel archives and—"

"Mr. Rizzo," she said, dragging out his name, "that will take a while. If you'll give me his name, and if you're certain he was active in the '90s, I'll have someone research it and get back to you. Of course, if we have an address and telephone number that was viable when he left the company, there's no assurance they would still be viable today. And even if they were, the company would not permit me to give out the information without receiving approval from the former employee."

"I'm aware, Linda, but it's a starting point. The man's name is Roy Dickerson, and as I mentioned, he was the magazine's promotion manager."

Rizzo provided Linda with his iPhone number and the office number, then ended the call. He leaned back in his chair and settled his eyes on a framed blowup hanging over the sofa. The relaxed face of his son, Matt, looked out at him. The seventeen-year-old boy's pose conveyed confidence and maturity as he leaned against a black VW Bug, the present Rizzo had given him upon his high school graduation.

Now that he was a junior at Fordham University and majoring in history, Rizzo couldn't be prouder of Matt's top-notch academic performance. In addition, Matt had secured his starting position at first base on Fordham's varsity baseball squad as a sophomore. He continued in the lineup at that position throughout his junior year.

Rizzo's thoughts led to his own baseball-playing excellence in high school. It set the groundwork for an offer of a baseball scholarship from Fordham University and a tryout with the Yankees. He turned down the scholarship, and nothing came of the tryout. Instead, he took the test for the NYPD. Even today, the question of what-if bothered him.

Rizzo opened his iPhone to the directory of contacts and found Jack Fields' name. After several rings, the voice answered with the usual sarcasm Rizzo had expected from the agent.

"You're calling me on my private number. My guess is you must be in deep shit again. What is it this time?"

Rizzo chuckled. He put the iPhone on speaker and set it down in front of him. "Oh, man, and I was going to ask you to join me for lunch at The Four Seasons. Now I'm not."

"You're too late, anyway. I've already eaten my peanut butter and jelly sandwich." Fields paused until Rizzo stopped laughing. "So, Luke, what's up? No long stories. I have a meeting with the boss-man in five minutes."

"First off, I need to thank you for the referral of Harry Fox, even though I don't have a clue where the hell to begin with this one. He give you any more information other than he needed to find someone who was in danger?"

"C'mon, Rizzo, you're selling yourself short. A major sleuth like you should be able to unravel the mystery."

Rizzo pictured Fields smirking. "He didn't tell you about the kidnapping of the woman? About the two Guidos involved? And making note of the tag number of the limo that carted her off to God knows where? Any of that?"

"Nope."

A long blast of horn-honking rose from the street, a taxi blocking traffic while picking up a fare.

"Isn't kidnapping a federal crime?" Rizzo said.

"Last time I checked, it was."

"And you're not interested in pursuing this with me?"

Fields went silent for a moment. Rizzo heard the agent's secretary, Rachel, on the intercom: "Jack, your meeting with Carter Brooke is about to start."

"Gotta go, Luke. If you get any more info, get back to me. Meanwhile, why don't you contact someone in the NYPD's Organized Crime Unit? Start there. Bye," and he ended the call.

The conversation with Fields had been a waste of time, except Rizzo was certain he'd hear from him in a few days. He knew he'd piqued the agent's interest, enough to expect a return call if Luke didn't call him first. Kidnapping was a felony offense, carrying with it a prison sentence of twenty years or more. He remembered as much from his police academy classes.

Rizzo pulled open the top drawer to the filing cabinet against the front wall and extracted a folder marked Important Contacts. Over the years on the job, he was meticulous about keeping a record of the names of those helpful law enforcement personnel he'd encountered during an investigation, and the nature of their interaction.

Lt. Bob Machado was his go-to guy in the NYPD's Organized Crime Unit. He was a serious-minded former undercover narcotics detective with more years on the job than he needed for retirement. Machado, twice decorated for valor, lived and breathed police work. Rizzo opened the folder and noted the number next to the lieutenant's name. He hoped the lawman was still on the roster.

A soft-spoken voice answered. "My goodness, it's Luke Rizzo. I thought you pulled the pin a few years ago."

"Happy to know I'm still in your address book. I retired, Bob, but not by choice. Seems I left my Mustang's window open while sitting on a plant during a drug bust. The bullet ricocheted off the post. Luckily, it found the fatty muscle in my ass and not my head. I vested out on three-quarters. I'm private now."

"Aha, not bad."

"Well, not the fun I had on the job, but it's been interesting."

When Rizzo said it, he flashed to the several cases in the past where he'd looked death in the face and escaped. Yeah, interesting.

"Look, you're busy, so I won't keep you. The reason for my call is exploratory. I got a kidnapping case. My client is an eyewitness. He says they forced the female victim into a black limousine. Happened in daylight on Third Avenue in the seventies. The two mugs snatching her were right out of central casting for a *Mafia* movie."

"Wow! Exciting. Did your client provide you with a description?"

"Yeah, and the limo's tag numbers. The driver was a short, bull-like character, dark hair, and wearing one of those Members Only jackets. The other thug wore a black, double-breasted, pin-stripe suit, white shirt with a black tie, and a gray Borsalino hat." Rizzo heard Machado chuckle. "What's so funny?"

"I was thinking, if your description isn't a cliché for a *Mafioso*, nothing is. The Borsalino is the interesting part. I suspect your client encountered one of the feared *capos* of the

Gambino family. His name is Sal Fusco, otherwise known as Sal 'The Hat' Fusco."

"No shit. Had Fox known, I'm sure he would have asked for an autograph."

"I'm not saying it was the *capo*. But if it was, take my word, Sal doesn't give out autographs. Only cracked skulls and orders for someone to be whacked. A real badass, he is. Let me have the tag number and I'll run it down. I'll call you when I have the info."

Rizzo recited the numbers.

"You alert the Feds?" Machado asked.

"Yes, today. Jack Fields, the SAC in the Manhattan field office."

"I know him."

"I expect he'll be calling me back soon for more details."

"Well then, how can I help?"

"You can't right now, thanks, but maybe soon. I called because I figured you should have a heads-up on the Feds. And I might need to impose on your good office for guidance if it gets to that point. I'll need more information from the client before I can justify snooping around."

"I'll help you all I can but try not to encroach on the Feds' territory."

"Oh, I know how that tune goes. Been there, done that."

"Keep me in the loop and, whatever you do, tread carefully if it does involve the Fusco badass."

"I will. Bye."

Machado's cautioning to Rizzo about encroaching on the Feds' territory produced a red-flag reminder. Several years ago, Rizzo got into a jam with Jack Fields and the FBI. He had flirted with being charged with interference in a federal investigation. The case involved stopping an international assassin. Rizzo got there first, to the chagrin of the Bureau.

Rizzo considered his next move. Harry Fox neglected to reveal to Fields the nature of his problem: Nicole Adams' kidnapping. Had he, Rizzo was sure Fox would not have knocked on his door.

He was glad he did. Nothing exciting had come his way since the San Juan drug trafficking bust last year. If it turned out this new investigation involved the mob and Sal "The Hat" Fusco, he'd be in for real fireworks, let alone excitement.

There was one drawback with this assignment. On his call to Fields, he referred to those snatching the woman as possible mob members. In doing so, he rang the RICO bell and invited the agent into the investigation. The fallout would relegate Rizzo to the role of spectator. He winced.

Chapter Three

Chelsea Area, Manhattan - Mon. A.M. 4/13

Monday morning, Rizzo boarded the packed R train at the West Forty-ninth Street stop, squeezing into the subway car before the doors closed behind him. Peak travel time on any workday morning was between eight and nine. Most mornings he avoided leaving during this period. Often, he was at his desk by seven-forty-five.

Rizzo surfaced to street level at Twenty-third, and after crossing Fifth Avenue, he stopped at the newsstand on the corner to buy a *New York Post*. He threaded his way between moving streams of pedestrians heading north and entered his office building. A man leaning against the wall opposite the elevator caught his eye. He wore jeans, a collared plaid shirt, and a brown sports jacket.

Before Rizzo could press the button to summon the elevator, the stranger approached. "Mr. Rizzo," he said in a lowered voice.

Rizzo turned and looked back over his shoulder.

The man reached out his hand and said, "My name is Roy Dickerson. Can we go somewhere to talk, someplace where we can't be overheard?"

* * *

Rizzo led the way across Twenty-third Street into Madison Square Park. They sat side-by-side on a bench facing the park's fenced-in dog run. The surrounding leafy-treed area provided some privacy, and the early hour meant sparse foot traffic passing their bench. A few dog owners, taking advantage of the city's rare amenity, romped with their pets within the pen. They were far enough away not to be a concern.

"So Mohammed has come to the mountain," Rizzo said. "What a surprise. You saved me a lot of time chasing my tail trying to find you."

Dickerson's face bore a worrisome expression. His scanning eyes took in the scene. "When I got the call from the magazine yesterday, I didn't know what to make of it. I knew the inheritance story was bogus. With exception of my brother, I have few close relatives, and no one well-off enough to leave an inheritance." A smile leaked from the corners of his mouth.

Rizzo knew he wasn't being clever with the inheritance bit, a cliché ploy used by every fictional investigator since Philip Marlowe, but it worked.

"When they said you were a private investigator and told me your name was Lucas Rizzo, I thought maybe you were working for Carmine D'Angelo."

"Who's that?"

Dickerson placed his laced fingers over his mouth, and dropping his voice, he said, "An underboss of the Gambino family."

"You mean Gotti's former mob? They still operating from Howard Beach? Didn't the Teflon Don pass away a while ago? Behind bars?"

"He did. Since then, there's been a few bosses, all indicted and jailed. The current boss is Carl Nunziata."

"And why would you believe they'd be looking for you?"

"I didn't until the magazine contacted me. That's what sent me worrying."

"Italian names can do that. Especially those with roots in Palermo, Sicily, like Rizzo. But now you realize I'm not working for them, right?"

Dickerson's head snapped up, and he jumped to his feet. He glared at Rizzo. "You aren't, are you?"

"No, no. Relax, for cryin' out loud. I figured you checked on me or you wouldn't have shown up here this morning."

Dickerson sat down and became quiet, his eyes locked on his feet. Before he lifted his head, Rizzo could see the man's emotional temperature easing. It was clear he was under a serious weight of worry.

"I did . . . check you out, I mean. My brother is part of the NYPD Joint Robbery Task Force. Thirty years on the job. When I gave him your name, he thought you sounded familiar. He researched it. Found a photo on the web of an official ceremony decorating you years ago. It was for stopping a crazy Cuban from bombing a restaurant. He texted me a copy. I spotted you in the lobby from the picture."

Dickerson had referred to the famous Palm Restaurant incident of almost a decade ago. Rizzo remembered it with a smile. The heroics got him a lifetime of free dining at Manhattan's premier steak house, and he never had to make a reservation.

"You wanna tell me why you're jumpy? You do something they didn't like?"

Dickerson's hand went to the back of his head. His face tightened while he massaged his neck muscles like someone rising from an uncomfortable night's sleep.

"It's my past involvement in a business. I'm no longer a partner, but the mob keeps me on their scope to make sure I don't go rogue."

"Why so? Was it a dirty business?"

"The company itself? No. How they used it? Yes." Dickerson removed his hand from his neck and peered out toward the dog run. He remained silent with a look of uncertainty.

Rizzo waited, then asked, "You think you could elaborate?"

"Crap, I say any more and they find out, I'll be a dead man in a heartbeat." His voice had become strained, the words squeezed out with reluctance.

"Okay," Rizzo said. "Let me give you two names. Tell me how you connect to them." He paused until Dickerson had time to compose himself enough to listen and consider. "The first is Harry Fox." Rizzo knew about their connection, but he was interested in hearing Dickerson's description.

The man's brow rippled for a split second as he gathered his thoughts. Normally, the recollection of an old business associate after the passing of several decades would be a challenge. Not so, in this case. Dickerson's role in extricating Harry Fox from an embarrassing entanglement with a Playboy Bunny made the recall easy.

"Advertising agency executive . . . Schweppes account. We worked together on a few joint promotions over the years."

"Good. Then, the second name should not surprise you: Nicole Adams."

Dickerson's eyebrows jumped. "Oh, God! Has something happened to her? We talked less than a month ago. She said everything was cool."

"Cool? They've kidnapped her. Definitely not cool. It looks like she got on the wrong side of the mob. I suspect you can shed light on why."

A wave of desperation splashed across Dickerson's face. Rizzo could see his eyes become moist—a tell he was experiencing a level of personal guilt. He closed them, took an audible inhale, then shook.

"But first," Rizzo said, "tell me how you and Nicole connected? Wasn't she a Playboy Bunny, once?"

"Yes. When they closed the Manhattan Playboy Club in the mid-eighties, she was out of work. Over the next ten years, she knocked around at various temp positions and short-term waitressing stints."

Dickerson paused while several people passed on their way through the park. He breathed deep a few times and continued.

"Around the end of that period, we ran into each other at a *Playboy Magazine* reunion. We exchanged numbers. I had left the magazine the year before, joining up with Pete Barone."

"What was your connection to him? From the publishing world?"

"No. He was a former college roommate, and about to open a sports bar on Atlantic Avenue in Brooklyn. Pete was financing the venture, or so I thought. He offered me a working partnership."

Rizzo wondered how Nicole had gotten entangled with the mob and was about to ask, but Dickerson continued his narrative, picking up speed.

"Nicole called me a short time later. She was looking for more substantial work than waitressing. She thought I might help her find something. I suggested a hostess position at our new place as a start. It would mean getting back into the restaurant business, but I told her I could train her on the managerial side. I said we had plans to open other bars in the New York area.

It could assure her of a well-paying career. She jumped at it." Dickerson drew in a breath and pushed it out between his lips.

"How did the mob get involved?"

"Pete Barone was already mobbed up. He was a mob associate." He wagged his head like he'd uttered something he found impossible to believe. "I had no idea he was the nephew of Carmine D'Angelo. His two brothers were low-level soldiers in the Gambino family. I remained in the dark about the mob's involvement in the business for a long time. Pete never shared the bookkeeping side with me. Over the next two decades, we built a small chain of five sports bars, three in Queens, and two in Brooklyn—"

"Let me guess. The mob did their laundering through the sports bars?"

Dickerson cast his eyes to the ground and nodded.

"And Nicole never knew?"

"Hell, no. She was like me. Our sole responsibility was the company's day-to-day operation. We ran the bars. She proved to be a savvy restaurant manager. After a few years, she became my assistant, overseeing the five locations."

"When did you find out about your silent partners?"

"Five years ago."

"Barone tell you?"

"Yeah, after I saw a guy coming out of his office. I recognized him from a photo in the *Daily News*. He was a well-known mob figure. Turned out he was Pete's uncle. They'd been in there for a while, behind the closed door. The next night, I asked Pete about it. He tried to toss it off as nothing. I pressed him, and he admitted to how the mob was using the bars. It shocked the hell out of me."

Rizzo smirked. "And you said you didn't want any part of it?"

Dickerson ignored the question. "Pete told me to calm down, no one got hurt. Then he reminded me of how well Time-Out Enterprises did with the bottom line. 'Hey, it's providing you with a fat bank account. Go along and don't make waves,' he said. I did for the next few years until I could no longer justify my role. I was worried about being a partner, and if things were ever exposed, it might look bad for my brother. You know, a lieutenant on the NYPD with a brother involved in a business laundering mob money. Pete offered to buy out my partnership share with a generous settlement. Providing, of course, I kept quiet. I agreed. Making waves would mean a death sentence."

"How about Nicole? You didn't tell her?"

"Yeah, I did. She'd been working for the company for the better part of nineteen years. At the time I cashed out, I felt obliged to let her know how Pete used the business for illegal activity. I told her she needed to get the hell out too. If she stayed, she'd be at risk."

"How so?"

"The son-of-a-bitch Barone made her life miserable. I laid it out for him at the get-go. Nicole was gay. The guy started hitting on her when his ten-year marriage headed for the toilet. Like he thought she was faking it. I kept reminding him to stop wasting his time. No surprise. He ramped up his efforts after I was out of the picture."

"You tell her the illegal activity was money laundering?"

"Not then. Before I left, I warned her again. This time, I spelled it out for her. If the operation ever came under the scrutiny of the Feds, she could become implicated. She said she wanted to hang in a while longer."

"Why?"

"For starters, we paid her sixty-five thousand a year, more than she'd ever made in her whole life. Then, nine years before this, we'd purchased a retirement plan for our employees. In one more year, she'd be fully vested. She was no kid and needed long-term security."

"And willing to risk it for another year?" Rizzo shook his head.

"Yeah. The last time we spoke, she said Pete had backed off after she threatened to go to the cops. I warned her, it was crazy trying to scare him like that. She said it worked. He stopped harassing her. That's when she told me everything was cool."

"But for how long?" Rizzo asked. "I'm guessing he continued, and she threatened him again. This time, the family got involved, and they decided it was *arrivederci* time."

Dickerson leaned forward with his hands covering his eyes. Rizzo could see his chest heaving in deep breaths.

Two women pushing strollers slowed when one of them noticed Dickerson's bent-over position. "Is he all right?" she asked Rizzo. "I'm a nurse. If you need help, maybe I can—"

"No, no, he's okay. He lost a bet to me. He's suffering from humiliation." Rizzo looked up at her with a broad smile. "Thanks anyway." The lady shrugged and moved on.

Dickerson raised his head, pushed back against the wooden bench slats, and folded his hands across his stomach. He gazed up into the bower of leafy trees above and gazed off into silence.

Rizzo grinned. "And, as they say, the rest is history. You realize now, you're at risk, don't you? The mob knows you're the one who told Nicole about their laundering operation. Perhaps you were right to worry about Italian-named people."

* * *

Forest Hills, Queens, NY - Mon. A.M. 4/13

The man's fate was in serious jeopardy, but all Rizzo thought about was what the hell happened to Nicole Adams. Dickerson had given him her address in Queens as the Boulevard Gardens Apartments at Sixty-eighth Road and Austin Avenue, building number 204. He found it on Google Search and learned the four-building apartment complex dated back to the sixties. Photos showed they had maintained it over the years. Ten years ago, the real estate company ownership converted it to co-op units.

Rizzo left his office and hopped on the subway at his corner. Forty-five minutes later, he arrived at the Sixty-seventh Street Station in Forest Hills. The neighborhood was upper-middle-class, made up mostly of the working millennial generation. He had judged none but the elderly and retired would be in their homes at three in the afternoon on a weekday.

Each building had underground parking that spilled out onto one of the four streets flanking the block-squared complex. Tended shrubbery sided the base of each structure, and benches and shrubs lined the walkways between. At the entrance of building 204, the tenant directory listed ten apartments for each floor, from A to J.

Rizzo pressed the 7-D buzzer for Nicole Adams several times but received no answer. These were not doorman-attended apartments, and Rizzo rode the coattails into the lobby behind a tenant with a key. He waited in the foyer until the tenant disappeared behind the elevator's closing door. Rizzo watched the numbers flip over and stop at the tenth floor before he pressed the button to recall the car.

Apartment 7-D was to the left of the elevator, on the opposite side of the corridor. To the right, coming from an apartment a few doors past the elevator, he heard a loud TV—a game show full of audience laughter. As he approached Nicole's apartment, he was relieved to see all the door locks were the original installation: the Yale brass single-cylinder deadbolt lock. Rizzo stood in front of her door, removed a small leather case from his jacket pocket, and unzipped it. He remained stationary for several seconds, taking deep calming breaths, and waited until he was sure the sound he heard came from the television, and not from the elevator. Satisfied, he knelt on one knee, placed the case on the carpeted floor, and took out two lock-pick tools.

As though struck by a bolt of enlightenment, Rizzo collapsed the second knee and remained kneeling, holding the tools to his side. His breathing became irregular as thoughts darted through his head. What the hell am I doing here? Am I out of my mind? What if she's in there? Dead? How do I explain breaking and entering? He sat back on his heels, holding still for several seconds.

His mind in a swirl, he missed feeling the gun barrel pressing into the back of his skull. He reached full awareness when he heard the words that accompanied it.

"Drop the tools, put your hands behind your head, and get to your feet—do it slowly."

Rizzo's body went rigid. He couldn't bring himself to grasp what was happening. For a half-second, he dropped his head forward, trying to evade the cold gun barrel. Instead, the weapon followed as though pinned to the back of his skull.

"Wait a minute. This isn't what it looks—"

"Get the fuck up. On your feet before I put another part in your hairline. I'm NYPD. You're gonna be a dead man if you don't do as I say."

"Holy shit, wait, wait, I'm getting up."

Rizzo released the tools and dropped them to the carpet, struggling to keep his balance as he inched up into a standing position.

"Now, bring your hands down and put them together behind your back."

Rizzo obeyed. "Oh, man, I'm a—"

"Shut your yap," the voice said as he jammed handcuffs around Rizzo's wrists. Once he had him secured, the officer holstered his weapon and told Rizzo to turn around.

Rizzo completed the turn slowly and the two men came face-to-face. Their eyes landed on each other, and their mouths dropped open in unison.

"What the—"

Before the officer could finish, Rizzo's tension released, and he let loose a staccato burst of laughter.

"Rizzo? I don't believe this. What the hell is going on? I haven't seen you since the Forty-first in the Bronx."

"That's me, Fisk," Rizzo said in between deep gulps of breath. "Glad you remembered, or I might be a dead man. Take these damn cuffs off and let me explain what's going down."

"I'd thought you'd vested out," he said, making no move to free Rizzo's wrists.

"I did. I'm private now. That's what this is all about."

"What the hell are you doing trying to break into someone's apartment?"

"Well, it's not what you think."

"So tell me, asshole."

Detective 3rd grade Cameron Fisk, now a member of the Precinct Detective Squad at the Twelve in Queens, listened while Rizzo described how his client witnessed Nicole's kidnapping off the street in Manhattan.

"There's a good chance the mob is behind it," he told Fisk without mentioning the reason they snatched her. "I came here thinking if I got a look around her apartment, I might find something that would lead me to her. Yeah, Dick Tracy here must be losing it. Before I hit the lock, I realized what I might find was her dead body. The possibility paralyzed me the moment before you tapped my head with your nine."

"I know who she is," Fisk said as he fumbled for the handcuff's key in his pocket and unshackled Rizzo's wrists. "I'm in the end apartment," pointing in the opposite direction. "Now and again, I run into her. My contact never amounted to more than a friendly nod. She wasn't the talkative type. Good lookin' but not social."

Rizzo massaged his wrists until he could feel normal circulation. "Well, maybe we can get a fast peek around her apartment? Together, I mean. See if she's in there."

Fisk took a moment before he removed his iPhone. "Yeah, we could do that. Let me call my Squad Commander, explain things. See if there's enough probable cause for a go-ahead."

"Works for me," Rizzo said.

Fisk ended the conversation after he had to wait five minutes until the call caught up with the Squad Commander. "We got a go," Fisk said, "and O'Shea says to say hello."

A smile came to Rizzo's face, pleased that one of his former NYPD brethren remembered him. He looked down at the lock-pick tools on the carpet and said, "Unless she gave you a key," Rizzo said with a wink, "I need to get to work."

"Go to it, Houdini."

Rizzo had the lock defeated in less than three minutes. He stepped back to let the detective enter first. Fisk stood to one side, turned the knob, and eased open the door. A well-decorated living room greeted them as sunlight streamed into the apartment from bay windows on one side.

"Miss Adams?" Fisk called out and waited before crossing the threshold.

Rizzo hung back. He hoped to hear a response. Silence blanketed the room, even after Fisk repeated his call-out.

"I guess we go in," the detective said and led the way into the apartment.

Rizzo let the door close behind him and stood in the middle of the homey-appointed living room. His eyes completed a 360 examination and, seeing nothing disturbed or out of place, he headed for the bathroom. Fisk took the bedroom. After Rizzo completed a search of the small compact kitchen, it was clear nobody had done any cooking there in the recent past. It was a typical one-bedroom layout, perfect for a single person. Rizzo and Fisk met back in the living room and produced the same headshake, saying they found nothing amiss.

"No dead body," Fisk said, smiling. "That's a break."

"And no sign showing she left under duress, or even in a hurry."

"Well, it appears you're still on first base," Fisk said and turned toward the door. "Let's lock it up. I gotta be on duty in an hour."

Rizzo reset the lock and looked back into the room. He shook his head and closed the door. He hoped he wasn't closing it on the life of Nicole Adams.

Chapter Four

Lower Manhattan - Tues. A.M. 4/14

The coffee shop across from the World Trade Center complex in lower Manhattan was near empty at the early morning hour of seven-thirty. Tourists would fill the shop once the 9/11 Memorial Museum opened to the public. Rizzo entered and let the door swing closed, shutting out the rushing sounds of the waterfalls at the two reflecting pools and the sorrowful memories they represented.

He walked to the rear and squeezed into the seat of a booth where his childhood friend, Vinnie Alcamo, waited. A half-filled mug of coffee and a partially consumed bagel with cream cheese sat in front of the low-level *Mafia* soldier.

Vinnie looked up and smiled. Dressed in a dark blue blazer over a white open-collared sport shirt, he reached across and enclosed Rizzo's extended hand within both of his. He shook it vigorously and asked, "Luke, *amicu*, how you been?"

Rizzo noticed the gravelly edge to the man's usual resonant voice. Vinnie was a heavy smoker, he remembered. Rizzo returned a warm smile. "Doing great, Vinnie. And what keeps you busy these days?"

"Oh, a little of this, a little of that." He turned and nodded toward the front of the shop, to the mammoth complex visible on the other side of the street. "This here project, you know, kept me hopping these last couple of years. My union, IBEW, done pretty good by it." He raised the coffee mug to his mouth and drank.

Rizzo's eyes landed on Vinnie's fingers wrapped around the mug. "Hey, you quit smoking."

"How the hell you know?"

"I don't see nicotine stains on your fingers. You used to chain-smoke like a chimney."

"I forgot. You're a detective. Good catch. Yeah. Been almost a year." Four stainless fingers tapped his chest. "Doc's orders."

"Good for you."

Vinnie Alcamo, when not breaking heads as an enforcer for the Gambino family, represented the family as one of the union negotiators for the International Brotherhood of Electrical Workers. Luke Rizzo had formed a close bond with Vinnie when they were teenagers growing up on the streets of Woodside, Queens. Vinnie wasn't a large kid, but "strong like bull," Rizzo liked to joke. No one within a radius of twenty blocks was tougher.

His two older brothers had carved out lives for themselves along diametrically opposite paths. Richie became involved with mob activities at an early age and met his demise—a rival mob-hit in Miami—before he reached twenty-five. The older brother, Frank, went into the seminary and became a priest. As contradictory as it might have seemed to Rizzo, he recalled one of the seven brothers of the former crime boss, Albert Anastasia, did the same. Salvatore Anastasia took the vows of the priesthood in Sicily instead of the vow of *Omertà* in Brooklyn.

Vinnie's father was a violent alcoholic. Rizzo often wondered how much family life had influenced the three brothers, and what factors could have instigated their chosen paths.

Vinnie, as a teenager growing up, was movie-star handsome by the standards of Rizzo's mother. She loved feeding him whenever Rizzo dragged him home for a pasta dinner. During Rizzo's years on the job, the two friends had politely kept their distance except for the occasional phone call on birthdays and weddings.

"How's married life?" Rizzo asked, aware Vinnie had recently remarried for the third time, this one to a struggling singer-dancer with limited success in Broadway Theater. Musicals had always been one of Vinnie's passions, an unusual dichotomy of taste for the rough-and-tumble guy he was—the aspect of his character Rizzo admired.

"Great. Lots better than the first two."

"Sorry I couldn't make the wedding."

"That's okay. You told me you would be busy down in Puerto Rico on business."

Rizzo grinned. "Maybe the next one, yeah?"

"Shit! There ain't gonna be no more. I mean it. This one's the last. Hey, you wanna order something to eat?"

"Just coffee. I'll get it," Rizzo said and walked to the counter. He returned to the booth, set the mug down, and sat. He leaned across the tabletop to lay his hand on Vinnie's arm. "I'd like to ask a favor," he said in a whispered voice. "Be straight with me. If you can't do it, or if it's too risky, say so and we'll forget it."

Vinnie's face held a vacant expression for a beat until it broke into a grin. "Who you want whacked?"

The question made Rizzo sit back and stifle a nervous laugh. "C'mon, bro, you know me better than that." He waited, thinking about the logic of Vinnie's response, and he felt his stomach do flip-flops. Did he mean it? Could he have someone removed? The look on Rizzo's face must have telegraphed his thoughts.

"I'm shitting you, bro. You'd be the last guy on earth to ask somethin' like that."

"Oh, you know it," Rizzo said with a quiet exhale of relief. "It's nothing exotic. I'm looking for help finding a kidnapped woman. About a week ago, my client saw her getting shoved into a black limo. The people doing the shoving didn't look like Yale alumni, if you follow me."

"Which family?"

"I'm not certain. Someone formerly associated with the guys making the snatch claims the Gambinos."

"I think I heard of them," he said, grinning. He jammed the remaining quarter of the bagel into his mouth, his jaws grinding like a piston in slow motion, his fingers laced together on the tabletop, his mind processing the information. Rizzo remained still, watching his friend.

"Tell me whatchu know," he said, taking a swallow of coffee.

Rizzo related the story of Harry Fox and Nicole Adams. He explained how Fox had witnessed the kidnapping outside D'Agostino's. When he described the two participants—a Borsalino fedora on one, a Member's Only jacket on the driver— he thought he'd detected a flicker of recognition on Vinnie's face. He reached the part of his narrative about Roy Dickerson's partnership in the sports bars with Pete Barone and paused, waiting for Vinnie to speak. Thus far, his friend had remained quiet throughout, his head tilted to one side, listening with intensity like a priest hearing confession. But Rizzo noticed the mention of Pete Barone's name caused Vinnie's eyes to flash with a wary look.

"You know this guy, Barone?"

"Oh, yeah. A real *stunade*. His uncle is Carmine D'Angelo, one of the underbosses of the family. Barone's not a heavy. He's an associate. I run into him from time to time at his bars in Queens."

"Were you aware the family is using his bars to wash their money?"

Vinnie laughed. "No shit! What a surprise."

"Yeah, well, when Dickerson got wind of it, he decided to cash out, leave the partnership. The woman, this Nicole Adams? Dickerson had hired her. She'd worked for Time-Out Enterprises many years, managing their five locations. Worried about her, Dickerson stupidly revealed the mob's laundering operation. He suggested she leave with him. She told him she wanted to stay one more year for their retirement plan."

"And she stayed?"

"Yeah."

"Not smart."

"I agree. Anyway, Barone had been hitting on her, getting nowhere. The dumb ass knew she was gay. I guess the *stunade* didn't believe it. She threatened to pull the curtain back if he didn't stop. He got pissed off. He told his uncle. They grabbed her and are holding her somewhere—if they haven't already dumped her in a New Jersey swamp."

Vinnie snickered. "And you wanna rescue her?"

"That's what my client hired me to do."

Vinnie finished the remains of his coffee. He rotated his head, stretching his neck muscles. Then he slowly rolled his broad shoulders several times, like someone preparing to lift a heavy palate off a truck's tailgate.

"Wadda ya want from me? I'll do what I can."

"Nose around. See if you can find out what happened to her. Barone would know, wouldn't he?"

"Probably. Then I find where they got her stashed and you charge in like the cavalry to save her?" He released a low, nasally snicker.

Rizzo wondered what he found so funny, but he let it pass when Vinnie's expression suddenly turned serious.

"I love you, my brother," he said, "but it ain't gonna happen."

"Why? Maybe I can make it happen?"

"Marone! *Goomba*, listen to me," he said, pumping his outstretched palms at Rizzo. "If she's stashed somewhere, you can bet your ass they're using a couple of tough *gavones* to guard her. They won't hesitate to put a bullet between your eyes. Let me see what I can find out. Okay? Then we go from there—if she's still breathing."

* * *

FBI's Manhattan Office - Tues. A.M. 4/14

"I hear you, Jack, but I don't think Rizzo would do much to interfere with the Bureau's planning," Bob Machado said. "We lay down the law before getting him involved."

The lack of confidence in Machado's tone produced a loud guffaw from the agent. Fields suspected the detectives of the NYPD knew about Rizzo's tendency to ignore territorial lines of the FBI.

"The Organized Crime Unit is aware of the Gambinos' money-laundering operation through Time-Out Enterprises. We've been on to it for a good while, waiting to get solid evidence. Once we do, you can throw RICO at them and close down the five sports bars."

"At this point," Fields said, "we don't know how the kidnapped woman fits in with the money-laundering scam. Maybe that's how Rizzo can help us once he finds her."

"Yeah. Then we shoot for both charges, money- laundering and kidnapping. Makes a stronger case all around."

"Yeah, that's a possibility."

"Why don't we call Rizzo, have a sit-down?" Machado said. "See what he knows."

"You want to contact him? The invitation coming from you might emphasize the gravity of the situation."

"But your invite would carry more weight, considering you have a longer history with him."

Fields recalled the difficulties over the years he and the Bureau had during the few contract assignments with Rizzo. "Yeah, but a spotty one. Okay. I'll call him. What's your schedule like?"

"I'm here all this week."

"Good. My office, okay? Then I can have one of my senior agents, Ralph Brancuso, sit in."

"Fine. Give me a yell when you set it up."

Fields ended the call and pushed the intercom button. "Rachel, ask Ralph to come in, please."

* * *

Jamaica Avenue, Queens - Tues. P.M. 4/14

The Dugout was alive with activity at ten-fifteen when Vinnie Alcamo entered. Inside the door, he shot a quick look around the horseshoe-shaped bar. He took in the three bartenders on duty and found his pal, Dominic Biondo. At six-four, two-forty, and built solid like an NFL left offensive tackle, the guy was hard to miss.

Vinnie spotted a stool close to him being vacated and moved in. "You leaving or going to the men's room?" he asked the man easing down from the seat.

"No, I'm leaving. It's all yours."

He sat and did an informal inventory of the bar scene: Twelve TVs located around the restaurant displayed live sports, from bowling to baseball to hockey. Four large wall-mounted screens aired the Mets' and the Yankees' games. Noisy patrons occupied every stool around the large oblong bar, watching smaller TV sets embedded in the fascia above the bar on the opposite side. A half-dozen six-seat high tops were clustered together on the left side of the restaurant, and for those patrons interested in food service, two rows of regular six-seater booths lined the right wall.

The kitchen was visible through the service opening on the back wall, where the wait-staff loitered, waiting for orders. The Dugout was, without question, the super sports bar of Queens.

Vinnie caught Dom's attention as the man bent over to pull out a cold mug from one of the ice compartments. The bartender looked up and flashed him a smile of recognition. He completed the delivery of the mug and bottle of beer to a customer at the far end, then hurried toward Vinnie.

"Hey, *come stai*?" Dominic shouted above the din. He reined up in front of Vinnie, wiped his palms with a dry bar rag, reached over, and grabbed him by the back of the neck to pull him close. He planted a kiss on his forehead, released him, and said, "Where the hell you been?"

"Busy as a son-of-bitch with the Trade Center project. How are you, man? No more headaches? Everything good?"

"Oh, yeah. Back to normal. We've been busy as hell too," he said, nodding at the large screens. "What with the baseball season just beginning and the Yankees and Mets fanatics doing their thing. What can I getcha?"

"A Bud, I guess."

"Draft or bottle?"

"Bottle, no glass."

Dom turned to the refrigerated box behind him and drew out a Bud, snapped off the cap, and set it on the bar in front of Vinnie. "So... business or pleasure?"

Vinnie hesitated before responding. Dom was the one employee in The Dugout—besides Peter Barone—who knew of his Gambino connection. The two friends had been associates in a crew working together doing "heavy lifting" for the family until two years ago. While they were putting the pressure on a reluctant account, a cop stumbled onto the scene as it was about to reach a bloody level. When Dom fled, he took the cop's bullet, the shot grazing his skull on the left side. He escaped further harm and capture with Vinnie's help.

The result was the pair became close friends. Dom recovered from the gunshot wound after receiving medical attention. He rehabbed for a month and suffered from frequent headaches. Thereafter, bartending at The Dugout became his full-time future.

Vinnie raised the bottle, and, tipping it toward Dom, he said, "*Saluti.*"

Dom waited until Vinnie returned the bottle to the bar. "So which is it?"

"Not business or pleasure. I'm doing a favor for a friend."

"Uh-oh! Better be a good friend. I mean, I can't count the number of times I seen a favor for a friend turns on you and bites you in the ass?"

"Not this guy. We've been buddies since we were kids. He's a private dick."

Vinnie let his gaze wander around the immediate area and then back toward the kitchen at the wait-staff activity by the order station. He couldn't spot anyone who appeared to be in the role of a manager. Vinnie looked back at Dom and asked, "Who's running this place now?" The silence that followed made him think Dominic was aware of what he was getting at. His friend's face took on a wary expression. Vinnie had guessed right.

Dom leaned across the bar, lowered his wide torso to the bar's surface, and rolled up his head and eyes toward Vinnie's face. "Anthony became the manager when Adams disappeared about two weeks ago," he whispered. "Then right outta the blue, she's back running the joint. Tried to ask her what happened, but she was in no mood to talk. I let it drop."

"And Barone said nothing to you about it?"

"Nope. He acted like he didn't know she was gone. But a little later, Sal Fusco comes in and sits at the bar like usual."

"Alone?"

"Yeah, always alone. I was curious, so I asked—innocent-like—if she was still on the payroll. Fuckin' guy goes ballistic. Almost bit my head off. 'Mind your own damn business,' he sez. 'She's a *boccalone*, a big mouth. Almost dumped her in the Hudson.'" Dom snorted. "Man, the sucker had fire in his eyes. Surprised the shit outta me. Not his ordinary chatty self." He stood erect and a smile settled on his face. "You know, I figured it was his sign not to push," Dom said with a note of sarcasm, so I shut up."

"Vinnie burst out laughing. "Man, you still got a big pair of *cogliones*. Is she here now?"

"Not tonight. She's at the Red Zone, the Atlantic Avenue store in Brooklyn. She'll be back checking on us before eleven."

"Barone here?"

"Yeah, in the office. You wanna see him?"

"Nah. Gimme another Bud. I'll talk to him if he comes out."

Dom stood still, his belly pressed against the ice chest under the bar, his attention fixed on Vinnie.

"What?" Vinnie asked. "There a problem?"

"*Paesano*, the word is out. She was in deep shit with the family when she disappeared. I don't know why, but I hear they snatched her off the street after she bugged out. Now she's back working. I haven't the foggiest what the deal is or for how long she's gonna be here. I'd be guarded if you talk with Barone. He's one big hothead."

"Oh, I will, *paesano*, I will. *Grazie*," he said.

Dom reached into the ice chest, pulled out a cold Bud, snapped off the cap, and set it in front of Vinnie. "Be right back," he said and slid down to the end of the bar, responding to a customer's signal for a refill.

Vinnie raised his eyes and locked them on the TV set in the fascia above the bar opposite him. Another Bud later, the Yanks' lead-off was at the plate facing the second relief pitcher Boston had used in the inning. Yankees were up by a run in the bottom of the eighth. Vinnie knew the result was inconsequential because it was still early in the season. Pride was the Yankees' only motivation. They hated losing to their division rival.

A hand landed on one of Vinnie's shoulders, accompanied by Pete Barone's voice. "Hey, hey, stranger, haven't seen you around in a long while. How ya been?"

Vinnie spun on his stool and shook Barone's proffered hand. Smiling, he said, "Hey, man, we all can't have cushy jobs like yours. A few of us gotta work."

"How's the Trade Center project coming? Things should be winding up soon. No?"

"In about another month, I'd say. Then it's on to a new contract. A big one out in the Rockaways the size of the Lefrak City."

"Wow! The union's gotta be happy about that."

"I see you're keeping busy here. How're the other four stores doing?"

"They're a mother of a gold mine," Barone answered, with no attempt to hide the braggadocio sound of his reply. "I pray every day they stay that way."

"Must be a bitch keeping on top of things, right? I mean, five locations." Vinnie immediately regretted his comment. He hoped Barone wouldn't think he referred to his mysterious absentee manager. The expression on Barone's face remained friendly. Vinnie decided no harm was done.

"We manage." A smile of self-satisfaction appeared. "We got a good stable of employees at all our locations. They know their jobs," he added, nodding his head in Dominic's direction, "and who signs their paychecks." Barone looked back over his shoulder as if someone waited for him, and said, "Hey, Vinnie,

I gotta run, but it's nice seeing you again. Kitchen's still open. If you haven't already eaten, tonight's special is the meat loaf. Outstanding." Barone turned and hurried toward the door.

"Thanks, Pete," Vinnie said, his words landing on the back of the departing proprietor. He looked up at the monitor and saw the game had ended. The Yanks held on for the win. Time to go, he thought. I'll call Rizzo tomorrow with the good news. At least, he assumed it was good news. But in his explosive and scary world, no one could ever know for sure.

Chapter Five

Chelsea Area, Manhattan - Thurs. A.M. 4/16

At seven-forty, Thursday morning, Rizzo slid the key into his office door lock. The iPhone in his back pocket vibrated, then rang with the beginning piano chords of Dave Brubeck's "Take Five." He grabbed for it, swung open the door, and hurried across the room, one hand holding his keychain and iPhone, the other grasping the bag containing his warm Egg McMuffin. Rizzo dropped the bag and keys onto his desk and tapped the speaker-phone icon once he saw Vinnie's name on the screen.

"Hey, *goomba, come vai?*"

Vinnie snickered. "It's nice you haven't forgotten your Italian."

"Yeah. Not much call for it. Nothing but Irish, Spanish, Poles, and Arabs on the PD these days. Italians are too busy becoming politicians. So whatcha got?"

Before Vinnie could respond, a thought popped into Rizzo's mind. It was only a few days ago he had coffee with his friend.

Could Vinnie calling this soon mean he got lucky or was the situation not so great? He hoped it was the former because he didn't figure Harry Fox would take bad news well.

"For starters, she's alive."

"Oh, great. You saw her?"

"No, but a reliable source told me she's back managing the five sports bars."

"No shit!"

"He doesn't know why it happened. He'd heard they grabbed her off the street and held her somewhere for a while. That's the word he got. The rest is a mystery."

"She's okay?"

"Yeah. My source wouldn't bullshit me. Went to The Dugout last night to speak with him. It's one of their Queens stores. He's a bartender. She wasn't there. Out checking on one of their Brooklyn locations. He assured me she's back working, business as usual."

Rizzo leaned back and his eyes lowered to the fast-cooling, bagged Egg McMuffin sitting on his desk.

Strange, he thought. Not the normal *Mafia* standard operating procedure when a threat of betrayal was the issue. He wondered if the story Roy Dickerson had told him was true. Maybe he never revealed to her about the laundering operation. Was it something different, something involving jealousy? Yeah, but jealous of what? Barone wasn't getting anywhere with her, according to Dickerson. She was gay. Unless he'd got it wrong.

"Luke? You still there?"

"I am, Vinnie. Sorry. Thinking about something."

"Well, now you can put away your Superman costume. No need to risk getting your ass shot off trying to rescue her."

"My client will be happy to hear that. Do you know if she spends more time at one of the restaurants than at the other four?"

"The Dugout's where the chain's main office is. You plan to visit her?"

"Far as I'm concerned, I found her. I'm done. My client might want to drop in."

"That's the smarter move, *paesano*. There may be more to this. And if there is, stay the hell away from the problem."

"Thanks, Vinnie. You're a pal. I owe you. Let's stay in touch."

"*Ciao*," Vinnie said and disconnected.

* * *

FBI's Manhattan Office - Fri. A.M. 04/17

"You take your coffee black, don't you?"

"Yeah," Rizzo said, smiling. "Hell, I've been here often enough. I'm surprised you forgot."

Fields ignored the jibe and spoke into the intercom. "Rachel, Mr. Rizzo takes his black."

"I know that."

The agent's eyebrows lifted.

"And the others?"

"The same." Fields stood, walked around his desk, and dropped into a chair facing the sofa.

Ralph Brancuso, the senior agent under Jack Fields, sat at one end of the sofa opposite Rizzo. Lieutenant Machado sat in a second chair, facing them.

"Okay," Fields began, "let's start with Rizzo. Bring us up to speed."

Rizzo pushed back into the sofa's cushion and slid his arm across the top. How many times, he thought, have I sat here answering questions? Or listening to the pontificating Fields hold forth on details of a contract assignment he wanted me to take on? Twice in the last year and a half, my life has been threatened, and one time it even endangered my wife's life. Tread carefully.

"Well, the lady, Nicole Adams, returned from wherever. That much you know. My source—someone within the family— said they grabbed and held her for close to two weeks. No physical harm. I'm guessing that because she's back to work managing the five sports bars again."

"Came back voluntarily?" Lieutenant Machado asked.

"My guy didn't know. When he visited The Dugout, the bar in Queens where their office is located, the bartender told him she was reluctant to say where she'd been. She snapped at him when he asked her. His quote was 'Business as usual.' Could mean anything."

"This source you got, he knows why you'd be interested in the woman?" Brancuso asked.

"Only that someone hired me to find her. He doesn't want to know any more than he needs to, and I don't volunteer any information either. I protect him and he protects me."

Rizzo stopped speaking when Rachel came through the door carrying the tray of four coffee mugs. She unloaded them onto the coffee table and left.

"Thanks, Rachel," Fields said before she closed the door. He then turned to Machado. "So that means we lose the kidnapping charge unless they're still holding her against her will."

"I don't believe they are, since she's back in their employ. My guess is they cut a deal with her. It's unusual, I mean, if she threatened to blow the whistle—and I'm not certain she did. They make people disappear for far less serious reasons than a threat of betrayal."

Machado turned to Rizzo. "Think you could get her away from the premises for an interview? Get a feel if she's there willingly or under duress?"

Rizzo raised the coffee mug to his mouth and took a sip. His eyes darted around the familiar surroundings of Jack Fields' office. He considered the question in light of Vinnie Alcamo's warning. "My source advised me I should let the matter go since

I've completed my obligation to my client. I know this guy for a long time. I'm sure he has my best interest at heart." He paused. A grin broke out as he scanned the three faces eyeballing him with perplexed expressions. "But when was the last time I paid attention to anyone's well-meaning advice?"

Laughter filled the room. When it subsided, Fields asked, "Can you set up a meeting someplace where she'd be free to talk?"

"It's a possibility. I have an idea how to make it happen. Give me a few days. My client might be the appropriate go-between. If we both end up dead, you'll know it didn't work."

"Ah, not happening," Fields said. "No client. He's not in the loop."

"Oh, of course. Sorry," Rizzo said, embarrassed he had to be reminded. "So you think Nicole Adams might be useful down the line?"

Machado nodded. "Yeah, that's why we need you to stay alive and involved."

Ralph Brancuso piped up. "And this time, I may not be there to save your ass like I did in San Juan."

"For which my wife and I are eternally grateful."

"Bob, if we find she'll cooperate," Fields asked, "can you construct a scheme that would enable us to nail down irrefutable proof of their money-laundering operation? Using her as access?"

Machado looked over at Rizzo. "That depends on what Luke finds in his interview with the woman. If she's ready to help, she could be useful. I'm sure we can devise something that makes sense. We'll be upfront with her about the danger involved. Maybe come up with a plan that would include Luke, you know, to mitigate her risk level."

"Whoa, slow down a minute," Rizzo said. "Right now, I'm simply a supplier of information on this. A conduit. If you want me to take an active role, it'll be on the usual contractual terms.

Ain't no way I'd go up against these Guidos without appropriate compensation."

"Go on," Brancuso said, smiling. "You're not afraid of these guys, are you?"

"You bet your sweet bippy, I am, Ralph. But I am crazy enough to take them on."

* * *

Rizzo stared at the lighted floor indicator, watching the numbers slowly flick by. He wondered if he should call Harry Fox with the news or wait until morning. *I'll do it later today,* he decided, as a hand took hold of his arm.

"Hey, buddy, you in a hurry?"

Rizzo turned to face Brancuso. "Not really, Ralph. Why?"

"Thought maybe you could stop by my office for a couple of minutes."

"Yeah, I got time. What's on your mind?"

"I'd like to talk more about this thing, about how we could use the Adams woman. Find a role for her that could provide the Bureau with the information we need."

"If you're considering something risky, like wearing a wire, forget it." The elevator door slid open and Rizzo stuck out his hand and laid it over the beam. "I don't think she's ready for anything that heavy."

"Why don't we take a few minutes and kick it around? I got a bottle of Johnny Walker Black in my desk drawer. We can sneak a taste while we chat."

Rizzo pulled back his hand to let the elevator door close. "I guess I can spare a few minutes. But, FYI, I don't drink."

"Oh, shit, I forgot. You're AA. Sorry. But will coffee do the trick?"

"Boy, you sure know how to sweet talk a girl. Let's go."

Rizzo followed the agent to his office. Seated opposite one another on the sofa, Brancuso again offered coffee.

"No thanks. I've reached my caffeine limit for today."

"Okay, then. Let's begin with an easy question. How well do you know the woman?"

"For God's sake, Ralph, I've never met her, spoken with her, nothing. She could be the incarnation of Lena the Hyena for all I know. Although from what my client tells me, she's a great piece of work. I mean, in her Playboy Bunny days."

"She's what, around fifty, fifty-five?"

"That'd be my guess."

"And she likes women?"

"Yep, that's the word."

"I'm trying to explore a bit about her, see if anything's there we can take advantage of—"

"Ralph, why don't you wait? At least until you meet her, before attempting to turn her into Mata Hari. We get her in, interview her and take her measure. Then we see if she's willing to cooperate, and in what way."

"Yeah, makes sense. It's . . . man, it's been bugging me, I mean. It'd be a damn shame to waste her valuable inside position."

"There's plenty of time for that."

His impatience reminded Rizzo of the first time he'd met the agent several years ago. Brancuso was the senior agent in charge of the Bureau's Albany office. He was brash, impatient, and ready to tear down walls to get things done. It was obvious to Rizzo he was the opposite of Jack Fields. Yet the two seemed to work together as a smooth team.

"You know, Ralph, I still owe you dinner for the rescue last year. We didn't get the chance before you flew off. Let's pick a date soon, you and the missus. Okay? You deserve a treat at The Palm."

"Woof, that's out of your pay grade, isn't it?"

"Hey, for you, nothing is off the table."

"Okay, bro. You got it."

Chapter Six

East River, Manhattan - Mon. A.M. 4/20

Rizzo watched the cable car of the Roosevelt Island Tram as it leaped from the station-berth on the Manhattan side to begin its journey across the river. Ahead, Rizzo could see the east-rising morning sun. Its rays bounced off the structural steel of the Edward I. Koch Queensboro Bridge, which paralleled the tram's cable lines.

Rizzo leaned his back against the railing that bordered the East River walkway while he delivered the news of Nicole Adams. Harry Fox, bent at the waist, rested his forearms on the railing and listened without comment.

Her mysterious re-emerging after an absence of two weeks had caught him short of breath. Fox became riveted by the story Rizzo related, about how Nicole Adams's life got embroiled with the *Mafia*. He listened with bug-eyed amazement as Rizzo described the circumstances in which Roy Dickerson hired Nicole for the company's original sports bar in Brooklyn, of her rise to a manager, and her eventual responsibility as general manager for the five-bar chain.

With reluctance, Rizzo fed him the details of the problematic attention she inherited from Pete Barone. His mouth went agape when he learned of the familial relationship of Barone with the underboss of the crime family. Rizzo neglected to mention the money-laundering operation and why the mob kidnapped Nicole. Harry, should they ever question him, needed plausible deniability. Rizzo invented a lie: Nicole made a threat to call Barone's wife and reveal what he was trying to do with her. The threat explained why she landed on the mob's shit list. Fox accepted it all without question.

Fox's sixty-eight-year-old eyes filled with excitement when he turned his head to gaze up at his messenger of good news. "You think it'll be all right we go there, to where she works?" he asked. "I mean, I wouldn't want to cause trouble if my sudden appearance became awkward for her." A gusty wind cruising downriver caught the brim of his battered felt hat. A quick hand saved it from a watery grave.

"Good catch," Rizzo said with a note of amusement.

"My, this is a windy spot."

Rizzo gave a furtive look around. He'd selected this location on many past occasions for backstairs meetings. Out in the open and impossible to eavesdrop, it was also scenic.

"Yeah, I'm thinking we should keep our visit to The Dugout casual. Not long and not too animated. No hugs and kisses. We'll stay for one drink. Then we leave like we just popped by on the way to somewhere else. We can't look like we suspect anything nefarious about her disappearance. They might be watching her."

Desperation appeared on his face. "We'll see her after that, won't we?"

"Certainly. I'll slip her my card before we leave the bar. Tell her to call my cell. I need to set up a private meeting with her anyway. Not in my office, but somewhere outside the New York metro area. Get the actual story. Find out if she's in any danger."

"Goodness, I feel like a character out of a John le Carré spy novel. Oh, the thug who threw me to the ground outside D'Agostino's? He knows what I look like. Am I in any danger?"

Rizzo had forgotten about that. Nicole's return now minimized the likelihood of Fox facing that risk. He represented no threat to the mob.

"Not unless you're someplace where he shows up. Then don't stick out your tongue at him. Besides, he was the limo driver, a low-level functionary," Rizzo said, trying to allay the man's worry.

Fox turned and took a couple of steps back when he saw the rising cable car out over the river. He pointed to it like a child spotting the Snoopy balloon at the Macy's parade. "Oh, my. I didn't know—"

Rizzo's hand shot out and pulled Fox back. Two teenage skateboarders coming from the north on the cement path careened in their direction, zigzagging left and right in polished skateboarder form. The kids would have taken out Fox if Rizzo's alert reaction hadn't averted a near-certain collision.

"Good lord," Fox said. "Do you think it was intentional?"

"Uh-uh. Couple of reckless kids, that's all."

Rizzo's stomach grumbled, reminding him he hadn't had breakfast. He'd left the house early, giving Flo reason to complain, "It's a Saturday, for Pete's sake. Will you be gone long?"

"Don't hold breakfast for me. I don't know how long I'm gonna be," and out the door he went.

Fox smoothed the ruffled arm of his sports jacket as Rizzo asked, "Did you have breakfast?"

"Only coffee."

"Let's walk. We'll head up to a neat little breakfast spot I know at Third and Sixtieth. They do fantastic omelets and poached eggs like no other place in the city. If blueberry scones are on the menu, order one. It'll knock your socks off. My treat."

The two men traveled west in silence. They covered the four avenue blocks at a fast clip before making the turn north. At the northeast corner of Sixtieth Street, they entered the Sunrise Café. The hostess seated them at a two-top against one wall. A nymphet in tight jeans and an orange scoop-top T-shirt, barely containing her small breasts, approached their table with an order pad. Rizzo sat back and watched Fox's eyes widen.

"Get you guys coffee while you decide what you want?" Her voice was Valley-Girl-Central, except this was the Big Apple.

Rizzo looked at Ms. VGC and nodded. "Black for me. Harry?"

"Same," he said, picking up the menu she'd placed in front of him.

Fox studied the list of breakfast options while Rizzo stared at him with wonder. How does a man so obviously conservative become rocket-speed enamored with a Bunny on first meeting at the Playboy Club? For certain, his reaction to their server, Ms. VGC, signaled the old guy hadn't lost his appreciation for sexy-dressed women. Was it that, or did his plummeting into the depths of sudden love signal something else?

"Harry, I'm curious. What was it about Nicole that made you fall into that romantic abyss? I mean, love at first sight is okay with romance novels. You're more the practical type. I wouldn't have guessed you'd be that flighty."

Fox set down the menu. His eyes rolled like someone remembering a titillating memory. A smile formed and Rizzo knew he had ignited a long-held, thirty-five-year-old feeling.

"I remember," he began, "my stupid taxi driver made me late for my lunch meeting. The cabbie annoyed me so much that when I sat down at the table, I didn't notice our assigned Bunny standing there. I pulled out a cigarette from the near-empty pack in my pocket and reached for my Zippo."

Rizzo recalled the confused and disoriented Harry Fox in his office that first morning. He could picture him as a young man in the same state of mind at the Playboy Club.

Before Fox could continue the tale, Ms. VGC returned. "Ready to order?"

"Give us a few more minutes," Rizzo told her. "His story is just heating up."

Ms. VGC's puzzled look lasted several seconds. "Oh, okay. No hurry," and walked away.

"Go on," Rizzo urged.

"Well, then I heard, 'Hi, I'm your Bunny Nicole.' I looked up, and she came into focus. She leaned toward me, and two pools of dark hazel eyes reflected my stunned image as she held a Bic lighter under my cigarette. Instead of drawing in, I stared. The Marlboro dangled between my lips. My throat constricted, and that was it. I'm embarrassed to say, that's all it took."

"A goner," Rizzo said with a smile. "You were smitten."

"You could say that. Something happened. What, I don't know. The skimpy Bunny costume played no role in my reaction. Had she been wearing a flannel shirt and combat boots, the effect would have been the same."

"And you returned later to wait for her to get off work? You didn't know if she'd brush you off, call the cops, or fall into your arms. A very romantic story."

"But not a romantic ending, I'd say."

Rizzo caught the nymphet eyeing them. He turned back to Fox. "Let's order before our server loses patience."

Fox chose the omelet and Rizzo the poached eggs. By sheer good timing, they found the blueberry scones on the menu. Harry was delighted.

"Told you," Rizzo said.

Back out on the street, Fox decided to walk up Third to his apartment. "Thanks for breakfast," he said and wandered north.

Rizzo flagged an approaching taxi and headed back to his office. While he rode south, he reconsidered the possibility of the danger Harry Fox might face if the mob had learned his identity. Fox witnessed the kidnapping in front of D'Agostino's. Would the mob care? Rizzo thought not. Then again, if they did, they might attempt to silence him. It was all conjecture, but he had to be prepared. Keeping Harry Fox safe became his priority.

* * *

West Hampton Beach, Long Island - Mon. A.M. 4/20

Waves rumbled on shore with the consistency and monotony of a metronome. Roy Dickerson liked to sit on the deck watching them crash, the white curling water rolling up the sand toward the house. Often, as an exercise, he would time each wave from when it crested and broke to the moment the next set of tumblers reached the same point. Their consistent tempo amused him. It was much like his daily routine. Of course, this wave-tumbling exercise was only possible at a time of day when the incoming tide was at its peak, like now.

Roy had finished a light breakfast and carried his coffee mug and a book onto the deck. The local radio station's forecast spoke of a cooler front, accompanied by light rain, to start around eleven o'clock. The conditions would force him to remain inside most of the day.

He'd pulled the novel from his brother's well-stocked bookcase. It surprised him that Keith, an NYPD Joint Robbery Task Force lieutenant, would be interested in reading Joe Wambaugh's police procedural thrillers. At least a dozen of the author's books lined the top shelf. All appeared to have been time-worn and reader-fingered.

His brother and his wife had parted ways a year ago, and their collegial separation agreement granted Keith the West Hampton beach house. She hated coming out to Long Island on the weekends and always complained about feeling isolated. It pressed on her. The nearest neighbor's house was a hundred yards up the shoreline next to the footpath slicing through the shrub from the road. "Go introduce yourself," he'd urged, but she never took the time in the four years they'd owned the house.

Keith had insisted his brother keep a low profile after learning of the circumstances under which Roy left the sports bar partnership. The West Hampton house was the safest place he could think of. He left his spare service weapon, a 9mm Sig Sauer, in the drawer of the bedroom night table for added protection.

Roy dropped the book onto the chaise lounge and set his coffee mug on the deck to one side. He reached to adjust the chair's back to a three-quarters slanted position when he heard the landline phone ringing. He turned and dashed into the house. No one, other than his brother, knew of his occupancy. The few exceptions were the town tradespeople he dealt with when he ordered deliveries purchased over the phone. He expected to hear his brother's voice when he picked up.

"Keith, what's going on?"

No one spoke. A faulty connection? Hang up, he'll redial. Before Roy could replace the receiver, he heard a scratchy voice say, "Wrong number," followed by a click and a dial tone.

Roy shrugged and went outside. He picked up the Wambaugh novel and adjusted the chair's back position. After lowering himself onto the chaise, he stretched out and opened the novel to the page he'd bookmarked.

* * *

"We sure he's here, I mean, at the house?" Angie asked for the second time. He removed his Mets baseball cap and wiped the perspiration coating his brow with his sleeve.

Mario could see the fat man's beige lanai shirt soaked with perspiration. His foul mood was getting nastier the longer they trekked over the soft, hot sand. The shirt hung over a pair of

Levi denim jeans, the wrong beachwear, Mario had warned. Angie bitched about the 9mm Beretta inside his waistband, jabbing at his ribs with each step. It was killing him. Every fifty yards, the toe of one of his sandals would catch in the sand, causing him to stumble.

"Leave the fuckin' things off. Carry them and walk barefoot." Mario said, raising his boat shoes in the air. "Like me, dummy."

Mario wore a lightweight linen Guayabera shirt reaching the knees of his khaki trousers. The shirt covered the Glock he carried in the belly holster strapped around his hips.

Angie continued bitching. "After this, the prick better be at the house when we get there."

Mario glanced back over his shoulder and shot an impatient glare at the sweaty man. "Hey, The Hat said he had a couple of locals stake out the place. Said the guy is always home. Never goes no place. Besides, he answered the phone, didn't he? It was the house phone, not a cell number."

"So why the hell did Fusco give us this job? He coulda used one of those locals when they were here at the house checkin' it out."

Mario dug his heels into the sand and came to a stop. He turned and threw up his arms. "*A fa nabila.* Hey Angie, you made ya bones last year. Ain't that right? Now you wanna question the *capo*'s decision like you were a Carmine D'Angelo?"

"Yeah, well—"

"C'mon, fuhgeddaboudit. Let's get this done and get outta here. We ain't had no breakfast and I'm hungry." Mario turned and trudged forward. Angie followed.

* * *

Roy turned the page of the novel and his vision carried over the top of the book. His eyes came to rest on two figures off in the distance, making their way along the beach in his direction. He lowered the book and stared. This was a weekday morning, he remembered, normally void of beachgoers. Not like the weekends.

The next moment, he swung his feet to the deck and fast-stepped into the house. He locked the glass sliders and closed the vertical blinds to block anyone from seeing in. He switched off the lights in the living room and moved to a corner of the slider doors. After several minutes, when he thought the walkers had enough time to reach the front of the house, Roy edged one of the plastic slats to the side. He peeked out. Two men, shuffling through the sand at the water's edge, came into view. They stopped for a moment and then continued.

Five minutes later, he peeked again. No sign of the men. A harmless pair, he told himself, out for their morning exercise. God, how he hated living like this: looking over his shoulder and flinching with every sudden movement, every loud sound. The tension grated on his nerves. He remembered Keith's service weapon. The bedroom night table. He considered retrieving it, then peeked a third time through the slats and saw no one. They've moved on, he decided. Dickerson went into the kitchen at the rear of the house and peered through the window over the sink. He saw dunes and scrubs. No boogie men.

The coffee carafe on the counter was still hot. He grabbed another mug from the cabinet and filled it, certain the coffee he left on the deck was ice cold. Out on the deck again, he gazed up and down the beach. He failed to see anyone. Once he settled on the chaise lounge, he picked up the novel and resumed his quiet morning of reading.

* * *

A hundred yards past the house, Mario had halted their sandy march, making note of the tide on its way out. He signaled to Angie to follow as he turned right and headed between a bank of dunes. The drifting sand at this point had built a series of high mounds, making it easy for them to hide and not be seen from the beach.

Mario dropped to his knees. Angie joined him, wearing a puzzled expression.

"Wadda we doing here?" Angie asked.

"Restin'. What else?"

Angie leaned back on his heels, wheezing. He removed his cap and used it to wipe the sweat from his brow. Mario watched and shook his head. His partner, besides being overweight, was also out of shape. Mario thought about the bodybuilding program he'd benefited from during those six years he'd spent upstate in Sing Sing serving a B-felony conviction.

"The guy went in the house before we got there. I saw him," Angie said. "Maybe we spooked him?"

"Probably had to take a piss."

"What if he doesn't come back out?"

"He makes it harder for us 'cause then we'll have to break in."

Two noisy gulls swooped down and perched on an adjacent dune. Mario looked over. He could feel a soft breeze kiss his face, drying the paint of sweat across his brow. The last year in Iraq before he got busted formed in his mind. He twisted around, taking in the yards of scrub and tall reeds filling the gaps between mounds of sand. The terrain appeared the same across the hundred-yard distance back to the rear of the house. We'll use that route. It'll give us good cover.

"You ready?" Mario asked.

Angie tried to light a cigarette with little success. "Yeah. This damn wind keeps blowin' out the match, anyway." He tossed the unlit cigarette into the sand and stood.

"This way. Stay low."

The two zigzagged between the scrub and mounds until they reached the back of the beach house. Mario whispered to Angie to go around to the other side. "Move up to the front corner. Wait there. If he's on the deck, don't move. I'll go out first."

Angie disappeared and Mario trudged forward. The Glock in his hand hung at his side as he peered around the building edge. He saw a figure stretched out on the chaise lounge. Mario raised the gun to his shoulder and stepped ahead. With his free hand, he grabbed the low wooden deck rail, swung himself up and over it, and landed in front of the stunned man.

"Roy Dickerson?" Mario asked quietly like he wanted to be sure he had the correct victim.

Roy bounced upright and attempted to stand. "What the hell's—"

"Don't move," Mario ordered, leveling the Glock at him.

It was Angie's leap onto the deck from the other side that turned Roy's face sheet-white with fear. His eyes widened and his body went rigid, frozen to the seat of the chaise.

Angie raised the Beretta as he slipped onto the deck. He stood behind his target and slapped the top of his head. "Try somethin', ya gonna be dead," as if the man needed another warning. For several seconds, the breaking waves out on the water created the only sound.

"Dear God," Roy said with a cry in his voice. "I never said anything to anyone. I mean, this is wrong, I'm telling you. Please, please, gimme a chance to prove—"

Mario stepped to one side and nodded. Before Roy could finish the sentence, two bullets entered the back of his head.

"Goddamn," Angie yelled as he jumped back, knocking off his Mets ball cap. "Ah, shit!" The second bullet had torn off the top of Roy's head and white matter splattered in the air, causing Angie to duck away.

Mario snickered. This was Angie's second whack job, and he didn't know what to expect with a kill shot to the skull.

"Quick, grab him under his arms. I'll take the feet. Let's get him into the water. The tide's going out. We sink him now, he'll disappear with the tide."

"Shit, we'll get wet," Angie whined.

"So take off your sandals."
"Yeah, but how 'bout my jeans?"
"Fuck your jeans. Roll 'em up. C'mon asshole, grab his arms."

Chapter Seven

Jamaica Avenue, Queens - Tues. P.M. 4/21

It was early enough when they arrived at The Dugout to find two adjacent vacant stools at the bar. The noise level was low enough so the bartender could hear their order without shouting.

"A Virgin Mary," Rizzo told him. "Lose the celery." Harry Fox selected a white wine.

The barman set the drinks in front of them and remained standing, staring at Rizzo. "Run a tab?"

"No, no," Rizzo answered, pulling two tens from his pocket. "Sorry. My mind was somewhere else. We're making a short stop, that's all."

The bartender picked up the bills and walked to a nearby computer register. He returned with four singles and a few coins. Before he could place the money on the bar, Rizzo's hand shot up. "No. That's yours, thanks."

"Thank you," he replied.

Rizzo glanced around. Two of the TV monitors embedded in the fascia above the bar showed two NHL hockey teams about to face-off. The remaining sets aired either a studio roundup of last night's baseball games or a replay of today's featured race from Aqueduct.

Fox leaned over and whispered, "You think she's here?"

"Well, I called a friend who spoke with someone who would know. He said she was scheduled to come in around five."

Fox looked at his watch. "It's seven-thirty now."

Rizzo nodded. His eyes roamed the restaurant to the various dining tables and booths. The bartender had taken a position over a nearby sink, washing beer glasses. Rizzo caught him looking over a few times between rinses.

He turned on the stool and continued his search for Nicole Adams. An alcove appeared to the right of the kitchen order station at the rear. He could see a door on one wall. After a few seconds, a male customer exited. Men's room. The ladies' room is gonna be in the same area. The manager's office—probably there, too.

"You looking for someone?"

Rizzo spun around. The bartender had returned and stood facing him. "No. The men's room, but I found it. Excuse me, Harry," he said and slid down from the stool. "Gotta tap a kidney."

He entered the restroom, washed his hands at the sink for several minutes, and re-emerged to discover a female standing at the computer located to one side of the rear order station. Her dressy attire said the manager.

Rizzo approached the woman. "Excuse me, miss."

She turned her head without moving away from the computer.

"Are you the manager?"

"Yes," she said, smiling. "Is there something I can help you with?"

"Well, I'm sitting at the bar with someone who knows you. He'd like to say hello when you have a moment. No, no, don't look over. Stay cool."

Her head snapped back, and she turned to face Rizzo. In a voice laced with suspicion, she asked, "What's this about?"

"Harry Fox."

"What?"

"He's sitting at the bar. He insisted on coming here to prove you were okay. You know what I mean. He wanted to see for himself."

Nicole Adams remained frozen, her eyes on Rizzo, her steady expression filled with uncertainty "Uh, I don't think that's such a great idea right now. Being seen with him, that is."

"I'm sure you're right."

"And who are you?" she asked, attempting to keep up a casual appearance. With wait staff buzzing about, her apparent discomfort said she needed to cut short their conversation.

"Harry hired me to find you," he said, keeping his tone cordial. "I'm glad to meet you, to see you're okay." Rizzo extended his hand, and she took it. "Call me for a private meeting, soon," he said, smiling. "Okay? I need to talk with you."

Nicole released his hand, palming the business card he'd slipped her. She cast her eyes at it and nodded.

Rizzo returned to the bar and climbed back on the stool. He picked up his drink and took a sip.

"Is she coming over?" Fox asked, failing to hide his excitement.

"Uh-uh. Not a good time." He bent his head toward Fox and spoke in a soft voice. "I gave her my card. She'll call me."

"You that pal of Vinnie's?"

Rizzo's head shot up. The bartender again. His grin made Rizzo think he was about to tell him he forgot to zip up his fly.

"Vinnie who?"

"Vinnie Alcamo. He was in the other night. Said he was looking to do a favor for a friend. You're the friend, I'm guessing."

Rizzo stayed silent, deciding if he should own up. Finally, after realizing the man was Vinnie's contact, he said, "And if I am?"

"Hey, no worry. I'm Dominic Biondo. A very good friend of Vinnie's." He emphasized the words, very good. Dom winked and reached across to shake Rizzo's hand. "Sorry about buttin' in. I knew right away it was you."

"How's that?"

"You're an ex-cop, right? Cops—or even ex-cops—are always easy to spot. You get what you came for? If not, maybe I can help."

"You did already. We came in for drinks. You served them."

Dom grinned. "Okay, I get it. But I'm here six nights a week. If you run into a problem, you know, maybe I can help. I'm here."

"Thanks. I appreciate the offer, Dom."

"Hey, my pleasure," and he made his way toward the end of the bar.

"What was that about?" Fox wanted to know.

"Finish your wine and let's get out of here."

* * *

Chelsea Area, Manhattan - Thurs. AM. 04/23

Rizzo picked up the phone on the first ring and pushed the letter he was reading to one side. "Lucas Rizzo, Investigations." He always answered the office's landline that way on. On his cell phone, it was "Rizzo."

There was a moment of dead air until a voice on the other end said, "Mr. Rizzo, this is Keith Dickerson, Roy's brother. If you're not busy, can I talk to you? In-person, I mean."

"Sure. When's a good time?"

"Right now, if it's convenient. I'm downstairs in the lobby."

"C'mon up. Fourth floor. It's a right off the elevator. Don't bother to knock."

Rizzo remembered Roy Dickerson had mentioned his brother was a lieutenant with the NYPD Joint Robbery Task Force. The unexpected visit launched Rizzo's red flag. He wondered if Roy had told the brother about the shady activities of his past partnership. If so, why would that bring him to his office?

The door swung open and a man in his late fifties stepped through. Rizzo noticed he was not in a suit, the signature of NYPD detectives on duty. Casually dressed, Dickerson wore an open-collar sport shirt under a light blue sweater, khakis, and loafers. His hair was silver-streaked, and age lines appeared below his eyes. His girth revealed a mid-life full of unchecked food intake and a lack of exercise, all signs of a law officer on the south side of a long career.

Rizzo stood, his hand outstretched, and greeted his visitor. He gestured to a chair to one side of his desk. "Have a seat, Detective. What's on your mind?" he said with a broad, welcoming smile.

Dickerson lowered himself into the chair and squeezed his body around. His face took on a grim expression. "He told me about your search for the woman he worked with."

"Yeah. He's been helpful, much as he can."

"I gather by the upbeat tone of that comment you're in the dark about what's happened."

Rizzo tilted back and laced his fingers against his chest. "I guess I am until you tell me." He waited.

"They murdered Roy," Dickerson said with a hiccup in his voice.

Rizzo's desk chair snapped forward. "Oh, good God!"

"Two bullets to the back of the head. The second one took off the top of his skull." When Dickerson finished the sentence, his eyelids closed, and tears streamed down his cheeks. "They found his body washed up on a beach in the Great South Bay."

"When?"

"Earlier this week. Tuesday. It must have been Monday when they killed him. He'd been staying at my beach house for the past few weeks—West Hampton on the south shore." Dickerson pulled a handkerchief from his pocket and blew his nose.

"Out there alone?"

"Yeah. The closest neighbor, a house about a hundred yards up the beach."

"Anyone report seeing anything, hearing shots fired?"

"The neighbors. Two men, according to what they told the Suffolk County police when they first arrived. Their vague description wasn't helpful."

Rizzo made a face. Suffolk County's reputation for being inefficient was notorious. Their history proved to be especially uncooperative with any NYPD investigation that spilled into their jurisdiction.

Dickerson looked at Rizzo. "He was uptight when he left the bar business. Afraid he'd pissed off his partner and he might try to seek revenge. I thought if he spent time alone at the beach, it would help him wind down and keep him safe. This is not what I imagined would happen. Had to be the mob, you think?"

"Sounds like a gangland-style slaying."

"But why? Why would the mob take him out that way?"

"Your brother became a threat to them. I warned him the day he came to see me. He never told you about the money-laundering operation the Gambino family ran through the sports bars?"

Dickerson's eyes jumped. "The Gambinos? Holy crap! No. He said his partner, Pete Barone, was dealing in some illegal shit. That's why he wanted to get out. I had no idea what was involved. And he never once mentioned the Gambino family. Had I known, I'd have dragged his ass out of the place."

The room fell silent, each man steeped in his thoughts. Rizzo was certain Dickerson was consumed with regret that he couldn't protect his younger brother. Rizzo's thoughts went to the meeting he had with Fields and Machado the other day. The case was getting stickier with the passing hours: a kidnapping, then a felony money-laundering scheme, and now a mob rubout. He wondered if Machado and the NYPD's Organized Crime Unit had gotten word of the killing. He could see it raising their interest in the sports-bar operation to a new level.

"I'd hoped you had more information about Barone's illegal dealings," Dickerson said. "Roy shared nothing with me. But tell me why he became a threat to the mob? Did he play a role in it?"

"No, that's not it. He learned of the money-laundering operation from Barone. Roy saw him take a meeting in his office with a Gambino family underboss, Carmine D'Angelo. He's Barone's uncle. Your brother pressed Barone for an explanation. He got it and paid for it, I'm afraid."

Rizzo related the tale of Roy's relationship with Nicole Adams. He explained about his hiring her, and why he stupidly revealed to her the mob family's involvement.

"Your brother tried to convince her to get the hell out. Instead, she used the info as a weapon to stop the sexual harassment from Barone. Barone fingered Roy as the betrayer. After he told his uncle, it was certain they would punish Roy."

Rizzo told him nothing of Nicole's kidnapping. It was more information than Fields would want him to let out.

"One question. How come they haven't taken out the woman too? Or is that still to come?"

"It remains a mystery. I'm trying to get a meeting with her, see if she's in any danger. One thing's for sure, NYPD's Organized Crime Unit is on to the family. It's a matter of time before they shut them down. Then bust them under the RICO Act for the money-laundering and Roy's murder."

"The bastards!"

"I'm sorry about Roy. Your brother was a good guy. He tried to do right by Nicole Adams, warning her to get out with him. She didn't use her head. Let's hope it doesn't cost her hers."

* * *

Chelsea Area, Manhattan – Thurs. P.M. 4/23

Angelo's, at the north end of Madison Square Park on Broadway, was Jack Fields' favorite luncheon place—Italian and overpriced. Rizzo never minded because the agent always picked up the tab. Fields, already seated when Rizzo arrived, greeted him with a level of sarcasm the man seemed to enjoy.

"Glad you found room in your busy schedule to come slumming with the Feds."

"Jack, you call—I find room. Especially when the Bureau's paying. We gonna talk business here or wait until we get back to your office?"

Fields scanned the small restaurant. It was early in the lunch hour. Diners occupied only five other tables. "We can do it here if you like. We're far enough away from the madding crowd not to be overheard."

"Aha! You've been reading Thomas Hardy. I'm impressed."

Fields chortled. "You're impressed? I'm amazed you know the source of the line."

"Hey, Mr. Ivy League. I read a book now and then."

"Boston U, thanks. And I'm happy I don't have to explain my occasional erudite references."

It occurred to Rizzo how far his relationship with the FBI agent had traveled, both personally and professionally. He flashed to their initial collaboration several years ago forestalling an ex-Stasi's assassination attempt. It was an adventure ending with hard feelings. Ultimately, their connection survived when Rizzo assisted the Feds to bring down a sex slave and drug-trafficking operation the year before.

Fields and the Feds were willing to include him again. The action and the occasional brush with danger was a jolt of adrenaline he needed—a break from his routine investigation business. Of course, getting double his daily rate was not a discouragement.

Fields, attired in the FBI's standard white shirt and blue conservative suit, looked relaxed, his all-business attitude set aside. Lately, in Rizzo's company, the agent had found it easy to laugh at himself.

The server arrived with two tri-fold menus. "Would you like to start with a beverage?"

"Just coffee," Fields said.

"Echo that," Rizzo said, and the man hurried off.

"Oh, I heard from Bob Machado about Roy Dickerson's murder. Damn shame. You think it was expected?"

"Well, yeah. I knew he was in deep shit after he told me he'd let on to the Adams woman the nature of the family's involvement. I warned him."

The server returned with their coffees and took their orders. Fields chose a small *Trecolre Salad* and a bowl of *Pasta e Fagioli*. Rizzo selected a cup of lentil soup and a Penne Pasta with eggplant, tomato sauce, basil, and shaved ricotta cheese.

Fields smiled. "Nice to see you're not obsessing over your weight."

Rizzo looked up, surprised. "Why? Should I be?"

"I'm jerking your chain. No. You look fit. You work out?"

"Not in a long while. The only workout I get involved with is at the range with my weapons. I must have a self-sustaining metabolism. My weight never changes."

"Lucky you."

Their lunches arrived, and they ate with a minimum of talking. When they finished and the server had cleared the table, Fields asked, "Have you arranged an interview with Nicole Adams yet?"

"I took Harry Fox to the bar in Queens, thinking maybe I'd catch her there. I did. But she became skittish when I told her why we were there. I guess bringing him was a mistake. But I introduced myself. Explained that Harry hired me to find her."

"Did you mention to her about Dickerson's murder?"

"No. I didn't know about it then. Not until this morning when his brother, Keith, came to my office to deliver the sad news. He's a detective with the NYPD Joint Robbery Task Force."

"I wasn't aware he had a brother. You tell him why Dickerson got himself killed, knowing about how the mob was using the sports bars?"

"Yeah. He was knocked out when I mentioned it was a Gambino operation. He had no idea. I figured he knew, and that's why he hid him at the beach house—like they wouldn't find him there. He suspected the bars were involved in something shady, but Roy never said it was a Gambino money-laundering operation. If he had, Dickerson would have done a better job at protecting his brother. Poor decision, the beach house."

"I should think he'll try to shake things up with the Suffolk County homicide investigation."

"That would be an uphill battle. The Suffolk County boys are notorious for not cooperating with the NYPD. He'd have a better chance taking on the investigation himself."

Fields shrugged. "How about the Adams woman? Will she agree to a meeting?"

"I slipped her my card. Told her to call me soon. When I hear, I'll set up a meeting, somewhere remote, between the two of us. I feel she'll cooperate, especially after I tell her about Roy."

"Were they lovers?"

"Not even close. She's gay. I thought you knew. It was something else. Yeah, there was an ocean separating them sexually, but I sensed they shared a tight, protective relationship going back a lotta years."

The server arrived and laid the check next to Fields. "No hurry," he said. "Whenever you're ready."

Rizzo noticed where he'd placed the check and smiled. "This guy knows how it works."

Fields reached inside his jacket pocket and pulled out his wallet. "How do they connect?" he asked as he placed his credit card on top of the check.

"Thirty years ago, both worked for Hugh Hefner, she as a Playboy Bunny at the club in Manhattan, Roy as the promotion manager of *Playboy Magazine*. He knew of her sexual proclivity back then. They became friends. She was a beauty. He'd used her in a few photo shoots for the magazine. My client, Harry Fox, was at the club for a business lunch with Roy. Nicole was their Bunny and Harry went ape over her. That's how the three connect."

Fields leaned back and smiled.

"What's funny?"

"You sure fall into the weirdest cases. They always seem to involve madmen. If it isn't an IRA fanatic, it's an ex-Stasi lunatic. Or a Russian FSB deserter. Now you have the Guidos from the New York mob to contend with."

Rizzo pushed his hands out, palms up, and broke into a grin. "Hey! What can I tell you? Ridding the world of its slimy underbelly is my life."

They stood and shook hands. The agent's face became serious. "You've taken a few chances in the past, my friend. You've been lucky so far. Let's hope your streak continues. Call me after you've interviewed the woman."

Chapter Eight

The Staten Island Ferry - Sun. A.M. 4/26

Rizzo arrived at the Whitehall Terminal at six-fifteen and picked up a coffee at the concession stand. Nicole would meet him aboard the ferry at six-thirty. He secured a bench on the main deck, starboard side, against the window, and waited.

The main deck was the least crowded, and at this early hour of the morning, he didn't expect tourists would pack the outside railings to take their photos. Those handfuls of Staten Islanders returning home from their overnight shifts in Manhattan were savvy enough to avoid the upper deck.

The forecast was for rain. It was foggy, and the low-hanging clouds appeared eager to release their moisture .

Rizzo checked the time. With one minute to go before they closed the gate, Nicole came up the ramp and climbed the stairs to the main level. Rizzo spotted her at the top of the landing and waved. Dressed not for work but her day off, she had on a pair of jeans, a tunic sweater that reached below her waist, and a pair of soft loafers. She wore no makeup and carried a light jacket. The image was of a woman in her early fifties still in possession of her youthful beauty.

"Boy, you cut it close. They closed boarding right behind you."

She grinned and sat next to him. "That was intentional. I'm being watched. Happens on my day off. I didn't want anyone following me when I came aboard."

"Smart move. Someone from the restaurant or one of Fusco's monkeys?"

"I don't know. They're never close enough to get a good look. I'm familiar with most of our employees."

Rizzo gazed around. "Let's go outside. At this hour, it shouldn't be crowded. And we'll limit the chances of anyone overhearing us out there." They exited and found an empty bench against the exterior wall, facing out to the water. "The trip takes thirty minutes. We'll have to get off on the other side for a short while before we can re-board for the return trip."

The ferry motored by the Statue of Liberty, her form silhouetted against the dim morning light as they headed out into the harbor.

"If it gets too cold or too breezy, we can go back in. There's rain in the forecast too."

"It'll be all right," she said, poking at the jacket on her lap. "I apologize for brushing you off so rudely the other day in the bar."

"No apology necessary. I understand. Since they're keeping you under watch, you're not exactly a free woman."

Nicole rolled her eyes. "Not exactly."

"Listen, I should tell you everything. Let me fill you in. To begin, Harry came to me after they rushed you off in the limo. He wanted me to find you . . . rescue you, he said."

"That's funny, because when we first met, he referred to himself as my Lochinvar. Harry's still the romantic."

"Well, seems my effort was all for naught. You turned up on your own. What the hell happened?"

"I'm not sure whose idea it was. They viewed me as essential to Time-Out Enterprises. They decided not to kill me. At least, not right now."

Rizzo flinched.

"With Roy gone, they needed me to manage the bars. Pete Barone is all but useless. They offered me a deal. If I stayed silent about the money-laundering part, they'd let me come back to the company as a principal, bump me up to a hundred thousand, and I would keep my accrued retirement plan. Like they say, it was a deal I couldn't refuse."

"Wow! Of course. Yeah, well, I didn't know about that. I continued my efforts to rescue you. I found Roy through *Playboy Magazine*. He described everything that went down between you and Peter Barone. I warned him then. I mean, telling you about how the *Mafia* was using the sports bars, it was—" Rizzo stopped when he realized he was about to employ the worn-out cliché, *the kiss of death*. He remembered she hadn't yet learned of Roy's murder.

"I feel terrible about it . . . what I did."

Rizzo lowered his head. "Nicole, I know you regret it. And that's why it's difficult for me to tell you what happened to Roy."

Nicole froze. Her eyes locked on Rizzo's face, fearful of expecting something she didn't want to hear.

"Barone made the connection. He was sure it was Roy who gave you the information. The mob handled it the way they always do when someone betrays them."

"Oh, no!"

"Roy's brother, Keith, tried to hide him. He sent him out to his West Hampton beach house, thinking he'd be safe there. You don't hide from these guys for long. They found him and—" Rizzo didn't finish.

Her body stiffened, then shook. Tears flooded her cheeks. Rizzo stretched his arm around her and eased her against his shoulder. She sobbed with uncontrolled shakes. "You gotta hold it together, Nicole. There's a lot more I need to say."

After a few minutes, she regained control. Rizzo offered her a handkerchief, but she pulled a tissue from her jacket pocket instead. They were halfway across the harbor, and Lady Liberty had shrunk in size. The sobbing eased, and she sat up and leaned back on the bench.

"My God! How does one live with something like this? If I hadn't—"

"Hey, stop. That's not gonna change anything. You did what you had to do to get Barone off your back. Believe me, Roy understood that. He said so," Rizzo lied.

She stared off across the harbor to the shoreline of New Jersey, just visible in the morning mist.

"Nicole, the Gambino family have been a major target of the NYPD Organized Crime Unit and the FBI for a long time. They're looking to put a crimp in this family's operation. They need something substantial to get them on. Washing dirty money through the sports bars is a federal crime, one they can use under the RICO Act to bust them."

The morning light grew stronger as the fog lifted. Her intense concentration remained directed out over the water. He could see the definition of Staten Island slowly coming into focus. They had ten minutes left before they reached the ferry port.

"Nicole? Did you hear what I said?"

She turned back to him. "I heard you, Luke. I was thinking about something I could do, I mean, if I were brave enough to do it."

"If you're considering going public, forget it." Her expression told him he'd guessed right. "They would whack you within a nanosecond. I have a better idea if you're open to hearing it."

She raised her head and looked him in the eyes. "What's involved?"

"Move closer. Let's talk."

* * *

Chelsea Area, Manhattan - Sun. A.M. 04/26

"Sorry Jack, about calling you at home," Rizzo said, "but I thought you'd want to know right away."

"You met with her already?"

"Yeah, I got back minutes ago," Rizzo said. "I'm in the office right now."

"Where'd you meet?"

"We caught the six-thirty ferry to Staten Island this morning. I wasn't aware, but on her day off, she picks up a tail everywhere she goes. She's a smart woman, though. She hung around the ferry dock until there was only a minute to go and aced out whoever was following her. He never made the boarding."

"Good move," Fields said. "Did he spot you?"

"No, I was already on board, tucked in a corner of the main deck. And she says she's willing to work with us."

"That's good news, but about her being tailed, that's bad. Gonna make it difficult to set up a meeting."

"I got a couple of ideas. You wanna hear them?"

"Shoot."

"We set it up out of town far from the madding crowd."

"Rizzo, you're too much. What do you have in mind?"

"I could drive her upstate, you know, to Saugerties in Ulster County. Remember the lieutenant, Tom Lange, who worked with us on the case involving the ex-Stasi lunatic? We could use his police station. At three or four in the morning, not many bodies around to bother us."

"That's a long drive. As I recall, it took us two hours. What else?"

"How 'bout the Seahorse Boat-tel out in Bay Shore? I'm sure Jackson Bell would find rooms for us until you got there. The drive out takes half the time to make it up to Saugerties, but it wouldn't be as secure."

"And how does either location eliminate the concern of her being followed?"

"Easy. I pick her up the night before, Saturday night. She leaves the bar late, heads home, parks her car, and jumps into mine. Nobody is following her going home. Sunday morning, they see her car still parked in the garage and assume she hasn't left."

"Might work. Better than waltzing her into FBI Headquarters or One Police Plaza in broad daylight. Let me knock it around with Bob Machado tomorrow. See what he thinks. I'll get back."

"Okay."

* * *

Howard Beach, Queens - Sun. P.M. 04/26

"You waited around at the ferry terminal a couple of hours on a hunch?" Sal Fusco said without attempting to hide the skepticism in his tone. The man he always considered slow-witted, useful as a gofer and nothing more, had shaken the image. It surprised him and pleased him that Vito Rossellini could think for himself. Perhaps he'd use the man down the line for assignments more important than running errands.

Fusco pulled a few scraps of bread crust from a small plastic bag on his lap and tossed them in the air to the flock of pigeons gathering around. The two men sat on folding chairs outside the mob's social club in Howard Beach. Up the street, amid the usual light vehicle traffic on a Sunday, a handful of neighborhood teenagers were throwing a football around in a loud effort to imitate a college practice session.

"Yeah, I thought maybe she hung back 'til the last minute on purpose. Ya know, to lose me like she did. I took a guess she was comin' back on the next ferry. So I stayed around."

"And you're sure he was with her when she stepped off the ferry?"

"To be honest, Sal, yeah, he was with her. But like I said, I wasn't sure if she knew him before or just met him on the ferry." Vito shrugged. "Alls I know is they was talkin' like old friends as they headed to the subway."

"And you didn't stay with her, but followed the guy?"

"Yeah, she took a different subway line than him. I shoulda stayed on her tail. I know. But I figured if my hunch was right, it might turn out to be somethin' you'd wanna hear about."

"No, no, Vito, you did good. You dropped the tail. No big deal. Sometimes hunches pay off, like this one." Fusco's next toss of crust landed in the circle of pigeons further back. "You mean you tailed him uptown to a building at Twenty-third and Fifth? Then what? Tell me."

"After he picked up a paper at the newsstand on the corner, he goes into a building on Fifth. Middle of the block between Twenty-second and Twenty-third."

"The Flatiron Building?"

"Uh-uh, the other side of Fifth. Anyway, I watched from outside the entrance 'til he gets in the elevator. I moved in real fast and see the numbers stop on the fourth floor. So, I mosey over to the directory in the lobby like I was tryin' to find a company in the building. Four names on the fourth floor. One was" . . . Vito paused like he was about to call this week's winning Lotto number . . . "Lucas Rizzo Investigations."

"No shit!"

A broad smile broke across Vito's face. "I did good, yeah?"

An errant pass by one of the teenagers landed and rolled up to the feet of the *capo*. Without getting up, Fusco gave the football a kick with the side of his foot and sent it toward the players. He watched until one boy retrieved the football and tossed it to the passer.

"Vito," Fusco said, "how 'bout you goin' back to the building and pay a visit to the shamus you saw goin' in? Go up to his office, ask a few questions, find if you were right about them being together. A good idea?"

Vito's face beamed with delight. "Yeah, boss. I can do that. I'll go there on Monday. Okay?"

"Yeah, and tell me what ya find."

Chapter Nine

Chelsea Area, Manhattan - Mon. A.M. 04/27

It was almost noon when Rizzo looked up as someone pushed open his office door. A short man wearing a dark suit, a black-collared shirt, and a solid white tie stood in the doorway. He looked like an actor making his first on-stage appearance in a production of *Guys and Dolls*. Now, here was a mobster, Rizzo thought, or someone playing one. In either case, Rizzo wasn't chancing it. He opened the top right-hand drawer where he kept his 9mm Glock 17.

"Hey, don't bother to knock. C'mon in."

"You Lucas Rizzo?" the short Marlon Brando imitator asked.

"Yep, that's me. How can I help you?" Rizzo got up and stood behind his desk, poised to grab the weapon.

Marlon Brando stepped forward. His eyes examined Rizzo and the surroundings. The clicking sound made by the closing door caused him to jerk around. When he turned back, an expression of tension appeared on his face. This *gavone* is an exposed nerve ending, Rizzo thought.

"You the one on the Staten Island Ferry yesterday?"

Uh-oh. That's what this is about. They saw me leaving the ferry with Nicole. Damn! It was stupid of me not to let her get off alone. Well, let's see how I can finesse this.

"Yeah, I took the ferry on Sunday. "Why?"

"How come you was over in Staten Island?"

"I had an appointment with a client."

"Who."

"Hey, pal, that's privileged information. I don't need to—"

"What was you doin' with the dame?"

"What dame? I was there alone."

"Wadda ya mean? You got off the ferry with a woman, didn't ya?"

Rizzo stared at him, maintaining a blank expression. Then a look of sudden understanding burst on his face. "Oh, you mean the woman I met at the ferry station on Staten Island. I wasn't with her. I mean, we chatted briefly before we boarded and a bit traveling across, but I wasn't with her."

"Ya sure looked like it when ya got off."

"Hey, if she's your girlfriend or wife, believe me, I didn't hit on her. No sir, I meant no harm. Matter of fact, she never even told me her name. A friendly exchange, that's all it was. Two people going in the same direction. Believe me, pal. You got nothing to worry about. Ask her. She'll tell you."

Marlon Brando stood motionless in front of the desk, internalizing, working his mind silly, trying to determine if the story Rizzo had handed him was legit. When he finally decided, he did an about-face and headed out the door without saying a word. Before the door closed, Rizzo called out, "Thanks for your understanding," and chuckled.

Rizzo sat down and turned the chair to look out the window. Despite his easy success at bluffing the Gambino mobster with the story, he felt rattled. There was no guarantee Marlon Brando wouldn't have second thoughts. He couldn't believe he'd been that careless in handling their departure from the ferry on Sunday morning. The Guidos were deadly serious about not trusting Nicole. He needed to keep that thought in mind. Had it not been for a not-too-bright mob soldier, that little misstep could have been costly. The situation with Marlon Brando might not have ended with a chuckle.

He picked up his iPhone and sent Nicole a text. 'Call me when you're alone.'

* * *

Jamaica Avenue, Queens - Tues. P.M. 4/28

The last server to leave had said goodnight and exited The Dugout by the front door. Before Dominic had the door locked, Pete Barone shoved through, sending the bartender back on his heels. "We're closed," Dom said, not recognizing who had pushed past him. "Oh, it's you, Pete. Sorry."

"Where's Nicole?" he asked without stopping. He slurred his speech like someone who'd been drinking heavily.

"She hasn't left yet. She's still in the office," Dom called out before the man disappeared into the dark shadows of the restaurant.

Aware of the already shaky relationship Pete had with Nicole, he decided to hang around until the man left. He finished stacking chairs on the four tops and moved behind the bar. After checking ice levels in the four refrigerated boxes, Dom looked up when he heard the rapid steps of Nicole coming from her office. Barone, in close pursuit, shouted something about her privileged position.

"It's gonna end soon," he yelled, "if I have anything to say about it. You can bet your ass."

Dom remained in front of the last refrigerated box, watching with concern. He'd witnessed these heated exchanges before, but this time Pete was drunk and could be dangerous.

Nicole approached the bar and stood at the server's end. Her shoulder bag hung over one arm and she held a light jacket in her hands. She'd been preparing to leave after Dom locked up, but Barone's sudden appearance at the office door delayed her.

Dom came around to the front and went through the motions of straightening each of the twenty-five stools surrounding the horseshoe-shaped bar. He kept the arguing pair in view as Barone's angry words continued.

"I don't want you talking to Sal Fusco when I'm not here," Barone shot at her. "He's a shithead, a stooge for my uncle."

"So should I ignore him when he comes into the office?"

Dominic worked around the bar, closer to where the argument was taking place. He stopped behind Barone and fussed with a stool placement like he couldn't get it to stand up straight. When he moved it again, the stool accidentally banged against Barone's leg.

Barone whipped around. "What the fuck you still doin' here, asshole? Take off!"

"Sorry about that, Pete."

"Don't you dare talk to my employees that way," Nicole shouted.

"Your employees? It's my motherfucking bar, you dumb bitch. You're lucky you're not at the bottom of the Hudson River swimming with the fish. And don't you tell me how to talk to—"

Barone's arm came up to strike her and Dominic's hand shot out. He caught Barone's wrist before the man could land the blow. Dom squeezed it like a vise and yanked the arm down. "Hey, Pete, cool down, will ya?"

Barone's free hand swung wildly at Dom's temple, but the bartender blocked it and grabbed the arm. With both hands immobilized, Barone attempted to knee him in the groin. Dom avoided the full impact by turning his hip. He felt his anger rising fast, and he worried he might lose it—but he didn't want to put a serious hurt on the man. That would not end well.

Dom held Barone's wrists and did a fast one-eighty spin, sending him sailing between two stools. Barone crashed into the bar chest high. His torso bounced off the top's curved edge, sending him into a half-turn before slumping to the floor. Barone remained in a sitting position without moving, his head pressed against the base of the bar .

Nicole's hands flew to her mouth. "Oh, my God! Is he hurt?"

"We'll see," Dom said as he approached the prone man. He bent down and reached under Barone's armpits, hoisting him to his feet. A dazed expression and a cut lower lip were all the damage Dom could find. "Sit for a couple of minutes," he told the stunned Barone as he lifted him onto the padded seat of a stool. Dom held him steady by a shoulder and turned to Nicole. "You ready to leave, take off now. Where's your car?"

"The usual spot, in the alley."

"Use the back door. You'll be okay. I'll get him to his car and lock up the place."

"You don't want me to wait?"

"No, you go before he starts up again."

Nicole's worried expression landed on his face. "Thanks, Dom. I'm grateful. Hope you'll be all right. Tomorrow, then."

"Yeah, if I'm still on the payroll."

Dominic felt guilty as he watched Nicole disappear toward the rear door. Whenever they closed up this late at night, he always walked her to her car. Tonight, Barone's drunken unruliness prevented him from performing a courtesy he valued. His relationship with Nicole had reached the friendly level of a good buddy. He respected her professionalism and the way she treated all the employees. He didn't give a damn about her sexuality. No one dared to refer to it around him. If they did, they made that mistake once.

He looked at Barone balanced on the stool. The man rolled his head, trying to regain a semblance of normalcy. "You okay, now?" Dom asked.

Barone stopped rolling. "Man, what's wrong with you?"

"Look, Pete. You were totally outta line. You might've hurt her bad, ya know."

"So what?"

"So what? Sal Fusco is what. He hears about you slugging Nicole? Man, I wouldn't wanna be you."

"Fuck Sal. And fuck you. You almost cracked my ribs."

"Hey, ya took a shot at me. No way I'm gonna let ya get away with that." Dom reached out to take Barone's arm and forced a smile. "C'mon, man, I'll get you to your car."

Barone shrugged away Dom's hand and slid down from the stool. He brushed off his trousers, glared back at the bartender, and bolted for the front door. "Shove it!" were the last words Dominic heard.

Chapter Ten

Long Beach, Queens, NY - Wed. A.M. 4/29

"Holy crap, Nick, it's seven-thirty in the morning." Sal Fusco moaned. "What's so goddamn important you gotta be calling me so early?"

"Sorry, Sal, but something happened at The Dugout last night."

Nick Lombardo, an IT and security camera specialist once employed by Cesar's Hotel and Casino in Las Valezs, now worked for the family. He and his crew installed and maintained the security cameras in all five sports bars. They could be found throughout the early morning hours reviewing the five security feeds of the previous business day and night. If they spotted any irregularities, Sal Fusco was the first-person Nick called. He'd been instructed to say nothing to anyone else. As one of the privileged few within the family, Nick had The Hat's' private number.

"Oh, yeah, wadda ya got?" Sal's voice came alive.

Nick waited a beat, thinking how to couch his words. He wanted to avoid coming off as ratting out someone—especially since the someone was the nephew of the family's underboss.

"Normally, I'd have second thoughts about bothering you with this, Sal. I'm not sure you'd even wanna hear about it. It doesn't involve theft or anything like that."

"Well, what the hell does it involve, Nick? Stop the bullshit. Tell me straight up."

"The Dugout. There was a fight there last night."

"Customers?"

Before he answered, Nick visualized the PTZ Dome Camera placements around the restaurant. They were over the front entrance and rear door, and two at each side of the bar where the argument took place, and over the high tops, four tops, and booths. He hesitated long enough to review camera placements in the event Sal questioned him about which cameras caught the action.

"No. Not like that. It involved Pete Barone and one of the bartenders. Dominic Biondo."

"Okay. What the hell happened?"

"Gimme a second while I boot up the flash drive. I made a separate copy of the incident. I'll give you a play-by-play."

"Wait, wait. Hold up, will ya? Don't be stupid. Get me the damn drive. I'll look at it myself. Gimme the bottom line . . . why you think I should see it."

Nick breathed in and squeezed the air out between his lips. Sal had a short fuse. He didn't know how the *capo* would react. "Well, what I'm guessing you'd wanna know, Sal, is this. Barone took a swing at the general manager and Dominic stopped him."

"The general manager? You mean Nicole?"

"Yeah."

"Damn! Get the drive over to me at the club—today."

"Right, Sal."

"And Nick, next time, don't second guess what I would or wouldn't wanna know. I wanna know everything. Okay?"

"Got it, Sal."

* * *

FBI's Manhattan Office - Wed. P.M. 4/29

The conference room was down the hallway from Fields' office. As Rizzo entered the 15x15 windowless meeting space, it gave him the impression an ex-math teacher had decorated it. It was a square-shaped room. The conference table in the middle was circular. A rectangular Parson's table occupied the wall facing the door. The round official seal of the Federal Bureau of Investigation hung over it. An étagère in one corner balanced the space like an illustration from a tenth-grade geometry textbook. He decided the FBI's Manhattan office, if nothing else, prides itself on form and function. It illustrated the rigidity of the Bureau.

"Sit anywhere," Fields said, making a large circular gesture with his hand. "Would anyone like coffee or a cold drink?"

No takers.

Lieutenant Bob Machado, Luke Rizzo, and Agent Ralph Brancuso took seats around the table. Jack Fields chose the chair polar opposite of Rizzo. Fields had placed yellow-lined pads on the table with Pilot ballpoint pens clipped to one edge. Rizzo knew this would be a working meeting.

Fields stood by his chair. He scanned the three faces like an obstetrician about to announce to proud parents they were going to have twins. He began, "I'm happy to report Luke had an interesting meeting aboard the Staten Island Ferry the other morning. A successful one, I might add. Nicole Adams has agreed to help us with our efforts to infiltrate the inner secrets of the Gambino laundering operation."

"If I can interrupt a second," Rizzo said. "What tipped her into cooperating was when I told her about the brutal murder of Roy Dickerson. I'm sure my limited persuasion skills alone would not have done the trick."

Brancuso smiled. "Such humility."

"Nevertheless, she's aboard," Fields said and sat down. "Before anything else, we need to determine who we should target to compromise, and what covert listening method we think would be safe and effective. And I can't overemphasize the safe part."

The room fell silent until Bob Machado said, "I assume the person in their operation that would produce the results we're looking for is Pete Barone. He's the source with the inside involvement and knowledge that would justify us to close them down."

"Well, it stands to reason if we use the woman for this covert assignment," Brancuso said, "we're limited to just those she'd interact with."

"You agree with that?" Fields asked Rizzo.

Rizzo nodded. "Sounds logical." His mind flashed back to his conversation with Roy Dickerson that day in the park. He remembered Dickerson indicated they kept him and Nicole at arm's length from the financial end of the business. Rizzo leaned into the table. "Yeah, Dickerson had mentioned to me their accountant for the five restaurants reported to Barone. He said Nicole had no contact with the numbers guy. Barone is the man who would know when dirty money flowed into their bank accounts, money the bars didn't earn."

"Then I guess that answers the question of who," Fields said.

Machado asked, "What's her relationship with Barone since she returned to the job? Is it strained, or what?"

The telephone call Rizzo had received earlier from Vinnie Alcamo popped into his mind. The call came mid-morning, about an hour before he'd left his office for the meeting.

Dominic Biondo had phoned Vinnie to describe an argument between Barone and Nicole Wednesday night at closing time. He wondered how much of this information he could share with the group without betraying Vinnie's confidence.

He looked at Machado. "Funny you should ask. I got a call this morning from my *goomba*. He told me he'd heard from someone who'd witnessed an argument at The Dugout bar between Nicole and Barone. It was ugly. Barone almost clipped her. My source felt I might wanna know that."

"Well, shit, that's not good news," Brancuso said. "Probably hates his guts now."

"She hated him before," Rizzo said. "But from things she told me on the ferry, Fusco is no fan of his. Maybe we can use that?"

"How?" Brancuso said.

"No clue, but I'll knock it around with her."

"Okay," Fields said. "Let's assume she can regain a peaceful relationship with Barone. The question remains, how do we catch him talking about the dirty money? If it's on the office phone, we'd need access after-hours to plant a bug. On second thought, too dangerous. If they got suspicious and went looking, it would be an easy find. And besides, he might be in the habit of using his cell phone for these calls."

"I guess having her wear a wire is out?" Brancuso said.

Machado shook his head. "No, forget it. That's risky. And besides, it wouldn't work. It requires her to be in his presence. She'd have to be there when he's on the phone talking about banking details."

"And that's unlikely," Fields said. "But how about this? A roving bug?"

Rizzo looked up. "What's that?"

"A remotely activated mobile phone," Fields said. "We can activate a phone without physical access. The Bureau has used it before."

"Is it legal?"

"Used to be you needed approval by the DOJ," Machado said. "No longer. I remember when US District Judge Lewis Kaplan ruled the federal wiretapping law was broad enough to permit eavesdropping. Even on conversations taking place near a suspect's cell phone."

"We can turn a cellular device into a microphone and transmitter," Fields added. "It can function that way whether the phone is on or off."

"Before anything, we need an eavesdropping warrant," Machado said. "It's the same as any other search warrant allowing a limited search and seizure of evidence. The law makes no distinction between listening to, monitoring, or recording a conversation. If we intend to target Peter Barone, we would name him as the subject in the warrant."

"No question, he's the key guy," Brancuso said.

"Oh, and something else we need to keep in mind," Machado said. "We're permitted to listen to conversations regarding criminal money-laundering activities. Any other criminal activity is also okay. What we can't listen to is any privileged conversation. They define this as any conversation between Barone and his priest, his attorney, his doctor, or his wife."

"I don't think he talks with his wife anymore. They've separated now," Brancuso said.

Smiling, Rizzo said, "But it doesn't include his banker, accountant, or any member of the Gambino family."

"No, it doesn't," Machado said. "If our undercover listener realizes the conversation is into the privilege category, he's supposed to stop listening."

"Yeah, sure," Rizzo said and laughed. "You guys ever used this type of bug?"

"We used one against the Genovese crime family several years ago," Fields said. "It was one of the first times we employed a remote-eavesdropping device in a criminal case. The technique was discussed in security circles for years."

Rizzo said, "I vote we go with it."

Fields turned to Machado. "Bob?"

"Makes sense to me. It's the safest route."

"I agree," Brancuso said. "I mean, all she has to do is leave the phone behind in her purse when he asks her to disappear because he wants to make a private call."

"Sounds foolproof," Rizzo said. Even if he checked her bag, all he'd find was her iPhone. What's involved in setting it up?"

"Easy," Machado said. "Her mobile provider remotely installs a piece of software onto her handset. We can have them do it without the owner's knowledge. Of course, we wouldn't do that. The software will activate the microphone when she's not using it to make a call."

"Unless there's a problem we've overlooked, let's go with it," Fields urged.

"Couple of questions," Rizzo said. "Who's her iPhone provider? Can every company install the software? Will they all go along?"

"We shall see," Fields answered. His eyes traveled to the FBI seal on the wall. "We shall see."

Brancuso turned to Rizzo. "She'll cooperate, you say?"

"We shall see."

Chapter Eleven

Atlantic Avenue, Brooklyn - Fri. P.M. 5/01

For reasons he would not admit to anyone, Sal Fusco chose The Red Zone to have his "discussion" with Pete Barone. Having it in a public place would remind him to keep his voice down—a necessity he found not to his liking. Another reason was he thought their kitchen was the best in the five-store chain, and the head chef was his grandson.

Configuration of The Red Zone was a near duplication of The Dugout sports bar. The remaining three bars—The Finish Line, The Half Court, and The Penalty Box—also followed a similar layout within the constrictions of their real estate.

Fusco tipped the Borsalino back from his forehead and gave Barone a stern look. "You don't know this 'bout me but I once studied lip-reading."

Barone cocked his head. "You're kidding me, aren't you?"

"Yeah, I'm bullshittin' you, but my point is it doesn't take a lip readin' expert to see what you said about me on the video."

"Hey, Sal, I was shitfaced. I didn't—"

"And I also know people say a lotta truths when they're shitfaced. You know what I mean?"

"But I—"

"I'm asking, you know what I mean?"

Barone took in a gulp of air and said, "Yeah, Sal. I do."

"And for that, if you wasn't Carmine's nephew, you'd be in a New Jersey swamp by now. *Capice?*"

The man's face paled. He cast his eyes down and remained silent.

"What's wrong with you? You ain't got no brains smackin' a woman like that."

"I didn't touch her," Barone said. His voice rose in pitch. "I meant to scare her. That's all."

"Bullshit. You took a swing at her. If it wasn't for Dominic, you'd a coldcocked her. Ain't I right?"

Barone slipped down in his seat and rested his hands across his stomach. "Yeah, I suppose."

Fusco removed the Borsalino, picked up his napkin, and wiped the inside headband. He repositioned the hat on his head and looked over at Barone. "I can't believe you had the balls to take a swing at Dom. You're goddamn lucky."

Barone shook his head. "Wadda ya mean?"

"Dom grabbed your arms to stop you. If he wanted to, he could a punched you into next week. It would take a miracle for you to come back. You got any idea how tough the guy is? Until he took one in the skull, he was the best in the family for handling the heavy liftin'."

Sal stopped talking when Frank Caruso, the bar's manager, approached their table.

"How were the spareribs tonight, Mr. Fusco?" he inquired. "You picked the right night to *mangia* with us 'cause when it's on the menu as a special, you can believe it's gonna be good."

Sal nodded. "*Mille grazie*, Frankie. Oh, would you tell our waiter another Anisette?" He looked to Barone. "You want another brew?"

"Nah, not right now."

"I'll take care of it," Caruso said and departed for the bar.

When the manager moved out of earshot, Sal turned his attention back to Barone. "So, what's with this hard-on you got for Nicole all about, 'cept she won't let you in her pants? How come you can't get along?"

"Oh, I don't know. She pisses me off. Sometimes she ignores my instructions about how I want things done. She acts like what I say don't matter."

"What the hell's wrong with her takin' charge? She's the general manager, isn't she? That's what we pay her for. I gotta say, she runs the five restaurants better than your first guy. These bars are busy all the time. What's to complain?"

The talk halted long enough for the server to place another Anisette in front of Fusco. He looked down at the *capo* for a second. "Is this okay?" and waited until Fusco muttered, "Thanks."

Barone shifted in his chair waiting for the server to leave. "Well, shit. I feel sometimes I'm not needed and—"

"Listen to me, you *ciuccio*. And by the way, you ever call me that again, I'll personally punch your lights out. Understand?"

"Yeah. Sorry, Sal."

"Listen, she's makin' you look good. Stop this ego crap, cryin' about your poor little hurt feelings. Who gives a shit? The company's makin' money hand over fist for the family and that's the bottom line. You don't worry about nothin' else. You hear me?"

A nod was all Barone could manage, but it was clear to Fusco his instructions were not happily received.

"Hey, *paesano*, sit on your ego and make friends with the broad. Who knows, maybe if you're nice enough, she'll let you go down on her."

Barone made a noise sounding like a harrumph.

Sal continued. "You wanna keep peace for the sake of the business. You know? She's a sharp broad and your uncle . . . well, he's high on her. Make a truce and work together. That's the smart way, right?"

"Yeah, I guess I can do that."

"Good. And Pete. I ain't sayin' nothin' to Carmine about this little dust-up. I don't need to tell him since you've agreed to put things right. Okay?"

"Okay."

"Good. Now, we won't drop you in a Jersey swamp. So let's have a nice piece of warm apple pie and ice cream. *Va bene*?"

* * *

West Side Manhattan - Sat. A.M. 5/02

Rizzo and Flo sat at the café table by the window sipping their first cup of coffee, struggling to revive from a deep sleep, a sleep following a Friday night of steamy lovemaking. In the past, they often preceded their nights of passion with silly "let's pretend" lascivious games. These antics always landed them in bed with the giggles.

Last night's connubial coupling began with a tender reaching out for each other. Later, as they lay in bed enjoying the afterglow, Rizzo gazed at Flo's partially closed eyes. There was something strange about the moment he couldn't explain. Now, in the morning light, as he studied her face again, the answer rushed to him like a bull charging the matador. He loved this woman more than he'd ever loved another soul.

He remembered Terri, his ex-wife, and wondered if there was a time when he felt that way about her—before his total immersion as a rookie cop on the job learning the ropes—before his fall into the habit of spending hours after his shift with other cops at the precinct's favorite watering hole—before the women who loved blue uniforms made themselves available for easy sex during his tour or following it—before booze took over his life— before, as a narcotics detective, the obsession with searching out crime and criminals almost punched his ticket for good— before he turned their marriage into shit?

When Matt came along, Rizzo imagined the child would make a difference in their relationship. It didn't. Booze, broads, and absenteeism still ruled, until he took the ricocheted bullet in his buttocks. By this time, Terri had endured enough and filed for divorce. Soon after, Rizzo vested out and opened his investigation office in Chelsea.

He'd met Flo at a time when he attempted to put all his self-destructiveness behind. An assignment for an English client sent him to Pennsylvania. There, a chance meeting with Flo, his Avis angel, as she stood behind the rent-a-car counter in the Pittsburgh International Airport, was the turning point. They went to dinner, and the same night fell into bed and in love. Two months later, she called to announce Avis had promoted her to supervisor. The promotion required she relocate to New York City, to their location at LaGuardia Airport. He was euphoric. Within six months, he realized life without Flo would be empty. They married the same year.

"What's got you so silent? You haven't said a word for the past several minutes. You've been sitting there with a wrinkled brow looking like a plowed potato field."

"Oh, nothing," he said, sounding vulnerable. "I was thinking about how lucky I am."

"Well, hon, that's not what I'd call nothing."

He stood and leaned over to land a wet one on her mouth. "Why don't you shower first, while I make breakfast? I can take mine after we eat."

Flo took a breath. "You're not planning to jump in with me, are you? I don't think I'm ready for more. Why, Lord, you sure got me all tuckered out."

Rizzo stepped to the counter, leaned back against it, and laughed. Flo's Kentuckian humor and use of the rural vernacular always tickled him. She was mother-earth-natural without a hint of insincerity or phoniness.

"G'wan, git in thar," he mimicked, doing his best to sound like Buddy Ebsen of the old "Beverly Hillbillies," TV Show. "I'll git started and rustle up yo favorite breakfast vittles."

"And don't burn the toast, Jed Clampett," she said before she disappeared into the bathroom.

Flo returned with her damp hair wrapped in a towel. Rizzo, in practiced fashion, had whipped up a breakfast of her favorite avocado, cheese, and ham omelet. He'd nuzzled two slices of bacon, done to a turn the way she preferred, to the side of the omelet. On a separate bread plate, he placed four slices of rye toast, golden brown. A small cup of mixed fruit completed the setting.

They finished breakfast with little more conversation than "How's the omelet?" Rizzo suspected it would change once he had the dishes in the dishwasher. Whenever Flo became quiet and thoughtful, he suspected something was up. She soon proved him right.

"More coffee?"

She lifted her eyes and stared as though she hadn't heard the question.

Rizzo raised the carafe. "More? There's plenty left."

"Oh, yes, thank you," she said, holding out her mug. "Half please." When he lowered the mug, she launched into what was on her mind. "Luke, hon, how is it the woman you tried to rescue mysteriously turned up? You said that, didn't you?"

Rizzo sat back with a knowing smile.

"I mean, do you still get credit? Does your client still pay you even though it wasn't you who found her?"

"Yes, sweetheart, I get paid by the hours I put in, not by the results. Although I do have an excellent track record for producing results. If I didn't, I'd find it hard to get clients."

"Then the case is, ah, how do you say it, a wrap?"

"Try 'closed.' In any event, with my obligation to my client satisfied, it's led to another contract assignment with the FBI."

"Oh, good God!"

He found it hard not to smile. She still hadn't recovered from the shootout in San Juan.

"Is this one going to be dangerous too?"

"No, my love. I'm serving as an advisor on this one. No active role."

Flo appeared satisfied with the answer. She drank her coffee while Rizzo waited. He predicted, because of her natural inquisitiveness, the subject would not rest there. She didn't disappoint.

"Let me ask you another question, okay?"

"Shoot."

"Why did the *Mafia* kidnap her? What did she do?"

The question caused Rizzo to hesitate. The case was ongoing. He wasn't comfortable providing her information that could be dangerous to possess if ever she— He didn't finish the thought. Too scary to contemplate. But then, the information was already out there, so why not.

"You remember, don't you, Nicole Adams was the general manager of five sports bars in Brooklyn and Queens? The *Mafia* owned the operation and one of the members ran the business."

"Oh, lordy, was she a gun moll?"

When Rizzo stopped laughing, he continued. "She didn't know it involved the mob when she accepted the position. The mob guy running the bars kept hitting on her even though the jerk knew she wasn't straight."

"The horny old man!"

"You might say that. But he wasn't old. Horny? Yes. Anyway, after she learned how the mob used the five sports bars, she threatened the guy. She told him if he didn't stop harassing her, she'd go to the Feds. Wrong! When she realized what she'd done, she took off. They found her a short time later and held her captive for a while."

"Then released her so she could go back to work?"

"A big surprise, yeah. Seems she was indispensable, a powerhouse of a manager."

"Imagine that?"

"Now she's back running the five bars."

Flo became thoughtful again. She scrunched her eyebrows, preparing her next question. "Well, what was she going to squeal about to the FBI?" She giggled at her use of a word that didn't fit in her vocabulary.

Rizzo rose from the table.

"No, don't go. Sit back down. Don't leave me hanging. What was it?"

He took a breath and pulled out his chair to sit. "Money laundering," he said.

"What's that?"

Rizzo got to his feet again. Flo looked up at him with an annoyed expression.

"I'll be right back. There's something in the bookcase that'll answer your question better than I can." He disappeared into the second bedroom and returned carrying an official-looking volume. He flipped the law reference to a page he had flagged and read:

> "Money Laundering is a term used to describe a scheme in which criminals try to disguise the identity, original ownership, and destination of money they have obtained through criminal conduct. The laundering is done to make it seem the proceeds have come from a legitimate source."

"In one simple sentence," he said, "it's the act of disguising the source of money gained through illegal means by mixing it with income of legitimate businesses."

"They do that through any business?"

"It has to be those dealing heavily in cash. It's hard to hide checks and credit card sales."

"Do they need to own the business to . . . what's it called, wash money?"

"Hmm, you thinking of going to law school?"

"No, smarty. I'm fascinated by the entire process. I never heard of it before. The *Mafia* must own a lot of businesses."

Rizzo recognized how much Flo enjoyed her rush of curiosity. Not wishing to spoil her fun, he continued to respond to her questions.

"They don't own them, at least not outright. It's through their incredible skill of persuasion they gain compliance of the owner to work with them." He snickered at his humor.

"The type of business they use? Well, it's all over the place. Their favorite is restaurant chains—then there are the motel chains, vending machine syndicates, garbage collection companies, linen supply for hotels. I've even come across several real estate companies that worked with them. Imagine all those million-dollar homes and property sold for cash to Arab princes. The businesses operate legally and generate justifiable income with deposits in banks all over the US. The mob's illegal cash is mingled with these deposits and nobody's the wiser."

Rizzo sat back and looked at Flo's amazed expression. "Okay, counselor, I rest my case. Now, I'll shower and dress. What do you say we take a bus uptown and spend the afternoon in Central Park?"

"Fantastic. Should I bring along one of your guns, in case?"

"Nah, you got me to protect you."

"You told me that in San Juan, and look how close I came to getting shot."

"Hey, you can't win them all."

"That's what has me worried, Sherlock."

Chapter Twelve

Forest Hills, Queens - Sun. P.M. 5/10

One week later, a lipstick-red Chrysler Sebring with the top down came out of the Boulevard Gardens Apartment garage and up the ramp to the street level. Nicole Adams, attired in jeans, a casual tee under a denim jacket, and a New York Yankees cap snugged tight on her head, sat behind the wheel.

Her companion, FBI Agent Anya Glikson, turned out in khaki pants and a collared golf shirt, occupied the passenger seat. She had a lightweight cotton sweater draped over her shoulders; the arms were tied across her chest. A battered fisherman's hat, pulled down over her short, spiky hair to protect her from the wind, challenged her to keep it on. The service weapon she carried sat at the bottom of the oversized straw purse on the floor between her feet.

Nicole traversed the heavy local traffic through Forest Hills. She steered the Sebring toward Queens Boulevard and followed it to the Long Island Expressway. Once they reached the L.I.E.—at twelve-forty-five on a warm Sunday afternoon—traffic moved along. A half-hour later, they were beyond the city limits and on their way to Long Island's South Shore and the ferry ride to Fire Island.

Glikson looked back over her shoulder. The breeze caused the brim of her hat to flap wildly. She pressed it to her head with one hand. "Damn, I should have worn my Mets cap." She pulled off the hat, folded it, and tucked it under one knee. "By the way, if your tail is still with us despite all the street traffic back there, I'd say he knows what he's doing. You ever spot him following you in the past?"

"One day last week, I got a glimpse of him on the subway ride down to the Staten Island Ferry to meet Luke Rizzo. He got off from the car behind. I'm not sure it's the same guy every weekend. I delayed getting on the ferry until the last minute. He was too late to make the closing gates. We sailed without him."

"I'm sure it pissed him off."

"I guess."

"But he never saw you with Rizzo, right?"

"No, he was already aboard."

"A smart play. Rizzo needs to remain an unknown."

"He's not with the FBI, is he?"

"He's private. The Bureau often contracts private investigators they trust. It helps them with situations agents can't touch." Glikson grinned. "You understand?"

Nicole nodded. She liked Rizzo, felt comfortable with him, and was willing to trust him if the FBI did.

The trip to Sayville was an easy drive. Earlier arriving weekenders had filled the main parking lot on River Road at the Sayville Ferry. Nicole found an enterprising homeowner nearby happy to rent space on their front lawn. The two o'clock ferry to Cherry Grove was already loading by the time they purchased their tickets.

* * *

Sayville, Long Island

Vito Rossellini, dressed in casual attire, leaned forward and squinted through the windshield of his Nissan Altima. He watched the unknown woman purchase tickets as he struggled to read the sign above the window. He remembered his glasses in his breast pocket and put them on. His focus sharpened, and he read Cherry Grove on the sign. The iPhone to his ear was on the tenth ring before Cheech Marino answered.

"Yeah?"

"Cheech . . . Vito."

"I know," he said, sounding annoyed. "I got caller-ID, you *Baccalà*."

Vito's eyes followed the two women as they strolled toward the covered waiting area and disappeared. "Cheech, listen, will ya. I'm following the dame. She left her apartment in her car this morning. Another broad was with her. They drove out to the Island and parked at the ferry dock in Sayville."

"So?"

"Well, that's the place where they leave for Fire Island. I seen them buy tickets to Cherry Grove. "That's fagsville, isn't it?"

"I think so. You gonna go with them?"

"Naah, I'm figurin' I'd stand out like a sore thumb, I mean, followin' them around that sissy place."

Vito heard Cheech laugh.

"Why don't ya drop the tail? Forget about it for now?"

"Yeah?"

"Come back in. We know where she'll be today. The broad with her is probably her girlfriend. Ya know?"

"You're right. But if I drop the tail, maybe Sal gets pissed."

"Don't worry. I'll tell him. Explain how she's off for some tit-ticklin' on Fire Island with her girlfriend."

"Okay. Good. I wasn't lookin' forward to sweatin' my ass off out there. I mean, tryin' to keep up with her. Ahh, I shoulda let you handle this weekend."

"C'mon, Vito. It ain't that bad. Hey, if you went over there, maybe some good-lookin' fairy takes a likin' to you and we'd never see ya again."

"Funny guy," Vito said and disconnected the call.

* * *

Cherry Grove, Long Island

Anya Glikson and Nicole Adams got off the ferry at the Cherry Grove slip and went into a summer-wear specialty shop at the end of the pier. "Did you make any males aboard the ferry that looked like they had an interest in us?" Glikson snickered.

"Not a one," Nicole said. "If there was someone following, we left him in Sayville."

"That's my feeling too." Glikson held up a short-sleeved tank-top to her chest. "She looked at Nicole and said, "Nice, huh?"

"You wanna look around?"

"We can't. No time." She dropped the tank top on the pile. "There's a water taxi waiting for us south of here. We'll leave the shop by the back door in case someone is watching."

After Glikson was certain everyone aboard the ferry had disappeared into the narrow, vegetation-lined streets, the two women made their way along the pebbled path down to the shoreline. Glikson spotted Ralph Brancuso crouched in the shadows aboard the water taxi tied up at a dock. She realized if the tail followed them this far, the guy would assume they were setting sail to another part of Fire Island. Deserted and left to fend for himself, he'd have to kill twenty-five minutes waiting for the return ferry to Sayville. She'd looked around but failed to see anyone suspicious.

"Jump aboard," the agent said. "Any problem with the tail . . . losing him?"

"I'm sure we dumped him back in Sayville. We didn't make anyone aboard the ferry with the aura of a *Mafioso*." Glikson chuckled. "When he saw we were heading to Cherry Grove, he probably chickened out."

Brancuso turned to the taxi driver. "We're ready."

The trip across the Great South Bay took thirty-five minutes. They tied up at the dock at the Seahorse Boat-tel in Bay Shore and entered the front office, where Fields, Machado, and Rizzo waited. On the way over, Brancuso explained to the women he would drive them back to Nicole's car in Sayville when the meeting ended.

* * *

Bay Shore, Long Island

Fields welcomed the ladies. He led them down a short corridor to a small, windowless room. The space was bare except for a table and enough chairs to accommodate the six of them. Rizzo gave Nicole a gracious smile, and he took the seat to the right of her.

"You can't seem to get away from ferries these days. At least you had sunshine on this one."

Nicole nodded. "It was a pleasant trip."

"Before we begin," Fields said, "would anyone like something to drink . . . water, coffee, a Coke?" He motioned toward a table in the corner. Six mugs, several bottles of mineral water, and a bucket containing an assortment of soft drinks buried in ice surrounded the coffee machine, all accommodations of Jackson Bell, the Seahorse's proprietor .

"I'm fine," Nicole said.

"Nothing for me, thanks," Glikson said.

Rizzo and Machado filled coffee mugs and returned to the table. Brancuso remained seated, looking down at a notepad.

"Okay, let's get started," Fields said. He shot Nicole a warm smile. "I'd like to thank you for coming out here for this exploratory meeting. Whether you agree to work with us on what we have in mind, I want you to know we appreciate your willingness to hear us out."

"I'm eager to be as cooperative as much as I can without getting myself killed."

"Our top priority, count on it. That's why we needed to conduct this meeting in secrecy. Away from the madding crowd, as Luke Rizzo is wont to quote."

Rizzo grinned, looked around the table, and saw three heads bobbing in unison.

Fields continued. "You, of course, already met Mr. Rizzo and Agent Anya Glikson. And you met Agent Ralph Brancuso on your sail over from Fire Island. I'm Jack Fields, the senior agent assigned to the FBI's Manhattan office. The gentleman to your left is Lieutenant Robert Machado of the NYPD's Organized Crime Unit."

A nod of acknowledgment came from each as Fields mentioned their name.

"Everyone in this room has your best interest at heart. We would never expect you to do anything illegal. What we'd like to ask of you is to facilitate us with a bit of eavesdropping."

A quizzical expression appeared on her face. "On who?"

"Before I answer that, let me assure you it will not require your presence in the subject's vicinity. Lieutenant Machado will elaborate on that in a few minutes."

Rizzo raised the coffee mug to his mouth. *If she wasn't confused before, she is now. Fields can't be brief. Instead, he conducts conversations as if they were seminar dialogues.* Rizzo braced for another long one.

Fields continued his narrative. "I'd be less than honest if I said there was little risk involved. The possibility is always a factor in clandestine police work."

Rizzo remembered the last time Fields used those words. It was during his final briefing before leaving for San Juan.

"In this scenario, however, should a threat occur, we would remove you from the situation and seclude you in a secure location."

Nicole remained silent. She turned her head, and her gaze met Rizzo's eyes. Rizzo saw a petition for assurance. He guessed her recent kidnapping by the mob had crossed her mind. Been there, done that.

"What Agent Fields means," Rizzo said, "should something not go as planned, we'd know about it on the spot. I'd be close enough to move you to a safe location. The FBI would then transfer you to a safe house and provide heavy security until the danger is gone." Rizzo noticed her face relax. While across the table, he saw the face of Jack Fields tighten.

"Uh, yes. That's what I meant," Fields said. "If not Mr. Rizzo, one of our agents would be close by." Fields shot a look at Rizzo and carried on. "Bob Machado can explain how the operation would go down, how we plan to accomplish the eavesdropping. Once Ms. Adams understands this, I'm sure she'll feel more comfortable with her role." Fields nodded at Machado to begin.

"Thanks, Jack." Addressing Nicole in his soft, less intimidating style, he began. "Ms. Adams, we are—"

"Lieutenant, please drop the formalities. It's Nicole."

"Oh, right. I'm sorry. Well, Nicole, we're prepared to use a listening device that's near-impossible to detect by anyone less than a sophisticated techie who's had prior experience with it."

"Who is it I'd be listening to?"

"No, no," Fields interrupted. "You're not doing the listening, Nicole. Oh, my," he said with a grin, "far from it. Let Bob finish with his description. We'll get to who's involved in a minute."

Nicole nodded and looked back at Machado.

"The device is referred to in the trade as a roving bug. You've no doubt heard about bugging telephones. Especially if you're a fan of detective novels. Well, we would place this bug on an activated cell phone. An iPhone, if you will. The FBI has used it before. It's perfectly legal."

"If you explain how it works, will I understand?"

"It's not complicated. Yes, you will."

Nicole leaned in and placed her clasped hands on the table's surface in front of her. "Okay then. I'm ready."

Bob Machado began. "The phone's mobile provider installs a piece of software onto the handset. This software places the phone in the diagnostic mode." Machado paused. "Okay, thus far?"

"Yes."

"Conversations in the immediate area of the phone are monitored over the voice channel. It allows us to listen in without being there. The software activates the microphone when it's not in use on a call." Machado captured her gaze. "Still with me?"

"Yes, go ahead."

"The software can be installed remotely, even without the owner of the cell phone's knowledge. This ability provides a level of additional security for the owner."

"How so?"

"Plausible deniability. Of course, that would have application nowhere but a court of law. But, in most other circumstances, the denial of 'I didn't know,' becomes more believable."

Rizzo rolled his eyes. The claim couldn't be more hair brained. The *Mafia* doesn't accept plausible deniability under any circumstance. Many a rat has taken two in the back of the head after screaming, "I didn't know!"

Machado continued. "Once we install the software, the cellular device can be turned into a microphone and transmitter."

"Isn't it the normal function of an iPhone? When I put mine on speaker, doesn't it serve as a microphone?"

"You're correct. But here's the kicker. You must turn the phone on to operate that way. With the installed software we use, the device can transmit conversations to a remote receiver without being activated."

A look of surprise crossed her face, then a smile. "Oh, I see where you're going. The phone could lie around anywhere. It would pick up the conversation and then transmit it wherever."

"Nicole, you're a fast study," Machado said. "Well, now that you understand how the device operates, I'm gonna let Agent Fields explain the scenario we have in mind for you and your iPhone."

"Okay," Fields said. "Let's start with the who question. Nicole, you share your office at The Dugout with Peter Barone. Correct?"

"Yes, when he's there."

"It's where he conducts business most of the time, isn't it?"

Nicole's eyes squeezed as she thought about how to answer. "I would say yes."

"Unless it involved Time-Out Enterprises' bookkeeping concerns? Isn't that true?"

"Well, anytime he's been on the phone in my presence, he's usually arguing with a supplier or distributor." She paused. "Once, I heard him on the phone with someone who sounded like a bank officer. When he realized I was still in the office, he asked me to go to the kitchen to see if the head chef needed anything. I thought it was a strange request until I understood he wanted me out of hearing."

"Has he ever asked you to leave the office, like when he was about to make a call?"

"Yes. Not every day, but often enough. A good deal of the time, I'm out checking on the other four stores. So it's not unusual for him to be alone in the office."

Brancuso jumped into the exchange. "I got a question," he said. "On those occasions when Barone asks you to leave the office, do you take your purse?"

"I keep the purse in my desk drawer, so, no. There's no reason to have it with me unless I intend to leave The Dugout to go to another store."

Fields glanced in Machado's direction with a questioning look.

Machado responded with a head nod and a grin.

"And that's why we feel the risk to you is minimal," Fields said. "It's not like wearing a wire." He wrinkled his brow and asked, "You understand how that works, don't you?"

Nicole laid her hand on her chest as if searching for the wired device that wasn't there and said, "Yes. I've seen a few movies where law enforcement used that type of device."

"Your iPhone doesn't touch your person while using the roving bug technique. And, the best part, you don't have to be present for it to operate. The fact of the matter is, unless you're absent at the time of the subject's conversation, we're sure the information we're interested in would not be forthcoming."

"Excuse me, Jack," Machado said. He turned to Nicole. "Before I forget, who's your cell phone provider?"

"Verizon."

"Perfect. The PD has a collegial relationship with their East Coast regional people. They'll cooperate."

"That's a plus," Fields said. "I'm glad you remembered to ask." His eyes searched the five faces around the table. "So can anyone think of anything else we need to ask Nicole? Anything we left out?"

"I have something," Rizzo said.

"I thought you might."

Rizzo slid his chair out from the table and turned ninety degrees to face her. "You had a bit of a donnybrook with Peter Barone the other night. True?"

She looked up. Her eyes held his for a long moment. "How'd you know about that?"

The corners of his mouth turned up. "I never kiss and tell, but that's the word."

"Yes, he got testy with me one night. We were closing up. He'd been out somewhere getting drunk. For whatever reason, he picked this night to go off on me."

"What reason? Can you tell us?"

"I can guess. The remarks he made, it sounded like he was angry I'd shown him up, made him look bad."

"Is he still angry?"

"Well, I don't know. The bartender there that night told me Sal Fusco, one of the, ah, owners, had a talk with him over dinner at another store. He's been okay since then."

"Thanks, Nicole," Rizzo said. "Jack, can I ask a few more questions?"

Fields looked at Rizzo, hesitated, then said, "Go ahead."

"Nicole, you hire the staff, right?"

"Uh-huh."

"Is Barone familiar with all the servers and bartenders?"

"The servers? Hardly. They come and go too often. But he knows most of the bartenders. They're his eyes and ears around the stores."

"That's not a surprise," Machado said. "It's often the way they work. Former mob soldiers." He turned from Nicole and looked at Fields, gesturing that he'd finished.

"Anyone else?" Fields asked. When no one spoke up, Fields looked at Nicole. "How about you? Have we left out anything you'd like to talk about?"

"The question I have is when can I expect this eavesdropping to start?"

"I'm sure we can be ready in about a week if our friends at Verizon play along." He paused for a second and smiled at her. "So am I to assume you're okay with this plan? Are you comfortable with your role?"

She brought her fingers up to her mouth, hesitated, and said, "I think so."

"Okay. Guess we've covered everything. Ralph, you're gonna drive them to Sayville, then come back for us?"

"Right."

"Nicole, we'll be in touch via Mr. Rizzo. And thanks, Anya. You were a great help."

"No problem. We'll check if our tail is still hanging around the ferry parking lot. Maybe offer to buy him a drink."

"See you back at the office," Fields said, smiling.

Rizzo gave them a friendly wave as they exited the room and headed to the front door.

Fields motioned for Rizzo and Machado to sit down.

Uh-oh, here's where the shit hits the fan. He could see sharp edges of anger in the agent's eyes.

"Rizzo, I swear. Sometimes I doubt you can tell the difference between bravery and insanity."

Rizzo assumed an innocent look. "What?"

"Don't cop to that pose. You know damn well what I'm referring to."

Rizzo lifted both palms. "Hey, I'll get a job there as a waiter. What's the big deal?"

"The hell you will. You'd stand out like a sumo wrestler at a debutante's ball."

Rizzo had never told Fields about Dominic Biondo, The Dugout's bartender. He figured if he could influence Vinnie Alcamo with the right amount of schmaltz, he could work something out between those two *paesanos*. The problem was he'd be unwilling to share the knowledge of these relationships with the Feds. While he wasn't committed to a vow of *Omertà*, he still had an obligation to Luke Rizzo's Code-of-Silence policy to protect his sources.

"I don't want to sound like I'm over-promising—"

"Then don't," Fields said.

"Right, but I'm gonna try to set up an alert system. I have the right conduits I can trust who can do this for me. If it can't be done, I'll call you."

"And who's gonna let me know if you end up under a concrete slab?"

"In that case, I'll have Jimmie Hoffa send you a telegram."

Chapter Thirteen

Belvedere Castle, Central Park - Mon. A.M. 5/11

The shadowed form leaned against the wall of Belvedere Castle and watched the bent-over man climb the hill toward him. The moon had fallen behind the 137-foot gray-granite tower, leaving Keith Dickerson—dressed in black from head to toe—in total darkness. Summit Rock at Eighty-third Street overlooked Central Park West and was one of the two turrets flanking the castle. Dickerson had chosen the site for his clandestine meet because the location was entirely sheltered from view—even in daylight.

Dickerson looked out over the trees that enveloped them. Central Park was a beautiful place, he thought, but like any other part of the world, it had an evil side, especially at night. New Yorkers knew enough not to linger in the park too long after sunset. The police allowed no one in the park between the hours of 1:00 am and 6:00 am. That's why Dickerson chose the Belvedere Castle to meet with Alfie. The likelihood of someone spotting him was nil, not even if a roving police patrol happened past the castle.

"That you, Lieutenant?" the man asked with a hint of uncertainty.

The illuminated hands of Dickerson's wristwatch displayed two-thirty. His snitch's outline formed before him in the darkness as he neared. "You're fifteen minutes late, Alfie."

"Sorry, Lieutenant, but trains from the Bronx don't run too often, at least not at this hour. I waited a long fuckin' time 'til one comes along."

Alfie was part of a crew of soldiers in a New York mob family other than the Gambinos. A three-time loser with a criminal history of robbery convictions, he was currently on parole. Three months ago, Dickerson's team had nailed him for an attempted B&E while carrying a gun. Dickerson cut a deal with the DA before he turned his snitch loose. Alfie had agreed to provide information he came across about the mob's activities if it pertained to a major robbery in the planning stages.

His sole option was to become the lieutenant's snitch. He knew they would charge him with felony robbery for his latest misstep. Caught with a weapon, he'd violated his parole. He faced serious time in a federal penitentiary, and that made the choice easy.

This night, Dickerson wasn't interested in the mob's robbery schemes. He wanted to get from Alfie the name of the shooter who put the two bullets in his brother's head.

During a previous meet, Dickerson had told Alfie about the murder at his beach house in West Hampton. He knew *Mafia* hitmen liked to brag among themselves when they've whacked someone—a macho confirmation. Dickerson guessed Alfie would eventually get wind of the culprit's name. When his snitch did, he would contact him through their pre-arranged signal.

Lucky for Dickerson, Alfie heard sooner rather than later. He caught a break thanks to the habit of loudmouth hitmenbraggarts who liked to embellish their stories. They ended up spewing pure fantasy, thus making it harder to believe them.

Dickerson pushed off the stone wall and shook Alfie's hand. "Okay, my man, Wadda ya got? Something good, I hope?"

"Yeah, it's good stuff. I got it from a guy who does his drinkin' a lot with the shooter. Sez there was two of them what did the hit."

"They weren't local, were they? They had to be from a family outside the state."

"No. They were local guys. Gambinos."

"Holy shit! Great! Names?"

"One guy is Angie Russo. He's the shooter, the one with the big mouth. The second guy is Mario Langella. I know Mario pretty good from a different crew. A mean bastard. He'd fuck over his best buddy if pushed. Wouldn't mind seeing him go down for this. Angie, he's a real *stunade*. Know what I mean? What I'm told, it's his second whack job."

"Good. Now where do they do their drinking?"

"Hey, Lieutenant, you axed me to find out who, nothin' more. I'm already holdin' on by my nuts. I can't get any more into this or I'll—"

"Bullshit, Alfie. Give me the name of their damn hangout. I'm sure the place is in the OCU's book. A raid ain't gonna come as a big surprise."

"Aww," Alfie groaned and smacked the heels of his hands together. "You know, Lieutenant, our deal was supposed to be strictly about robbery scuttlebutt. This is way out—"

"I don't give a rat-fuck, Alfie. It was my brother they killed. Remember? The place and location? Now!"

Alfie threw up his hands. "Oh, God damn it. It's called Ruby's up on Hunts Point Avenue in the South Bronx. Near the—"

"I know where it is. And so does everyone in the Forty-first Precinct. I'm sure it holds a special place on the precinct's desk blotter. A nasty-ass neighborhood."

"Can I go now, Lieutenant?"

"Yeah, you go ahead. But be careful, Alfie. There's a lot of bad shit out there. I need you to stay alive, you know?"

"I'm with ya, Lieutenant."

Alfie turned to leave when Dickerson's call stopped him. "Hey, I'm sure I don't have to remind you, this meeting never happened. Unless you're looking to have one of your *goombas* put one through your mouth. *Capice*?"

"*Capice*, Lieutenant."

* * *

West Side, Manhattan - Tues. P.M. 5/12

The bar at Joe Allen's was elbow to elbow with the usual after-theater crowd. The level of chatter made it impossible to hear the person next to you unless you leaned in close. Rizzo didn't mind. It gave him an excuse to steal an occasional smooch from his Avis Angel.

Flo reached over and patted his hand. "Hon, I'm awfully glad you invited Vinnie and Carla to have drinks with us tonight. She's such a sweet person, and so pretty."

"His best wife of the three," Rizzo said with a grin. "And this one has real talent. The duet she did in the first act with the lead was terrific. I remember seeing the original version of this show. The person playing her role back then wasn't nearly as good."

"I liked her a lot. And him," she said, rolling her eyes. "So ruggedly handsome. Too bad they couldn't stay longer. I enjoyed talking with her."

"She has an early morning call, but we'll see them again."

He was happy Flo liked Carla. When Rizzo told her about receiving Vinnie's invite to his wife's dress rehearsal, he wisely omitted what Vinnie did for a living. Except to say he was a union representative, which he was. Muscle for the mob was all but in the past. And it wasn't appropriate to mention.

"You two were huddled in conversation for a long time. What were you talking about?"

"Just guy stuff."

"I can't believe you know him since you were kids. That's amazing and so unusual. It's nice you kept in touch."

Rizzo smiled. "Yeah, my mother used to say he would grow up to be a movie star."

"Well, he's handsome enough, and my, he looks strong."

Rizzo started to say, "Only on the outside," but caught himself. He didn't think Vinnie would want him to share the latest report he'd received from his pulmonary surgeon. Stage-four lung cancer was a deadly prognosis. Rizzo had difficulty processing it. He knew what it meant.

They'd arrived at the bar after the rehearsal around ten-forty-five. The two women women had been sitting on stools while Rizzo and Vinnie stood behind them, talking. The ambient noise level was at its peak, so when Vinnie told him about the surgeon's report, Rizzo missed hearing him. "What did you say?" Rizzo leaned in and Vinnie repeated himself. This time, the words fought back from exiting his throat.

Cancer had progressed rapidly since his initial examination. The preliminary diagnosis was only six months ago. The doctor was hesitant to say how long he had, and Vinnie didn't want to know.

Recalling how difficult it was for Vinnie to tell him the news, Rizzo swallowed hard. He sat staring at the bartender while he prepared different cocktails and placed them on a tray at the service end. His eyes followed the hands of the mixologist, but his mind was preoccupied with a confusing assortment of images.

The image that bothered him most was Vinnie's face while he spoke of his terminal condition. He thought about his friend's chosen path in life and the ever-present possibility of a final exit—not unlike the one of his brother Richie. The mob rarely accorded their members a happy ending. Rizzo decided if Vinnie had to die before he completed a full life, at least now it wouldn't be in a fusillade of bullets. Small comfort.

Rizzo felt Flo's hand land on his arm.

"Where are you, hon? You haven't said a word in a while."

He turned to her and noticed her empty glass. "Another Big Jack?"

She thought a moment, then asked, "What time do you have?"

"Twelve forty. Why? You got a date?"

"Yes, with my handsome husband. He promised to fly me to the moon tonight."

Rizzo struggled to transition from earthly thoughts of Vinnie's condition to the stratospheric delights his wife had offered. Despite the million miles separating the two, he couldn't hold back smiling. "You know you can't accomplish that unless you're under the covers in bed?"

"So?"

Rizzo flagged the bartender. "Joe, cash me out, please."

* * *

Chelsea Area, Manhattan - Wed. P.M. 5/13

"Yeah, I'm heading back to the office now. Be there in ten minutes. Meet me in the lobby." Rizzo ended the phone call and paid the lunch check at the door. He exited the Lantern Coffee Shop, sucking on a mint he'd picked from the bowl on the cashier's desk. The treat countered the lingering taste of the sautéed onions that smothered the cheeseburger he'd consumed. Rizzo loved his sautéed onions.

He found Keith Dickerson leaning against the wall in the lobby. Rizzo remembered the man's brother, Roy, standing in the same spot when he and Rizzo first met a month ago.

Dickerson, attired in a suit and tie, indicated the detective was on duty. During their silent elevator ride, Rizzo noticed the man's mouth turned down at the corners, making him appear angry. His steely gray eyes, heavier pouched than the last time he saw him, gave him an aura of worry and determination. Rizzo was sure this would not be a social visit.

"Take a seat," Rizzo said, gesturing to the sofa. Instead, Dickerson sat in one of the two new armchairs at the ends of the coffee table. Rizzo circled behind his desk, checked for messages on his phone console, and looked up. "Coffee?"

"Thanks, but no. I'm wired as it is."

Rizzo scooted around from his desk and dropped into the chair opposite his visitor. "What's going on? What's got you so uptight?"

Dickerson lowered his head and stared at his hands folded in his lap. He looked up. "I've thought long and hard before deciding to come here."

Rizzo's "uh-oh" antennae launched him into a state of red alert. He remained silent and waited for the man to continue.

Dickerson's eyes fixed on Rizzo's face, his elbows perched on the chair's armrests, hands laced in front of him, torso tilted forward like he didn't want Rizzo to miss a word of what he'd say. "What I'm gonna tell you is something I've thought about doing since Roy's murder a month ago. It opens me up to all sorts of liability if you ever decided not to keep it confidential."

"Then maybe you shouldn't tell me."

His body jerked back like someone ducking a right cross. "You saying you wouldn't keep quiet?"

"Well, depends on what it is."

The noise from Fifth Avenue's busy traffic activity bled its way into the room. Dickerson's heavy breathing came through his nose, a characteristic of a person on the heavy side. His wide brow creased as though he felt pain.

"Hey, whatever it is, it's clear you haven't done it yet. Right?"

Dickerson issued a soft "No."

"Then, damn it, there's no culpability until you do whatever it is you're sweating over. So, tell me already. Let's hear what it is."

"But if I—"

"Keith, stop the bullshit! I can guess what's running through your mind. Talk to me about it. Now!"

Dickerson spread his hands and ironed them along his thighs. Confusion invaded his eyes, and then with a sudden burst of energy, he popped out the words, "Oh shit, okay."

A tight smile tugged at the corners of Rizzo's mouth. He felt like he'd defused an active bomb.

"I got a snitch in my pocket," Dickerson began. "He's part of a crew in a mob family. Not the Gambinos. His crew has been heavy into truck hijacking, big box-store looting, shit like that. He's been reliable with his info."

Rizzo flashed to his years on the job, when Rabbit Valez, his snitch, proved to be such an asset. "How long you been running this guy?"

"Oh, more than a year now."

The trouble with snitches, Rizzo thought, they're often the source of third-hand information and not the most current actionable kind. He remembered several of Rabbit's tips turned out to be week-old drug deals .

"How does he figure in this?"

"I asked him to keep his ears open for any talk among the dogs who liked to brag about their exploits. You know, like maybe a recent hit they pulled off."

"He'd be privy to that shit?"

"Sometimes. He was reluctant at first, but I squeezed him. Damn if he didn't get back to me a week later with two names."

"Hired guns? Out-of-state family?"

"No, local. The Gambino crew."

"That's crazy," Rizzo said. "A hit like that is always contracted out. Then they can't connect the local bosses to it. And you think his info is on the money?"

"No reason to doubt him. He said they even mentioned Roy's name. I got him to tell me where they hang out. A bar up in the South Bronx."

"You know what they look like? Do they have records? Have you checked them out?"

"That's the problem. If I search them on any official link, I leave my identity."

"So, what's the big deal?"

"This is where it gets sticky." Dickerson looked away. The corner file cabinet held his eyes for a moment.

Rizzo's open palms shot out in front of him. "Don't tell me. Let me guess."

"Well, shit, I wouldn't be the first on the NYPD to use a throwaway."

"No, you wouldn't be. But you might be alone as a first-grade detective lieutenant with a long, distinguished career behind him to be that stupid. And with only a few more years to go before retirement."

Dickerson's face reddened.

"Tell me, why in God's name are you here? I mean, if that's the route you intend to take? What the hell do you want from me?"

"I need to go up to this bar in the Bronx. Take a look around. See if I could ID them. I wanted to hire you to go with me as my backup."

Rizzo stared at him with complete disbelief.

Dickerson didn't seem to notice. "Then go back alone another night and do them both as they left."

A thought struck Rizzo. "Just as a matter of curiosity, what's the name of the bar in the Bronx?"

"Ruby's."

Rizzo didn't change his expression. He'd guessed right. "Okay, now tell me the names your snitch gave you."

"Angie Russo and Mario Langella. Russo was the shooter. He's the one my snitch said did the bragging. Said he knew the other guy, Mario, from a time before in a different crew. He hated him."

"You've never been to that bar, Ruby's?"

"No, but I've heard about it."

"Well, I've been there," Rizzo said with a note of confidence. "And I've met this Mario guy. I can see why your snitch hated him." Rizzo got up and walked to his desk. "I'm gonna tell you something about the time I met Mario." Rizzo leaned over and flipped the pages of his desk calendar as though trying to find the right date. "I made a trip up there looking for a bad guy that used the bar as his hangout. Sound familiar?"

Rizzo returned to his chair while Dickerson remained silent. He watched Rizzo. His eyes tracked him like he was a blip on a radar screen.

"I had someone with me as backup," Rizzo went on. "Not anyone experienced. He was a monster Rastafarian buddy. Mario, with arms the size of a boa constrictor, and another *gavone* with a loaded nine, didn't like us the minute we walked in. They asked us . . . no, not asked, they showed us the damn door before we finished our Coronas. I don't doubt they would receive us in the same cordial manner if we entered their inner sanctum of dirtbags today."

"You think my plan for revenge wouldn't work?"

"No. I'm also certain you'd end up with a snarly body snatcher slipping a toe tag on you while you're laid out on a slab in the Bellevue Morgue."

Dickerson leaned back and pointed his chin to the ceiling. He closed his eyes and released an audible sigh.

"Keith, it's not an impossible situation. You can get your revenge."

Dickerson came out of his reverie and looked back at Rizzo. "How?"

"We do it the legitimate way. We nail them with your snitch's testimony."

Dickerson jumped to his feet. "No way. This guy would take a .45 in the mouth before he had time to testify."

"Yeah, but who says they couldn't break down Angie or Mario during interrogation? A lot tougher birds than them were made to sing."

A loud horn blast rose from the street. Dickerson jerked his head around and looked toward the window behind Rizzo's desk. The traffic noise became a low murmur again. He sat down and turned to Rizzo. "I hope you're right."

Rizzo flashed him an uncomfortable grin. Yeah, I do too. "Okay, for starters, here's what I need you to do. You know your West Hampton neighbor's name?

"MacDougall."

"Get their number. Call them. Find out if the Suffolk investigators ever followed up with them about seeing any strangers. I'm betting they didn't contact them again."

"They that bad?"

Rizzo shrugged. "If I'm right, and they spotted someone, ask if we can come out, speak with them, show them head-shot photos. Meanwhile, see what you can get on the computer. Download the files for both Mario and Angie."

A look of understanding crossed Dickerson's face. "If we get an ID from MacDougall, sketchy as it might be, with my snitch's input, we might have enough probable cause to bring in the two of them. And they won't require my snitch to do a face-to-face."

"That's my thinking. I'll run it by my guy at the OCU, but you never can tell. He might feel it's not enough."

Chapter Fourteen

West Hampton Beach, Long Island – Fri. A.M. 5/15

"I don't understand," Dickerson said. He held up the baseball cap by the bill with two fingers and looked at it like something that fell off the back of a garbage truck.

"What?" Rizzo said from his bent-over position. He'd been examining a faint shoe imprint he found near the wicker chaise lounge on the deck.

"This," Dickerson said. His nose wrinkled like he'd gotten a whiff of a bad smell. "It doesn't belong to Roy. No way. He was a Yankees fan. Yeah, from the day he was born. Hated the Mets with a passion."

Rizzo rose and ducked when two seagulls swooped past his head. The gulls' cree-cree-cree faded quickly, and in seconds they were out of sight. He walked to where Dickerson stood and stared at the cap dangling from the man's fingers. "Where'd you find it?"

"Under the lounge, caught between one of the leg struts. Probably blown there by the wind. I never saw it when I came out here weeks ago to meet with the police."

Rizzo shook his head. "It's obvious they didn't either. Drop it on the chair—carefully. I hope there's a plastic baggie in the kitchen large enough."

"You think this could be evidence?"

"I got a hunch it belonged to one of the two killers. If it did, we've hit the mother lode."

"DNA?"

"You bet." Rizzo shook his head. "How dumb-ass sloppy of the locals. If you told me the Seventh never came here to investigate, I'd believe it. You find anything else they missed when you came out? Besides the cap?"

"I found a mess on the deck . . . blood, skull fragments. But they saw it too. Made me wait for forensics before I could clean it up."

Dickerson set the cap down and disappeared through the opened sliders and into the house. Rizzo looked around, taking in the beachfront scenery. He listened to the rolling waves lapping ashore not fifty yards from the deck. The salty scent in the air tickled his nose. He sensed a peaceful feeling produced by the cool afternoon breeze and the steady sound of breaking waves. Suddenly, a shudder passed down his spine. The tranquility he enjoyed at the moment, juxtaposed against the reality of a brutal murder that took place right where he stood, struck him as weird.

Dickerson returned with a large size baggie and held it open. Rizzo picked up the cap, pinching the fabric at the top of the crown, and dropped it in.

"The sweatband looks saturated."

"Beautiful," Dickerson said, smiling.

"That, along with the MacDougall's photo verification this morning, made coming out here worthwhile. You think? Let's get this to the Seventh. Should make it a ground ball for the Suffolk investigators. Now, aren't you glad you don't need a throwaway?"

The smile disappeared from the man's face and his eyes glazed over. He lowered himself onto the chaise lounge, still holding the bagged cap. The change in the man's mood was dramatic.

"What the hell is going on?"

"Rizzo," he said, "I've been around long enough to know ground ball cases are rare. I've seen stronger evidence than this go south." The raised baggie dangled from his fingers. "Yeah, I've seen surer things hit a wall all because some ambitious ADA wants to prove how fucking by-the-book he can be."

"Yeah, but—"

"No, Rizzo, I'm not saying we don't have a good shot, that there isn't enough to indict those two sons-a-bitches. I hope we do—no, I pray we do. But keep in mind, I'm not ready to dump my throwaway yet."

* * *

Fordham University, The Bronx - Sat. A.M. 5/16

"How did Carla's opening night go?" Rizzo asked as he turned off the Bronx River Parkway at the East Fordham Avenue exit.

"The show got great reviews, and she got nice mentions in most of them. By the way, how come you didn't ask Flo to come with us? She doesn't like baseball?"

"I would have, but this is her one Saturday a month to work."

"What's your son's position?"

"First base. Matt's played it ever since his freshman year in high school."

Rizzo steered the rented Mustang along Southern Boulevard. He reached the main vehicle gate of the Fordham University campus and cruised into the baseball field's parking lot. The gate attendant directed him to go straight two aisles and make a right, where he would find ample parking.

The lot appeared lightly filled, which meant Houlihan Park's limited one thousand-seat grandstand capacity would not require them to sit elbow-to-elbow. It was the Rams' last game of the season, the third of a three-game series with the University of Massachusetts. The contest was meaningful solely to the pride of the players on both teams.

"Let's grab seats on the first-base side," Rizzo said as they entered the fence-enclosed ball field. "That way we can watch Matt up-close."

They climbed the stands and at mid-way, sat down a few yards past the first-base bag. Vinnie's eyes scanned the infield diamond. He studied with intensity the players warming up as they fielded ground balls and tossed them to Matt at first base.

The tight smile on Vinnie's face appeared to Rizzo as if he imagined himself as a part of the action on the field. Vinnie looked over at Rizzo with a wistful glint in his eyes. Something had occurred to him.

"Remember those softball games in the schoolyard when we were kids, sliding into second base on that damn concrete?"

"Oh, yeah. We didn't call it Raspberry Field for nothing. You were pretty good with the bat, as I recall."

"Not even close to your swing."

Rizzo smiled. "Fun days, they were."

Vinnie watched in silence the many times the ball popped into Matt's glove. He appeared to be engrossed with the athletic tosses Matt made around the infield, and the graceful and competent stretches he would execute to reach an off-line throw.

"Does your son get nervous knowing his father is in the stands?" he asked Rizzo. "I know I would."

"Not anymore. He's grown comfortable with his playing skills. My presence doesn't bother him at all."

It occurred to him Vinnie's question had an underlying sadness to it. His friend hadn't posed it out of idle curiosity, but more as a recollection of what his early childhood lacked. Rizzo never met Vinnie's parents. The singular piece of information about them came secondhand from another neighborhood kid: his father was an abusive drunk. Nor had Rizzo known Vinnie's two brothers, the whacked mobster, and the priest. He had no idea what amount of positive familial influences impacted Vinnie's life. If pressed, Rizzo would say nothing good.

The game began and proceeded with quickness through the early innings, allowing for a fair amount of action on both the offense and the defense. When the last out was made at the top half of the ninth, Fordham claimed a 4 to 2 victory. Matt played an errorless first base and went two for four at the plate. Before he ran through the tunnel to the Rams' locker room with the rest of the team, Matt came over to hug his father and be introduced to Vinnie.

"What a great kid," Vinnie said later as they climbed into the Mustang. "You gotta be damn proud of him."

"Oh, yeah, I am. There were rough times early on, especially when I was drinking and pulled every kind of serious shit behind Terri's back."

"How'd it affect your relationship with your son?"

"Well, before the divorce, his mother was none too kind with her comments about me. The things she'd say did a job on him."

"He seems okay now."

"After we divorced, I joined AA."

"That help?"

"Oh, yeah. I met Flo about a year later and got religion. He and I reconciled. It's been a fantastic relationship since."

"Hey, thanks for inviting me today. I enjoyed the hell out of it."

They were on the Bronx River Parkway headed back into the city when Vinnie asked, "How's the Adams woman doing?" Vinnie made a face, a conspiratorial expression.

"Bro, you'd know better than I since you keep in touch with Dominic."

"Yeah. He tells me she's found her footing after the donnybrook she had with Barone. He's come around to accepting her. Fusco had a chat with him."

"You told me about it," Rizzo said.

"So you keep in touch with her?"

"Well, it's kind of—"

"Look, *paesano*, you don't have to tell me what's going on between you and her. But let me give you a little insight on the situation." Vinnie's expression turned troubled. "I don't believe things are aces with her. From the rumblings I hear, she's there because of Carmine D'Angelo."

"You think something is going on with them?"

"No, that's not what I mean. Yeah, she's there because D'Angelo wants her there. Fusco mentioned to Dom that Carmine likes the job she does. And he's told Barone as much."

"What's the problem then?"

Vinnie lowered his voice like he feared being overheard. "Sal Fusco. He's the problem. I'm telling you this because I don't want you to get dirtied by any of the fallout."

"Man, this sounds big-time serious."

"It is. And you gotta keep it to yourself."

"Oh, I will."

Vinnie stared out at the passing scenery along the parkway. It was clear to Rizzo the man struggled with a decision. Finally, Vinnie turned in his seat to face him.

"Fusco's angling to take over from D'Angelo. He's looking for any reason to bad mouth him to the don."

"Wait. I shouldn't be asking, but how the hell did you come to know this? I mean, this is really inside baseball shit."

"You're right, and you shouldn't ask. But I'll tell you anyway because I want you should understand it ain't fairy tales I'm giving you."

"You sure you wanna tell me? I don't have to know."

Vinnie continued as if he hadn't heard Rizzo. "Dominic has always been a favorite of Sal Fusco. He loved the way he came through for the family back when we were doin' the heavy lifting, breaking heads. I mean, before Dom lost a slice of his."

Vinnie had told Rizzo that story some time ago. He was amazed how Dominic had survived and carried on with his life.

"Fusco envied Dom's size and toughness. But for whatever reason, he often takes Dom into his confidence. He likes to schmooze with him at The Dugout bar."

Rizzo's head swiveled back and forth while he listened to Vinnie and concentrated on staying in his lane.

"And Dom shares things with you? That's how you found out about Fusco's scheme to replace D'Angelo?"

"Yeah, but it doesn't mean shit to you. What you should be careful about is your relationship with the woman."

"How does Nicole Adams fit into whatever he plans to do?"

"She's a club. He's gonna use her against D'Angelo. Consider for starters, an underboss keeps a woman around who threatened to blow the whistle on their operation. I mean, that's a major no-no. I'm sure Fusco's got other clubs."

"And then what?"

"When he gets enough ammo, he's gonna ask for the don's permission to have D'Angelo whacked. Then he steps up to become underboss."

"And what's all that got to do with me?"

"You were seen with her on the Staten Island ferry ride, and Fusco doesn't believe it was a coincidence."

* * *

One Police Plaza, Manhattan - Thurs. A.M. 5/21

Bob Machado grinned as he leaned back in his desk chair. "You two will be happy to hear this. I got a call from Detective Sergeant Bryce of the Suffolk Major Crimes Unit. He wanted to convey his thanks to you guys for turning over the cap and photos to the Seventh Precinct."

Machado remembered the earlier phone call from the Seventh's commander. The call came to let him know how pissed he was that Rizzo and Dickerson had gone back to the house without notifying them. But when he learned the Seventh would be a part of the task force to take down the Gambinos, he was mollified.

"They get a hit on the DNA?" Dickerson asked.

"Yep. Belongs to Angie Russo."

Rizzo nodded to Dickerson, who smiled.

"We got the report this morning and now Suffolk can haul his ass in for questioning."

"He was the shooter," Dickerson said."

"How do you know that?"

"That's according to my snitch."

"I suspect they'll be able to squeeze Russo to give up the second guy, Mario Langella," Rizzo said. "Not that they'll need to. The neighbors' ID of the photo should add enough to probable cause to bring him in."

"They're both losers," Machado said. "I doubt either wants to do lengthy jail time again. Should be enough an inducement to rat out whoever ordered the hit. And Fields will have a predicate for a RICO charge against Carmine D'Angelo. Won't that make him happy?"

Dickerson's expression grew stony as he cast his eyes to the floor.

Machado noticed. "What's bothering you?"

"I was thinking about something."

"What?"

"I was thinking if the mob ever got wind of Angie Russo's bragging. I mean, there could be two dead soldiers at this point. They wouldn't hesitate to remove them both."

"By God, you're right," Machado said and reached for his phone. "I should call Suffolk. Get 'em to move fast on the arrest warrants. Can your snitch tell us where they live, where we can find them?"

"I'll try to contact him tonight. See if he knows. Sometimes he's hard to reach."

"Bob, Suffolk should send their guys to check out Ruby's in the South Bronx," Rizzo said. "They might find both of them there . . . if it isn't too late."

Chapter Fifteen

The South Bronx - Sun. early A.M. 5/24

The Suffolk County investigators had nothing more than mug shots to ID the two killers. Rizzo agreed to help out and tag along to the South Bronx. His encounter with Mario Langella wasn't that long ago. He assured the detectives he'd be able to spot him coming out of Ruby's even from fifty yards.

They'd arrived a little before midnight at the Forty-first Precinct with signed arrest warrants for Langella and Russo. Now, parked on Hunt's Point Avenue fifty yards up from Ruby's on the opposite side, they had an unobstructed view of the door. At the early morning hour of one-thirty, an occasional vehicle went by. The night was eerily quiet.

Rizzo remembered the last time he'd staked out this infamous mob hangout. He was searching for the killer of his snitch. The killer also worked for a gang of sex-slavers, and he knew where they were holding two kidnapped sixteen-year-old Mexican girls. Rizzo's companions on that plant were from

Florida. The second girl, Rosita Fuentes, was the sister of one of the Floridians.

This time around, Rizzo had the company of two Suffolk County detectives from the Major Crimes Unit. The driver, Detective Ira Rubin, leaned back and stretched both arms, trying to shake the tightness in his neck and shoulders. "Damn, I forgot how tough it is sitting this long in one position."

Detective Wayne Falbey turned to face Rizzo in the back seat. "You're sure he's in there?"

"That's what the bartender told my contact when he called him. The source is golden, believe me. The bartender said Langella stays until two or two-thirty Friday and Saturday nights. He's a creature of habit. We should see him walk through the door any time now."

Rizzo thought about their decision to make the two arrests separately—Mario Langella upon leaving Ruby's and Angie Russo when he arrived at his apartment. He and the detectives had discussed it earlier.

They'd watched Russo leave the bar a little before one as the bartender had predicted. A second pair of Suffolk detectives followed Russo home to his apartment; it was the address listed on his driver's license. Rizzo assumed they had him in cuffs by now and were on their way to Riverhead, Long Island.

Rizzo turned to peer out the back window at the unmarked car from the Forty-first. He'd noticed it parked on the other side of the avenue when it arrived about an hour ago. The precinct's duty officer had offered the Suffolk detectives back-up. They declined out of professional pride. The DO nodded, smiled, and dispatched one anyway.

The Forty-first on Longwood Avenue, known as an "A" house, dealt with the abundance of crime and prostitution that saturated the South Bronx neighborhood. Despite the detectives' decision to go it alone, the duty officer also arranged to have an RMP make a pass around the block every fifteen minutes. At one o'clock, the Forty-first's unmarked detective's car had taken a position up the avenue, but close enough to offer assistance if needed.

While he was on the job, Rizzo had spent a few years assigned to the Forty-first precinct, nicknamed Fort Apache. He knew how protective they could be when their officers went to make an arrest. The bad guys of this neighborhood were off-the-charts violent. Guns were everywhere. Rizzo was happy the precinct maintained their guarded arrest practice.

At two-thirty-five, a pair of figures appeared at Ruby's opened doorway. A streetlamp towering overhead bathed them in a pool of light. Rizzo recognized Langella as soon as he stepped out.

"That's him," he said. Rizzo squinted for a moment before the second man came into focus. He recognized him as Nelly, the one who had flashed a gun during his original visit to Ruby's.

"That's a problem," Rubin said. "There's two of them."

Rizzo leaned over Rubin's shoulder and said, "Let's take a minute. In the past, they traveled in their own cars. See if they split up and which way they go."

The two men reached the curb together and stepped off. They crossed the avenue and appeared to be heading toward an alley between two retail stores.

"Enough," shouted Falbey. "We can't lose them. Go! Now!"

Rubin put the vehicle in gear and sped off. They screeched to a stop before Langella and Nelly reached the other side. Falbey leaped from the vehicle, his weapon drawn, and shouted, "Police, face down on the ground. Now!"

Langella and Nelly froze with bewildered expressions.

"I said, down on the ground," Falbey repeated. This time, he gestured with his weapon. The two men remained fixed, determined not to comply.

The next moment, the Forty-first's unmarked vehicle drew abreast of the scene. The driver's door opened and a beefy, sandy-haired detective stepped out. He stood at least six-five, because when he leaned across the top of the vehicle, his torso covered half of the roof. "Langella, you and your pal do as you're told if you know what's good for ya."

Langella turned his head. "Casey, what the fuck's goin' on here?"

"You're being arrested, asshole. Stop whining and get your face down. You too, Nelly."

The two men lay prone on the ground, close to the curb. Rubin straddled Langella. He jacked his arms back, and in a smooth, practiced movement, had both wrists locked in cuffs.

Falbey walked over to Nelly and tapped him on the hip with his foot. "You can get up."

Nelly didn't move.

"I said you can get up," Falbey repeated.

The man rolled over into a sitting position and looked up. "What's goin' on?"

"You're not being arrested. You're free to leave."

"But, I don't—"

"Where's your vehicle? Get the hell outta here before I come up with a reason to book you."

Nelly hoisted himself up, stood for a moment, and brushed off his shirt and pants. He looked down at Langella. "Hey, man, you hang tight. This is a shit-box mistake, for sure."

Langella closed his eyes for a moment. "Yeah, bro, a mistake," he muttered. "Make sure you tell The Hat about the mistake."

The words fell on Rizzo's ears like a loud gunshot. He slipped up behind Falbey and whispered, "You heard what he said about The Hat, didn't you? Remember it."

"Yeah. Why?"

"It's the nickname of a Gambino *capo*, Sal Fusco."

Falbey nodded. He turned to Nelly and waved him off. Without wasting a moment, the man headed toward the alley and disappeared into the dark.

Rubin motioned to Falbey to help get Langella upright. When they had him stabilized and leaning against the vehicle's rear fender, Langella turned his head and stared into Rizzo's face. "Hey, I remember you."

"Never saw you before in my life," Rizzo said. His words carried little conviction.

"Oh, yeah, you're the guy. The prick I threw out of Ruby's a couple of years ago. Yeah, you're him, all right. You and that raghead Rastafarian."

Rubin knelt and wrapped restraints around Langella's ankles, tying them so he couldn't take a step. He opened the vehicle's back door. Together, he and Falbey edged the man into the vehicle and a seated position.

Falbey approached the Forty-first vehicle with the two detectives. "Hey, thanks, guys. I'm not sure this wouldn't have ended in some nasty business if you hadn't been here."

"No sweat. Sometimes a familiar voice is all you need. Happy to help." Casey looked across at Rizzo. "Hey, Rizzo, you need a ride back to the Station House?"

"Yeah, I'd appreciate it," Rizzo said.

Before Rubin could close the door, Langella leaned out and looked up at Rizzo. His bottom lip curled, and with a sneer in his voice, he spit out, "So that's your name? Rizzo, huh? Well, pal, you're a dead man."

Langella managed to pull his head back a second before Rubin slammed the car door closed. "Shut the fuck up, dirtbag," the detective said.

* * *

Jamaica Avenue, Queens - Mon. A.M. 5/25

After blowing into the dark liquid for several seconds, OCU's Detective Artie Franks took a swallow of coffee from the McDonald's container. He set it down on the edge of the platform lining one side of the surveillance van. The monitors and recording equipment took up most of the platform's surface. Franks removed his headphones and laid them across his lap. He extended his arms up, laced his fingers behind his head, leaned back, and stretched. He'd been sitting in one position for over an hour .

"Artie, be careful with the coffee cup. At least put the lid back on while you're not drinking. That's all we need," Detective David Dowd said. "One spill on the recorder and the Feds will have an earthquake-size conniption."

"Shit, we've been at this every day for almost two weeks. The most significant thing we've gotten thus far is him screaming at a dumbass supplier for not delivering enough bar napkins."

A folding floor-to-ceiling partition behind the driver and passenger seats protected the gray van's security from anyone seeing in through the front windshield. The two small windows on the back doors were treated to provide one-way visibility. Each day, they changed the van's position on the avenue in proximity to The Dugout in order not to become conspicuous. The pair of detectives at night used a similarly equipped van, that one a midnight black vehicle. Every third day, they swapped vans, the black one used during the day, the gray one at night.

"This surveillance is so haphazard," Franks said. "I gotta believe we get anything useful, it'll be a minor miracle. The guy is never there. When he is, he's alone. The broad is off somewhere else with her cell in her purse."

"Give it time. It's been less than two weeks."

"Yeah, and how many of those days were they both there at the same time?"

"Come off it, Artie, you're sounding like my wife when she bitches about me working nights."

Artie snickered, picked up his coffee, and removed the lid carefully. He looked over at Dowd. "What I can't figure is why we start the morning shift at eight o'clock. The damn place doesn't open until ten."

"Did you forget she always arrives before they open the door? The exception is Wednesday. Then it's at noon. What if Barone got there early? What if he had a meeting set up with Fusco or D'Angelo? And we missed recording it because we weren't there?"

"We'd be looking for a new career."

"You bet your ass, we would. Put your ears back on."

For most of the morning, before Dowd took over the earphones, Franks listened to busy sounds: papers rustling, a drawer opening and closing, the woman on the phone speaking to someone who sounded like a manager of one of the other stores, a server calling in sick for his night shift. Once, an employee stuck his head in to inform her about the scheduled special for the night's menu. Franks assumed it was the chef speaking.

A little past one, the office door closed with an audible clunk sound. Muted ambient noises of a busy bar and restaurant passed through his headphones. Franks heard her speak to someone named Anthony. She told him she was off to The Red Zone store in Brooklyn. He heard the sound of clicking heels, then the noise of the safety bar on a metal door being pushed. A whooshing of air followed and ended with the metallic ringing of the back door as it slammed closed. He lost the signal once she was in her car heading toward Atlantic Avenue.

Chapter Sixteen

Chelsea Area, Manhattan – Wed. P.M. 5/27

Luke Rizzo stared at the telephone console on his desk, attempting to make sense of the phone call. It was close to six when the call came in. He had slipped his Sig Sauer into his belly holster and zippered up his cotton lightweight jacket over it. He was ready to leave. Halfway to the door, the phone rang. Tempted to let it go to the message line, he decided it might be important. Maybe Fields with an update on the schedule for the arraignment of Mario Langella and Angie Russo.

Rizzo lifted the receiver. Nothing but dead air. Then he heard a click when the call disconnected. A couple of thoughts crossed his mind. The caller realized he had the wrong number and hung up before having to apologize. Or the caller was a robot telemarketer who experienced a glitch in the connection. Or the caller wanted to confirm Rizzo was still in the office and not somewhere else.

Rizzo unzipped his jacket and removed the Sig Sauer from his belly holster. He pulled back the stainless-steel slide on the 9mm Luger to make certain a round was chambered. He tapped the bottom of the 12-round magazine as a gesture of acknowledgment and headed for the door.

Before he pulled it open, Rizzo remembered the Russian hired gun sent last year by the sex-slaver, Umberto Salazar. The gunman had entered through the fire exit into the corridor of the Flatiron building's fourth floor. He'd flashed his weapon as Rizzo stepped out of the office. The gunman called to him. Rizzo turned, the Sig Sauer still in his hand, and got his shot off first. He hit the man in the left shoulder, wounding him.

What killed him, Rizzo remembered with a smile, was the man tripped at the top of the stairwell during his flight. He attempted to regain his balance by reaching for the handrail with his good right hand. He missed. The move found him turned around. He fell backward and down the stairs. During his descent, his head bounced off each of the fourteen steel-edged steps and arrived dead at the mid-floor landing.

When Rizzo first moved into his new building, he took note of the location of the fire exit. Now, he never failed to look to the far end of the corridor as he stepped through his office door, some of the time holding his weapon at his side. The door locked behind him while he kept his focus on the fire exit. Once inside the elevator, he holstered the weapon, zippered his jacket, and patted his belly. "Looks like you and I are going steady again."

* * *

West Side, Manhattan – Wed. P.M. 5/27

At six-fifteen, Rizzo pushed into the subway car packed with home-bound riders. Nothing unusual for peak travel time on the northbound N train. His hand grasped the center pole and joined four other hands steadying their owners during the ride.

His eyes fell on the faces of those closest to him until he surmised none bore the look of someone preparing to do him harm. He swiveled his head left and right to take in those travelers within striking distance. They, too, appeared harmless, occupied with their devices or musing with anticipation of what they planned to do for entertainment that evening. He became convinced killing him on the subway was not on the menu.

At six-forty, Rizzo ascended to street level at Forty-ninth and Seventh Avenue. The busy intersection, a block and a half from his apartment, was still sunlit thanks, to Daylight Saving Time.

He crossed to the west side of Seventh Avenue and came to an abrupt stop before his foot hit the curb. *What the hell am I doing? If someone's following me, I sure as hell don't want the guy tailing me to my doorway. Bad enough they're onto the location of my office.*

Rizzo slipped into the flow of foot traffic heading north. He walked at a quickened pace until he reached the corner of Fiftieth Street and turned west. Glancing over his shoulder, he caught a glimpse of Marlon Brando in his "Guys and Dolls" getup. The man started across the avenue and continued west on the opposite side of Fiftieth Street.

As Rizzo neared the Avis garage at the corner of Ninth Avenue, he noticed that his not-very-tall shadow bobbed up and down on his toes. Brando had difficulty keeping Rizzo in his view from behind all the parked SUVs lining his side of the street.

Rizzo reached the garage entrance, waved to Marie behind the counter in the glass-enclosed office, and hurried to the rear of the garage, passing Ernie, the attendant on duty. Ernie had just stepped out of a compact Ford he'd moved to a ready-to-pick-up position and looked up. "Hey, Luke. You order a vehicle?"

"No, Ernie. Just taking a shortcut. The back door and gate open?"

"Yeah. It was this morning."

Many times in the past, after he'd returned a vehicle, Rizzo exited the Avis garage using the back entrance. He'd cut south through the service alley of a restaurant on Forty-ninth Street. From there, he had less than a one-block walk east to his apartment.

"Good. See ya, buddy. Oh, Ernie, someone comes in looking for me? You don't know what they're talking about. Okay? Tell Marie, same thing."

Ernie nodded. "Gotcha."

Because of Flo's supervisory position at the Avis La Guardia Airport location, everyone at the Ninth Avenue garage knew Rizzo. This was the first time the garage came in handy to lose a tail—not the sort of adventure he'd share with his wife.

After the short walk, Rizzo arrived at the front of his apartment building. He hopped up the Brownstone's four steps and looked back, but the inept soldier was not in sight. Eluding the faux Marlon wouldn't sit well with the man's ego. Rizzo needed to be more vigilant in the days ahead.

He opened the door to the foyer area and was greeted with the aroma of Italian cooking coming from the rear apartment. At that moment, the bouquet of simmering spaghetti sauce wafting under his nose made the decision for him where he and Flo would dine that night. He was confident the restaurant he had in mind was out of Brando's league. At least, he hoped so.

* * *

Lower Manhattan – Wed. P.M. 5/27

"For Christ's sake, slow down, will ya?" Rizzo had to issue that admonishment to the driver a few times before they exited the taxi at Mulberry Street. The ride downtown to Little Italy was a trip from hell. The cowboy driver cut off four other cabbies and ran intersections as the lights changed from yellow to red. In a high-test city like New York, jumping the light was standard practice. But the numbers of times the driver placed Flo and Rizzo in danger were far too many for a seven-mile cab ride.

They were ten minutes early for their eight-thirty reservation, but Emilio, the host of La Luna, seated them right away. Earlier diners had vacated tables, which allowed them to occupy one in the middle of the restaurant. They took chairs facing the entrance to watch for Vinnie and Carla.

"I'm glad you thought to invite them to join us," Flo said. "I'm surprised Carla was free and not performing."

"Oh, she performed today. On Wednesdays, she does the matinee, and another actress does the evening performance."

Rizzo looked at his watch, and moments later, Vinnie and Carla appeared at the restaurant's entrance. Emilio spotted them and rushed to the door. He embraced Vinnie and planted a wet kiss on Carla's cheek. The enthusiasm of his greeting signaled to Rizzo that Vinnie and Carla were no strangers to La Luna.

"*Paesano*, nice you come back to La Luna," Emilio said. "Too long we don't see you. I didn't know you were the other people on Mr. Rizzo's reservation."

"Yeah, he doesn't like to admit he knows me."

"Oh, no, I'm sure that is not so," Emilio replied, sounding as though he believed the remark was serious. Vinnie bellowed with laughter, and La Luna's host joined in.

Emilio pulled back the chair to seat Carla. Rizzo signaled him over to whisper in his ear, "Tell our waiter a bottle of Chianti, and to be sure to give me the dinner check."

"Mr. Rizzo, you might get an argument for that," Emilio said.

"Do it anyway, okay?"

Emilio nodded and walked to the bar. When he returned, he carried a bottle of Ruffino Classico Chianti Riserva to the table. He handed it to their server, who removed the cork and offered it to Rizzo.

Rizzo waved him off and said, "*Bene, bene.* If that's the usual choice of my friend here, I'm sure it's fine. I'm not having any, thanks."

Soon, an assortment of Italian fare blanketed the table. The variety of aromas filled their senses and contributed to the amiable mood at the table. Their conversation covered the early success of Carla's play and the great reviews she'd garnered for her performance.

Vinnie again remarked about Matt's playing ability on the diamond, lauding the boy's cool demeanor in the batter's box. Rizzo smiled with a father's pride.

Close to ten-thirty, two men entered the restaurant. Both wore black double-breasted suits, one with a white shirt and yellow silk tie, the second with a gray mock turtle barely visible in the restaurant's subdued lighting. Without waiting for Emilio to seat them, they passed Rizzo's table and headed to a vacant one against the back wall. The man in the mock turtle nodded to Vinnie as he went by.

Rizzo caught Vinnie staring. In a low voice, he said, "I thought La Luna was not popular with the boys."

"I thought so too."

"You know them?"

Vinnie glanced at the two women engaged in dissecting the difference between two makeup brands. His eyes cut back to Rizzo and he subtly signaled with a shake of his head not to continue.

Emilio returned to their table and drained the remains of the Chianti bottle into the three glasses.

Rizzo looked at his watch and then at Flo. "We should get home. It's an early rise tomorrow. Work, remember?"

"You're right," Flo said. "Let me go to the ladies' room . . . powder my nose."

Carla jumped up. "I'll go with you."

When they were out of range, Rizzo repeated his question. "You know them?"

"The first guy. He's connected to one of the other New York families. I assume the other one is too."

"I ask because I'm being tailed these days by a goofy *gavone* who dresses like he's Marlon Brando."

Vinnie chuckled. "That's Vito Rossellini. He's one of Sal Fusco's gofers. He's harmless unless he has a gun pointed at you."

"Which I hope to avoid."

"Well, I warned you Sal's not buying the coincidence bullshit with you and Nicole Adams on the ferry. You'd better be up on your tip-toes and watch your back."

Rizzo motioned to the late arrivals in the rear. "Well, if you're seen in my company by one of the Gambino boys, like in this situation, you should be on your guard as well. No?"

"Something to consider," Vinnie said with a grin.

* * *

Jamaica Avenue, Queens – Fri. A.M. 5/29

Detective Franks couldn't believe what he was hearing:

"What the hell you mean the computers were down? And you had no backup? Fucking amazing. It happened last month too, although I didn't call you on it. I figured this month's statement would show a correction. With you being the bank's president, you should be watching this account like a hawk? Right?"

"I'm sorry, Mr. Barone. I was on vacation last month. My senior VP didn't catch the error and—"

"Hey, Mr. Schuster, it's not only last month. This month's statement was shortchanged an easy fifteen grand too. That doesn't sound like a coincidence to me. We feed money into this account through at least two dozen businesses in four different states."

"I know that—" Schuster started to say, but Barone cut him off again.

"Fuck, you think business just lightened up? The waste management company in Pennsylvania alone is good for at least ten grand a month. The vending machine syndicate across the river? Another five grand a month. You got someone in the bank, maybe, bleeding this account, not worrying because the deposits are an illegal activity, and no one's gonna bring it to your attention?"

"Mr. Barone, I can't imagine how—"

"You can't? Well, I can. And a certain someone else might come to the same conclusion. You need to do a top-to-bottom investigation and get back to me—fast!"

The call ended and Artie Franks removed his headphones. He turned to his partner, Dave Dowd, and said, "Hey, we just nailed it. Listen to this," and he hit the play button. The recorded conversation played back in its entirety. When the two OCU detectives finished listening, they looked at each other wearing smiles.

"Whaddaya say? Think it's enough?" Franks said.

"I don't know, but you better put your ears back on. He could be on the phone right now with the underboss."

"You're right," Franks said and slapped on the headphones.

What sounded like a chair slamming against the wall was followed by a light tapping sound on the office door, followed by a woman's voice.

"Is it safe now?"

Franks looked over at Dowd. "She's back." Then he heard, "Yeah, come in. I'm leaving anyway." The voice sounded aggravated. "You gonna be around later?"

"I'm going to The Finish Line store for about an hour, but I'll be back afterward."

"Maybe I'll see you," he said before the office door closed behind him with a click.

Dowd listened to the playback. He took out his iPhone. "I better call Machado. Let him know what we got. This has been a bonanza of a day."

"Yeah. Now we can wrap it up and get outta here."

* * *

One Police Plaza, Lower Manhattan – Fri. P.M. 5/29

"Yeah, it's fantastic stuff, Dowd. You guys did great."

Machado looked over at Jack Fields, who sat across from him. "You want it played again, Jack?"

"No, but I would like a USB flash drive sent to my office soon. I'd like to get Carter Brooke's reaction."

"You hear that, Dowd? Shoot me the drive and I'll messenger it over to FBI headquarters."

"No problem, Lieutenant."

"Oh, and I'm sure you guys don't need to be reminded," Fields said, leaning in toward the speakerphone on Machado's desk, "protect the original file with your life. For certain, the mob's lawyers are gonna claim we monkeyed around with it."

"You got it," Dowd said. "Er . . . Lieutenant, how soon you want us to wrap this up?"

"Not yet, Dowd. We're going to stay with it for another week. They've lit the fire. Let's see who comes running out of the flames. You can't tell. He might talk with someone else about something we can grab them on."

"Okay, Lieutenant, we'll keep the ears on."

"Don't forget the flash drive for Agent Fields."

"I won't. Bye, Lieutenant," Dowd said.

"It's good you're keeping the door open. I'm sure we got enough, but more couldn't hurt. We never got this type of hard evidence against them before. Nothing but rumors."

"You're right," Machado said. "Anytime I've worked a RICO in the past, I always looked to expand the case. You never know what or who will pop up out of the woodwork. Matter of fact, I can see either Schuster or the Senior VP getting whacked over the missing money."

"After I speak with Carter Brooke, he may want us to bug Schuster's phone. As soon as we determine which bank it is and where it's located, you think your boys can get in there to plant one?"

"I should think so. We can come up with a ruse."

"He'll be especially guarded now. The mob scared the bejesus out of him."

Machado smiled. "And for good reason."

Chapter Seventeen

Chelsea's West Side – Sat. A.M. 6/06

The taxi dropped Rizzo at the door of the Landmark Tavern at one-fifteen in the morning on Saturday. Vinnie had called earlier on Friday to say it was urgent they meet somewhere with Dominic that night after he closed up The Dugout. Rizzo had no inkling of what was going down, and Vinnie refused to talk about it over the phone.

Rizzo suggested the iconic Landmark watering hole in Chelsea, on the far West Side, to meet. He knew the bar stayed open late, and it was unlikely they would run into any *goombas* there. The Landmark Tavern had been a stronghold of IRA supporters and dock workers going back many years.

He pulled open the heavy oak door to this century-old establishment and entered. The odor of stale beer replaced the smell of the Hudson's oil-slick waters. A scattering of neighborhood regulars occupied stools along the lengthy mahogany bar. The tables were unoccupied except for one at the rear.

After acknowledging Vinnie's raised arm with a wave, Rizzo stepped to the bar to order a Virgin Mary. He walked with the drink to the table where his two companions waited.

"Hey, I should be in bed at this hour," he said and dropped into a chair. "Last time I was here, sex trafficking of teenage Mexican girls was the subject. I hope this is nothing as serious."

Vinnie nodded at Dominic as if to say, "You tell him."

"How about life-threatening?" Dom said. "That serious enough?"

"Oh, shit! Whose life we talking about?"

"Well, it could be a double-header. Nicole and you."

Rizzo's head jerked up. "Okay, guys, you got my attention."

Vinnie cleared his throat and looked at Rizzo with a forced smile. "Dom's been hearing rumblings about the arrest of a couple of guys in the family. Seems someone thinks you played a part in it."

"Langella and Russo," Rizzo said, dropping his voice to a whisper. A scowl appeared across his brow as he leaned back in his chair. "I guess I'm not surprised."

"No disrespect intended," Vinnie said, "but what the fuck were you thinking? You couldn't let the Suffolk cops handle it without you putting in your two cents?"

The space between Rizzo's dark eyebrows and hairline pinched with annoyance. "Hey, did you forget I wear the white hat?" he said, struggling to keep his voice low. "Remember, I work for law enforcement, and that whack job was a cold-blooded massacre."

"Yeah, but you didn't have to be there when they grabbed Langella. He recognized you."

"I know that. Suffolk asked me to come along to ID him. Not a smart play, I realize now." Rizzo drew in a deep intake of air and squeezed it out through his lips. "Ah, screw it. What's done is done. I'll handle it."

"How?" Vinnie said. "You gonna leave the country?"

Rizzo didn't respond. After several seconds of staring into his Virgin Mary, he raised his eyes and looked at Dominic. "So, what's going on with Nicole? How'd she come to be on the soon-to-be-dead list?"

"It's Fusco," Dom answered. "He's still convinced she's involved with you. It's driving him up a wall."

"That's what I told you three weeks ago," Vinnie said.

Rizzo nodded. "Yeah, I know. Is she in any immediate danger?"

"Not sure," Dom said. "He came in last night. Sat at the bar for an hour, flapping his mouth, asking if I noticed anything different about how she was acting. He's frustrated. He can't stand Barone, but he doesn't trust Nicole. He hasn't said so, but he wants her gone."

Rizzo closed his eyes for a moment. He considered how vulnerable Nicole was after the OCU bugged Barone's conversation with his banker. The Feds hadn't made their move yet, but when they did, it would be time for her to disappear. It wouldn't take much for Fusco to make the connection.

Rizzo looked at Dominic. "Can I ask a huge favor of you?"

"Ask. If I can do it, I will."

"Give me a heads-up if you sense things getting too hot for Nicole with Fusco. I don't want to wait too long and be shut out before I can take defensive action."

"Oh, I will. I like the broad a lot. She's been a good pal to me. Don't wanna see her come to any harm. Whaddaya have in mind?"

"Make her disappear, and I mean into deep hiding."

"What about you?" Vinnie said. "How do you plan to protect yourself?"

Rizzo shot him an exaggerated grin. "Carry two guns?"

* * *

West Side, Manhattan - Sat. A.M. 6/06

West Forty-eighth was an eastbound one-way street. Rather than circle the block to get to his building, Rizzo exited the taxi at the corner of Eighth and Forty-eighth. He turned and walked west, stayed close to the curb and away from doorways. A lone man on the sidewalk of the city at three-thirty in the morning was often the target of a desperate mugger. Rizzo had an innate sense of caution, something acquired by any savvy person who grew up in the concrete jungle. Keep moving and look like you know where you're going—the rule most New Yorkers followed.

Twenty yards ahead, in the splash of light from the nearest streetlamp, Rizzo caught sight of a head poking out from the doorway of a building, two up from his own. He stopped, reached into his shoulder holster under his windbreaker, and waited. Rizzo wasn't certain what he saw was a person. Moonbeams, in the waning hours of the night, flickered through the few trees lining the street, causing lively, moving shadows. Was it only that?

He had his answer when a bullet sailed past his ear and shattered the windshield of a vehicle parked on the opposite side of the street. The Sig Sauer came out of his holster in a flash. He held the nine-millimeter out of sight as he darted across to the other side to take cover behind a parked car. Thank God for alternate-side-of-the-street parking, he thought. Saturday's schedule was in his favor until seven this morning. The gunman—whoever he might be—was left out in the open.

Crouched low, Rizzo could see the man at an angle through the car's windshield. He expected the guy would soon realize his vulnerable position and make a move.

The way the shooter behaved surprised Rizzo. The man inched to the curb, stopped as if testing the water, and waited for Rizzo to react. When none came, he continued into the street with a purposeful step, stopping again when he reached the middle.

The streetlamp above cast enough light to allow Rizzo to ID the shooter. He was the other half of Ruby's pair of thugs. "Nelly, what the hell you think you're doing?"

"Gonna' kill you, motherfucker."

"Listen, bro, you don't have to do this. It ain't gonna end well. You gotta know that."

"Oh, I know it. It's gonna end with you dead." He walked casually to the front of the car, stopped, raised his weapon, aimed across the car's hood, pausing like he had all the time in the world.

Rizzo saw him smile. With lightning speed, he brought the Sig Sauer up with a two-handed grip and fired off two quick shots. They both hit the shoulder that supported Nelly's weapon. His painful yowl sounded like a wounded panther. The impact of the bullets spun him around. His hand released the gun and he tumbled face-down to the ground.

Rizzo was on him in a millisecond. He kicked the gun under the car and reached into his windbreaker pocket for the plastic ties he routinely carried. Straddling the wounded man's body, Rizzo dropped to his knees and landed on Nelly's back. A loud explosion of expelled air followed before the man passed out.

After securing Nelly's two arms behind him, Rizzo stood and called 911 on his cell. Minutes later, two RMPs from Midtown North, lights flashing and siren wailing, tore down Forty-eighth from Ninth Avenue.

Both RMPs pulled to the curb on the opposite side, nose to rear, and two uniforms from each emerged with weapons drawn. Rizzo stood beside his attacker's inert body; his Sig Sauer placed on the pavement at his feet. He faced the approaching officers with his hands over his head. "Retired NYPD," Rizzo called out to the Patrol Sergeant who had his service Glock trained on him. "I checked him. He's alive, but we're gonna need a bus soon. He's bleeding heavily."

A second officer went to work patting down Rizzo.

"No other weapons," Rizzo said. "You'll find the shooter's under the car. I kicked it there."

"Okay. You can lower your arms."

"The officer pulled on surgical gloves, picked up Rizzo's Sig Sauer, and placed it in the trunk of the first RMP. He fished out the other weapon from under the car and secured it in the trunk of the second RMP.

The last two officers had been scanning the area, and finding no other shooters, came back to examine the unconscious Nelly.

"Sarge, he's alive, but he may bleed out."

"Call for a bus," the sergeant replied. He turned to Rizzo. "Okay, what the hell went down here?"

"Sergeant, my name is Luke Rizzo, NYPD narcotics detective, retired. I'm a private investigator. My ID is in my wallet in my back pocket. Okay I reach for it?"

The sergeant nodded. He took the wallet from Rizzo and examined his driver's license and concealed-carry permit. When he pulled out the laminated Lucas Rizzo Investigations license from one slot, he grinned. "This situation relates to an investigation of yours?"

"In a way. He's a low-level hood from the Bronx. I helped get two of his *Mafia* pals arrested for a whack job they did on the brother of an NYPD Lieutenant Dickerson."

"Keith Dickerson. Yeah, I heard about that."

Rizzo motioned with his head. "So bozo here, looking for revenge, waited in a doorway for me to come home. I live in the brownstone over there," he said, pointing. "When I got close, he stepped out and took a shot at me. I made a beeline across the street and ducked behind a car."

"That vehicle where he's down?"

"Yeah. He must have thought I was unarmed because he followed me across with no concern about cover. He closed in, stopped, and raised his weapon. I got off two shots aimed at his shoulder. I didn't want to kill him."

The sergeant shook his head. "Man, that's a tough shot. You always hit what you aim at?"

"Most of the time."

"Lucky for him," the sergeant said as he holstered his Glock. "Okay, Rizzo, that's good for me. You're gonna go through the complete story again anyway when the suits get here. Why don't you wait in front of your brownstone?"

While the officers cordoned off the area around the car, the EMS ambulance arrived, loaded the wounded man, and took off with lights flashing and siren wailing, once again destroying the early morning tranquility.

Rizzo sat on the steps of his brownstone and thought about Nelly's attempt on his life. He'd discovered his full name was Nelson Gomulka, a non-Italian, which told him the man was not a made *Mafia* soldier but a mob associate. Nelly's threat to avenge the arrest of his pal, Mario Langella, hadn't worked out as he'd planned. Still, as Vinnie and Dom had warned, Rizzo had lit a lethal fuse with the Gambino guns. And he knew it.

It took the detectives from the Eighteenth Precinct almost three hours to complete the investigation and interrogation before they released him. Thank God there wasn't a dead body. Waiting around for a medical examiner to do his thing might have added another hour.

Rizzo slipped into the apartment in stocking feet, trying not to wake Flo. He checked the time. Six-fifteen. He stripped to his underwear in the living room and left the rest of his clothes on the sofa. On tiptoe, he entered the bedroom and slid under the sheet on his side. When his head hit the pillow, Flo turned to adjust her position.

"I didn't hear the alarm," her sleepy voice said. It was set for her once-a-month working Saturday. "That time already?"

Rizzo's head poked up. "No, sweetheart. You have forty-five minutes before the alarm. Go back to sleep."

"Why are you so late? What time is it?"

"Time to get some sleep. I'll tell you all about it tonight when you come home from work."

"Okay," she mumbled and closed her eyes.

His eyes stayed open for another hour.

Chapter Eighteen

Fort Lee, New Jersey – Wed. P.M. 6/10

Barone paced back and forth in front of the fireplace. "They banged on my door shouting, 'FBI, open up.' At four-thirty in the fucking morning. I was in a dead sleep when I heard them yelling. I thought I was dreaming. Scared the shit outta me."

"You got no warning, no phone call requesting you come in and report to them?" Carmine D'Angelo asked.

"Hell, no. It was a complete surprise. I couldn't believe it."

D'Angelo's arms rested on the cushioned armrest of his desk chair. He cupped his chin with one hand and furrowed his brow. Barone stopped moving and remained quiet, not wanting to disturb his uncle's thoughts. He was aware his arrest had put his uncle into an indefensible position with the don. As the family's underboss, he had the ultimate responsibility for the performances of his *capo*s, and all the people under them.

"Did they say what they were arresting you for?"

"No. I asked the lead agent, but he refused to say. The son of a bitch ignored the question and told one agent to cuff me. He said they had probable cause for a court-issued warrant for my arrest. When I got downtown, I would find out."

The underboss looked up. "Did they take anything from you?"

Barone restarted his nervous rant. "Their stinking storm troopers, and those from the NYPD, all decked out in riot gear, ransacked the apartment. Collected all of my electronics—my desktop computer, my laptop, both iPhones, and notebook. Took files from my cabinet. They were in my home office over two hours."

"Sit down, Pete. Your pacing is distracting. I gotta figure this out."

Barone walked to the wet bar and picked up a glass tumbler. He grabbed a handful of ice cubes from the bucket on the bar and filled the glass halfway with Black Label scotch.

"The two soldiers Fusco sent to dispose of your former partner? Were they made men?"

"Yeah, I believe so. I heard one of them made his bones last year. The other guy's been around a while. I'm sure he's made."

"You figure we can count on them to respect their vow of *Omertà*?"

The order to whack them, Barone remembered, came from Fusco, but it was his uncle who set it in motion. If the Feds ever got down to the basic responsibility for the killing, they could indict the underboss on the charge. Barone silently acknowledged the RICO Act put Carmine D'Angelo in a shit-pot full of trouble between the money-laundering charge and the killing of Roy Dickerson.

"I sure as hell hope so,"

"You called Donnie Napoli, of course?"

"Right after I got downtown. It was about eight-fifteen. He'd already arrived at his office from home. He came right away.

The bastards kept throwing questions at me, but I told them I'd say nothing until my lawyer arrived."

"That was wise. The less you say, the better it is. Best you let Donnie do all the talking. When did they release you?"

"The next morning. They kept me overnight until Donnie returned to post bail. My court appearance for the indictment hearing is set for two weeks from now."

D'Angelo fingered his temples and rolled his head. "Pour me a glass of red wine," he said and pointed to the wet bar. "Maybe it'll help with this damned headache."

Barone started toward the bar and stopped after taking a few steps. He turned to his uncle, and with a crestfallen expression, he said, "Carmine, I am deeply sorry about all this. You know that, don't ya?"

D'Angelo nodded. "Get the wine, Pete."

Barone filled a wineglass halfway from an opened bottle of Chianti Classico. He handed D'Angelo the wine, raised his tumbler of scotch, and said, "*Saluti.*"

"Yeah, saluti. These next few weeks I'm thinking we're both gonna need a lot more than Chianti and scotch."

"Carmine, how the hell could this happen? I've been extremely careful anytime I talked with the bank. I never used the landline in The Dugout office. If I called from there, it was always on my iPhone. And I was always alone. Same from my apartment office."

"You have someone search for a bug in The Dugout?"

"Not yet. I got a techie coming soon to check on it."

"Have him check your apartment, too."

"You think they could have—?"

"I don't have any idea, Pete. Do it, will you?"

"Okay Carmine, I will. I'll let you know if he finds anything."

"If he does, then find how it was done and who did it."

* * *

Chelsea Area, Manhattan - Monday, P.M. 6/15

"I'd come up to your office, Jack, but I've got somebody on my ass these days. They shouldn't see me going into your building. Same thing for One PP."

"Well, is it safe to talk on this phone?"

"I would say so unless they've discovered how to tap into my cell. I've stopped using my landline."

"So what's the emergency?"

"I've got inside info."

"About what?"

"Fusco is making noises like he wants to remove Nicole Adams—for good. We need to get her out soon. Make her disappear."

"Is the danger immediate?"

"You busted Pete Barone for money laundering last week with that bank conversation you got on tape. He's out on bail, but it won't be long before he connects the dots. My gut tells me Fusco is already there."

"Okay, Rizzo. I'll call Machado. See if we can work up a plan. "I'll get back," he said and hung up.

An hour later, "Take Five" chimed. He grabbed the iPhone, pressed the accept button. "Rizzo," he said, without looking at the caller ID readout.

"Fields. We came up with a plan to get her out without raising notice."

"Already?"

"Yeah. I didn't know, but Machado had been working on one for a while. It's a viable plan. I like it."

"Okay, I'm listening."

"Text her right now. Say you'll meet at her apartment tomorrow night when she gets home."

"Oh, good God! Another late night."

"What?"

"Nothing. I'll tell you later."

"Okay, here's the deal. She's gonna disappear this Saturday night. Right after she finishes work. Nobody will be the wiser until Monday morning when she fails to show."

"Man, that's five days from now."

"Right. Didn't you say things were looking toxic?"

"Okay, what else?"

"Brancuso suggested she call in sick for a couple of those days. Being home might relieve her of the feeling she's sitting on a live explosive."

"Yeah, but they're keeping an eye on her. It's bound to invite her shadow to stake out her apartment."

"No big deal. If she takes off, say Thursday and Friday, and then goes in on Saturday, the stakeout would be meaningless. She's home in bed getting better."

Rizzo thought about it. "Yeah, it could work."

"You said the bartender agreed to keep watch over her at work, didn't you?"

"Yeah, but he's not around when she's out checking on the other stores. Wait a second. She doesn't have to leave the office to do her checking. She can stay there all day Saturday and use the phone to talk with her managers.

"Okay, then. That's the scenario I want you to propose when you meet with her."

"And what do I say when she asks where the Bureau is sending her?"

"To a hotel at JFK. Tell her to pack light clothing. In the morning, she flies down to the Caribbean. Charlotte Amalie on St. Thomas. It's a guest house. The owner is a friend of Brancuso. He's a retired CIA agent. She'll be in good hands. We'll make all the arrangements. Get a pen and paper. Write down this information. She'll need to know about her apartment, her car, and how we plan to deal with all the obligations she'll leave behind."

For the next ten minutes, Fields dictated the full list of commitments the Bureau was prepared to handle.

"She making the trip alone, unprotected?"

"There'll be two agents with her. She'll have nothing to worry about once she leaves The Dugout Saturday night."

From your lips to God's ears, Rizzo thought. "How long will she be in St. Thomas?"

"Until things cool down. Then we can talk to her about the WITSEC program if she wants. Who knows, she may opt to stay put under her new identity."

"Sounds like a plan," Rizzo said.

"I hope she signs on to it. By the way, what was it you started to bitch about? Something about late nights?"

"Oh, right," Rizzo said with a chuckle. "It's about the sleep I've been losing. A disgruntled *Mafia* associate, ten days ago tried to take me out. I haven't told my wife about it. I hope she forgets it was early in the morning when I crawled into bed."

"What happened?"

"It was late one night on my way home. The guy was upset I played a role in the arrest of his good buddy—the dirtbag that killed Lieutenant Dickerson's brother."

"No kidding. What happened?"

"He flew one past my ear when I was on my street heading to my apartment. I put two in his shoulder. He lives because I let him. The dumb ass wanted to settle the score. They carted him off in a bus. He's a three-time loser. He won't show up again. That's for sure."

"How come you said nothing of this to me?"

"I don't like to brag."

Fields chuckled. "Yeah, sure, Mr. Humility. Call me tomorrow after you've had your chat with Miss Adams."

Chapter Nineteen

Sands Point, Long Island – Tues. P.M. 6/16

The house was set back on four treed acres with a gravel driveway the length of a football field. A three-story mansion backed up to Long Island Sound in the upscale town of Sands Point. The drive from Little Italy in Manhattan to the western edge of Nassau County took less than forty-five minutes.

Fusco leaned over the front seat. "I don't know how long I'm gonna be, Gino. Park here on the circle unless one of the don's men tells you otherwise." He removed his Borsalino and placed it on the seat.

The *capo* stepped out of the limo, gazed up, and gawked at Don Carl Nunziata's residential opulence. Fusco approached the front door with the reverence of someone about to receive communion. He looked back, hesitated, then stepped forward. His hand reached for the brass door knocker, but before he could take hold, the door flew open.

"Hey, Sal. Great to see you."

He was jolted for a moment by the sudden greeting. Tommie, one of the don's trusted bodyguards, produced a warm smile. The man had headed a crew some time ago under Fusco's authority, with outstanding success. The anxiousness Fusco experienced during the ride out of the city slid into neutral.

"Tommie, how ya doin'? The don's expecting me, ain't he?"

"Oh, sure, Sal. Carl's in the library waiting. You're right on time."

The *capo* followed the bodyguard over the marbled floor of the vestibule, past the curved staircase on the right. He was conscious of the clicking noise his leather heels made on the hard, polished tile.

Fusco could see a large family room ahead, where French doors opened out onto a terrace, offering a panoramic view of the Sound. Lights, scattered about on the water, blinked like liquid stars. Before the two men reached the open room, Tommie stopped at the double doors of the library and pulled them open. "In here."

"*Amicu nostro*, come in," the don said and approached Fusco with an extended hand. They shook and Carl Nunziata nodded to Tommie, who closed the doors and disappeared.

"Carl, thanks for taking the time to meet with me. Like I said in my note, couple of things have gone sour you should know about, things that are gonna cause the family a lotta problems."

The don gestured to one of two wing chairs flanking a large square coffee table in front of a white leather sofa. "Sit down. We'll talk. First, something to drink? What's your pleasure? Wine, Scotch, beer, soft drink? What?"

"Maybe a glass of red would be nice."

The don walked to the wet bar behind the sofa. He returned with two glasses, one of Chianti and one of Pinot Grigio, and handed the red one to Fusco.

"*Saluti*," Nunziata said, and raised his wineglass.

"Health and a long life," Fusco replied as he lifted his glass.

They remained silent for several seconds before Fusco remarked, "Carl, this sure is a beautiful home. I'm honored to be invited here to talk."

"My pleasure, Sal. At least we can speak without the worry of being overheard. I assume what you wanna talk about is sensitive?"

Fusco swallowed the saliva that had collected in his throat. He brought his glass up to his mouth and held it. "Yeah, Carl. I haven't shared my thoughts about what's happenin' with anyone else because, well, they'd be my personal thoughts and unofficial without you hearing them first."

"I appreciate that, Sal." Nunziata flashed a pleasant smile. "Sometimes these young Turks forget how it goes. They go running their mouths until they end up . . . well, shall we say, quieted? You've always been a good soldier, Sal."

"Your words mean a lot to me, Carl. I pray never to do something stupid that would cause you to change your opinion. That's why I asked for this meeting."

"Okay, tell me. What's got you so concerned?"

"To start, you're aware they picked up the two guys for whacking the former manager of our sports bar company? The man became a liability because Carmine's nephew, Pete Barone, opened his yap to him about our money operation."

"Yes. Unfortunate. Where does their arrest stand?"

"They're being held out in the Suffolk County lockup waitin' for their trial."

"Are they made men? Will they honor *Omertà*?"

"I'm pretty sure one will. The other one, I don't feel so good about. I can't figure how the hell he got to be made. Some damned *cidrule* musta sold him a button. Who knows? Anyway, he was the shooter."

"Who ordered the hit, or did they act on their own?"

The question came as a surprise. If the underboss hadn't discussed it with the don before the hit took place, he was certain D'Angelo had to be on shaky ground.

"Carmine did," Fusco said. "But before he gave the order, he never checked on the target's background. Turns out, his brother is an NYPD lieutenant in a major robbery unit. The hit brought out the cavalry. You know how that goes." Fusco was aware he'd lit another hot coal under D'Angelo's coffin.

"And you don't trust the shooter to stay silent?"

"Not really. After the hit, he went braggin' about it to his drinkin' buddies."

"That's not good. We both understand how this could end up if he talks to the Feds. Is there a way to get to him?"

"I don't think so. They have them both locked up tight with no bail."

The don looked up and shook his head. In a quiet voice, he said, "No, Sal, there's always a way. I'm sure you'll find it."

Fusco felt the power of the don land on his head with all its weight. Nunziata's renowned silent demeanor was nothing more than a deceptive façade. He used it to hide an ultra-violent nature. Fusco had his orders, and he'd carry them out.

"Not to worry, Carl. I'll take care of it."

"I'm sure you will, Sal."

Fusco's expression turned grim. "I hate to say this, but that's not all the bad news."

Nunziata raised his eyes. "What else?"

"Carmine's boy, Barone, got wiretapped while he talked with the president of one of the banks what handles the money laundering deposits. Seems the account came up with a major shortage and Barone chewed the ass off the bank president. The Feds got the whole conversation on tape. They arrested Barone, but he's out on bail."

The don placed his wineglass on the coffee table and leaned back in his chair. "This is un-fucking-believable. How come this is the first I'm hearing about it? When do you believe Carmine was gonna fill me in?"

"To be fair," Fusco said, "the shit hit the fan last week. He's still tryin' to figure it out himself."

Carl stayed silent for several minutes, massaging his hands like someone forming a plan. When he stopped the exercise, he looked over at Fusco. "Barone is not a made member, is he?"

"No. Carmine's nephew is an associate."

"And a liability to become a cooperating government witness." His brow rippled with concern. "Maybe it's time for Carmine D'Angelo and Peter Barone to go. That way, it might be easier for me to deny knowledge of the hit and the money operation. Of course, the Feds won't buy any story I tell them, but at least without direct evidence, they'll have to work harder to implicate me. You can handle the arrangements?"

"Consider it done, Carl. I'll find a way to catch them together."

"Do it soon."

"Gotcha."

"Oh, and Sal, be sure you don't use anyone from within the family. Call the Maranzano brothers in Chicago. You make the deal through an intermediary, and I'll go along with anything you agree to."

* * *

Carl Nunziata stood at the library door, watching Tommie escort Sal Fusco to the front entrance. He didn't feel comfortable about this situation. Every man has his breaking point, he acknowledged, a point where the survival instinct overpowers loyalty. He didn't trust Fusco. It was apparent he had designs on becoming underboss. After all, the way to get ahead in the mob remained the same as it had been since the nineteenth century in Sicily; you kill the guy above you, and you take his place.

Tommie closed the front door after Fusco's limo departed. The don motioned to him to come back into the library.

"Close the door," he said and walked to his chair. "I wanna ask you something."

Tommie nodded and stood by the chair Fusco had vacated. "What's up?" he asked Nunziata.

"There's an opened bottle of Pinot Grigio in the box of the wet bar," he said, holding out his wineglass. "Pour me a half. Have one too."

"I'll pass, thanks," Tommie said and stepped behind the sofa. He returned with the don's half-filled glass and handed it to him. Tommie dropped into the second chair, looked over at Nunziata, and watched him raise the wine to his lips.

The don set the glass on the coffee table and looked up with a faint smile. "Fusco's gone?"

"Yes."

Nunziata fell silent for several moments before he asked Tommie, "You remember the guy they call The Mob's Assassin, a freelancer from the West Coast? He's an expert at removing unwanted people. Worked for the St. Louis and Phoenix families in the past. Last I heard, the guys in Rhode Island contracted him for a removal."

"Yeah, I guess he's still in business. Why?"

"Think you can get in touch with him?"

Tommie looked down at Fusco's empty wineglass. "I'll phone Al Scalisi up in Providence."

"Good. No rush. When you contact the assassin, see what's his availability. Get back to me. We'll arrange for a time in the future to talk about it."

Chapter Twenty

West Side, Manhattan - Wed. P.M. 6/17

Rizzo waited until she finished her second Jack Daniels to tell her why he was late that night after Nelly took a shot at him. Keeping it from her all this time had created a headache filled with guilt. He completed his scary narration of the event that put Nelly Gomulka in the hospital and then on a path to prison. Flo listened without comment. She held her breath the whole time. Moment to moment, he'd take a bite of Joe Allen's famous prime rib roast, then continue.

"Oh, good Lord, you mean to say he attacked you in the dark and shot at you?"

"Yeah. Never gave me a warning. Imagine that."

"Damn it, Luke, don't be flip. He could have killed you."

"You're right. That was his intention. It didn't worry me."

"You can't be serious."

"Oh, but I am. Not to sound smug, but it's not for naught I spend those many hours on the practice range. It's what keeps me alive. I rarely miss what I shoot at."

She looked up; her nostrils flared, and her eyes burned with anger. "How long before someone shoots you when you're not looking? Does your target practice improve your ability to see behind you . . . grow eyes in the back of your head?"

"No, my love, I depend on my experience and a sixth sense to avoid those kinds of situations. And I never go anywhere without being armed with at least one weapon." He stopped speaking when he realized she wasn't listening.

Flo remained silent. Her bottom lip quivered. Rizzo expected her to break out in tears. Had they been home, instead of at Joe Allen's, he was certain she would have spiraled into a break-down.

At nine-thirty, the bar scene was quiet. Tables of theatergoers in the dining section had emptied by seven. The dining area now hosted a few late arrivals. Seth, the server, wandered by, and when it appeared he would stop at their table, Rizzo shook his head to wave him off.

Rizzo was conflicted. But for his good conscience, he might have continued his plea for understanding. He appreciated how difficult it was for anyone outside law enforcement to comprehend the driving need to bring a criminal to justice. Its attendant dangers came with the package. He accepted that. Flo couldn't.

The disturbing effect this last close call had on Flo reached a new high. He had to lessen her level of worry somehow.

Seth looked over and Rizzo raised his hand, motioning for the check. "Flo, you ready?"

She lowered her moist eyes. "What time are you supposed to meet her?"

"I need to be at her apartment by eleven-fifteen. She leaves the restaurant between ten and eleven."

Flo took the napkin in her hand and patted the corner of her eyes. "Will you be late?"

"No, sweetheart. I'm certain I can finish prepping her in a little more than an hour. I should be back no later than one, one-thirty."

"No one else but you can do this?"

Rizzo dropped his chin to his chest and blew out a puff of air. "Flo, listen to me. This is what they've contracted me for . . . to serve as a liaison in situations where the police or the Feds can't risk being seen. In most instances, like tonight, the danger is nonexistent."

In a voice barely audible, she asked, "Then why are they trying to kill you?"

Seth arrived with the check and placed it in front of Rizzo. "Take your—"

Rizzo covered the folder with a credit card before the man finished. "We're in a hurry, Seth. Sorry for the rush."

"Be right back," he said and dashed off with the card.

"I've got a car waiting at the Avis garage. I'll walk you home first. You gonna be okay?"

"I'll be fine," she said. "Will you?"

* * *

Forest Hills, Queens, NY - Wed. P.M. 6/17

It was five minutes after eleven when the buzzer sounded, releasing the front door lock. Rizzo rode the elevator to the seventh floor and found Nicole standing in her opened doorway. He exited the car, and she waved to him. She was unaware of his former visit to her apartment, and he decided to keep it a secret.

He entered the living room and took a seat at one end of the sofa.

"Can I offer you anything to drink?"

"I think not. Thanks, anyway."

Nicole remained standing for a second with a questioning look. "Am I going to need a stiff drink to face what it is you're going to tell me?"

Rizzo smiled. "Sit down. You're gonna like it."

She dropped onto the other end of the sofa and adjusted her back against the throw pillows. "Okay. I'm ready."

"To begin, and I'll start with this not to scare you but to explain why all this is necessary."

"They want to kill me."

Her light tone and bluntness surprised him. "Well, I realize it comes as no surprise, but the update is Sal Fusco may want to do it sooner rather than later. That's according to an insider's message from a person in the know."

"Wow!"

"Yeah, wow. So here's the scenario worked out by Jack Fields at the FBI. Hold your questions until I finish."

Rizzo laid out the details one by one. He began with her calling in sick tomorrow and Friday. He told her Dominic had agreed to keep an eye on her until she left at her normal time on Saturday.

"By the way, he's been your watchdog from the get-go."

"I know. I wasn't aware he'd been colluding with you, though. He's been a fantastic friend."

"Two FBI agents will meet you when you pull into your garage. They'll escort you up to your apartment to pack. When you're ready, they'll drive you to a hotel at JFK. Your flight leaves in the morning to St. Thomas at nine-ten. The agents will be with you on the flight."

Her eyes widened with each piece of information. The description of the Charlotte Amalie guest house and the owner's former CIA affiliation brought a smile to her face.

"It's called The Galleon House, and it will serve as your safe house for an indeterminate period. Don't worry about expenses.

The Bureau will pick up everything. That includes an appropriate tropical wardrobe and whatever else you will need."

"What's going to happen to this apartment and my car while I'm gone?"

"Don't worry about your apartment, car, your bills, or other obligations you leave behind. The Bureau will forward your mail and bills to St. Thomas. You can take care of them from there. Don't forget your checkbook and bank card. The car will remain in the garage. Before they leave you, be sure to give the agents the keys to your apartment, mailbox, and vehicle."

"Sounds like a hell-of-a-vacation."

"After things settle down, they'll talk to you about the WITSEC Program."

"What's that?"

Rizzo explained what he knew about the program and she reacted as he expected she would.

"Oh, my. It doesn't strike me as something I'd want to do."

"You won't need it," he said. "It's a program they offer to criminals who agree to become a state's witnesses. You aren't in that category—those who need a deep cover for the rest of their lives. You don't quite fit into the description."

"Any idea how long I'll be in hiding?"

"My guess, based on the whispers I've heard, the mob will probably lose interest in you after a year or so. They face larger threats than you on the horizon."

"Well, I'll have to stay alive for the next three days. "Won't I?"

Rizzo nodded. God, I hope so, he thought.

* * *

West Side, Manhattan – Thurs. A.M. 6/18

Rizzo entered the apartment, surprised to find Flo still awake and stretched out on the sofa. She had the television tuned to TCM, and the channel aired the classic musical *That's*

Entertainment. Donald O'Connor was at the end of his famous "Make Them Laugh" routine, and Flo's face beamed with a wide smile. She looked up when Rizzo came in.

"Oh, Luke, honey. You missed it." Her smile remained. "I love this movie, especially Donald O'Connor's performance with that funny dance number he does."

"I remember it. We've seen the movie a dozen times. He never gets old, does he?"

Flo got to her feet and held out her arms. "Sugar, I'm glad you're home."

Rizzo entered her embrace, surprised when she pressed her lips harder than he could ever recall. When they came apart, he asked, "You wanna stay up and watch the rest of this or go to bed? I'm wiped out."

She pulled back and looked at him, her eyes filled with love. When she spoke, her voice went full Kentuckian. "C'mon," she said, and took him by the hand, "ahm gonna put mah sweet honey to bed."

Flo led the way into the bedroom, all the while gripping his hand as though she would never let it go. They stopped at the side of their king-size bed, and Rizzo reached up to her face and cupped it in his hands. "You're not mad at me anymore?"

The question went ignored, while Flo giggled, raised her arms between his, and took hold of his shirt collar. "If you don't get these clothes off pronto, ahm sure gonna get mad at you again and bust you one in the gut." She had the six front buttons undone in a flash and yanked his shirttails free of his belt. After dropping the shirt to one side, she worked on his trouser belt and button, and then unzipped his fly.

"Wait a minute," Rizzo said, struggling to keep from laughing. "I can undress myself."

"Y'all be quiet, ya hear? Ahm in charge now," and she pushed him into a sitting position on the edge of the bed. She knelt on a knee, lifted his legs one at a time, and removed his shoes and socks. She stood and looked down at him with an affected, fierce expression.

"But, I—"

"Shush up, and lift your damn hips," and taking hold of his trouser cuffs, she pulled and pulled until she had them clear of his feet. With deliberate casualness, she dropped them on top of his shirt and kicked his shoes into the pile.

Rizzo leaped to his feet when he saw Flo's hand heading for his jockey shorts. Before she could object, he slid them down to his ankles, stepped out, and flipped them in the air with his toe. Buck naked, he folded his arms, faced his wife, and said, "Now you." Before he could get his hands on her, she pushed him back onto the bed.

"No, no. Ah told ya, ahm in charge, ya hear?"

Until this point in their marriage, Rizzo had never heard Flo sing a note of music other than when she hummed along to a TV program's theme song. With no warning, Flo's soft voice let fly with a song from the Broadway musical, "Gypsy."

"Let me entertain you, let me make you smile; let me do a few tricks . . .," she sang, in the sweetest tones he'd ever heard her vocalize. At the end of each musical phrase, she punctuated the lyric with a slow, teasing removal of an item of clothing. A half-dozen lines into the song, she reached for her panties, the last piece of clothing to come off.

Rizzo sat mesmerized, not only by her vocal performance but by his exposure to a side of her personality he'd not seen before. It was a captivating mixture of discovery and eroticism.

The panties dispensed with, Flo came forward and locked his knees between hers. She bent and they embraced in a long, loving kiss before she forced him back to lie flat on the bed. Straddling him, she lowered herself and carefully guided him into her. The physical pleasure Rizzo experienced during the next several minutes was without equal. Their bodies gyrated in sexual harmony, and all the while Rizzo could hear Flo softly humming the melody of "Let Me Entertain You."

Chapter Twenty-One

Jamaica Avenue, Queens – Thurs. P.M. 6/18

"Where's Nicole?" Pete Barone asked as he climbed onto a bar stool." It was the first time anyone had seen him at the restaurant since his arrest.

"Flu" Dominic answered. "She called this morning and spoke with Anthony. The doctor gave her a Z-pack. She should be okay in a day or two." Dom figured Barone bought it because he shrugged instead of going off on a tirade, as he did whenever an employee called in sick.

"Well, at least the manager's here. Where is Anthony?"

"In the kitchen," Dom said, nodding his head in that direction.

Barone turned to look back. "Hey, I haven't eaten a damn thing since yesterday afternoon. Have the kitchen make me up a steak sandwich, will ya? Make it on Italian hero bread with melted *Gorgonzola*, and fries."

"You want a beer?"

"Shit no. I've had enough to drink to last me into next week. A cup of coffee, black."

Dom moved off toward the burner with the full carafe, picked up a mug, and filled it. He placed the coffee in front of Barone and watched him blow into it before taking a sip.

Barone raised his eyes as if a thought had popped into his head. He scrutinized Dominic with intensity. "You sure you lock up this place every night before you leave?"

Dominic's head jerked up. The question sounded to him like, 'You cheat at cards?' "Bet your ass I lock up. I always double-check them before I leave. Why you asking?"

"Naah, never mind."

The barman stayed silent, his eyes fixed on Barone's face. Seconds later, he turned and walked back to the kitchen to put in the order for Barone's steak sandwich.

"Tell them to toast the bread, not just warm it," he called after him.

Dom wondered why Barone had asked about locking up. He sensed it bothered the man because his tone was laced with suspicion. Dom decided he'd wait to revisit it. He knew the Feds had arrested Barone. Not sure why, but it didn't require heavy brainpower to assume the question about locking the doors related to his arrest.

Minutes later, Anthony arrived from the kitchen with Barone's lunch. "How's it going, Pete?" he said in an upbeat tone as he slid the hero platter in front of him.

"Thanks, Tony."

Anthony winced. He looked at the man and shook his head with disdain. Barone was aware Anthony hated to be called Tony. Dom figured he did it on purpose as a reminder to Anthony he was a subservient employee. That's something Nicole wouldn't do, Dom thought. He never saw her cop a demeaning attitude with any worker.

"Will you need anything else?"

Barone, with a mouthful of hero, shook his head. Anthony turned and hurried toward the kitchen.

Dominic walked toward the end of the bar. The lone customer, his eyes staring at the TV set on the opposite fascia, watched a championship bowling match. Dom refilled his beer glass and asked, "Who's winning?"

"Lewinski," the man said. "Them Polacks sure roll 'em good."

Dominic chuckled. "Maybe it's something in the water?" He turned and saw Barone holding up his coffee mug.

Dom arrived with the carafe and set it down in front of Barone.

"Sal Fusco been in this past week?"

"Haven't seen him in a while," Dom said. He refilled the mug and returned the carafe to the burner.

"He's pissed over the bugged conversation I had."

Dominic's face went blank. "What conversation?" His instincts told him to be careful. Barone's earlier question about locking up was no doubt connected to this conversation.

"Ah, forget it. Forget I mentioned it."

Something's going on that I'm not aware of and probably shouldn't be, Dom thought. "How's the hero?"

"Good," Barone said. He brought the coffee mug to his mouth and then lowered it without drinking. "You're aware they arrested me, aren't you?"

Dom hesitated. "Yeah, I heard about that. You're out on bail now, right?"

"You know why?"

"No, and I'd rather you didn't tell me. The less I know, the better."

"Well, I'm gonna tell you, because it might have to do with you."

"Hold on, bro. I can't imagine what you mean, so be damn sure of your info before you accuse me of anything."

"I'll spell it out for you. Someone tapped into a phone conversation I had with my banker. I was in the office when I had it."

"They bugged your phone?"

"No, there was no bug on my phone. I was on my cell. The device was somewhere in my office."

"You have Nick Lombardo, the IT guy, come check it out?"

"Not yet, but what worries me is this. If someone got in to plant a bug, how the hell did he get past the locked doors?"

Dominic had to be circumspect with his answer if he didn't want to cast suspicion on anyone. "The only ones with keys to The Dugout are me, Nicole, and Anthony. Oh, and Sal Fusco. I lock up every night but Wednesdays. Anthony locks up that night. Nicole uses her key to open up in the morning, not to lock up at night."

"Nick's coming in next week. He's gonna check the office."

"You know, Pete, the NYPD has techies who can defeat any kind of lock. If they wanted to, they could get past any door to plant a bug. Locked or not, it doesn't matter. Same with the Feds."

Barone cocked his head and stared at him as if he'd never heard about that.

"You sure you weren't on the office phone?" Dom said.

"No, damn it. Fusco is pissed at me. He thinks I shoulda called from somewhere else."

"Pete, all I can say, I make damn sure I double-check the doors every night after I lock up. Same with Anthony."

"There's gotta be an answer, and I'm gonna find it."

"I hope you do," Dom said in a tone ringing with insincerity. "Hey, you being arrested, is it gonna affect what happens here, to the restaurants, to the employees?"

"No, so don't go looking for another job. They can't close the business until they go through a long legal process. And then, they'd need a conviction first before they can make it happen."

Dom nodded. "Well, that's a break," he mumbled.

When the last morsel of the hero disappeared, Barone slipped from the stool. Dom was busy with the bowling fan, but he noticed the pissed-off man exit the front door without a word. Dominic looked up at the monitor with the bowling contest and grinned.

* * *

Forest Hills, Queens, NY – Sat. P.M. 6/20

At ten o'clock, Dom escorted Nicole to her car. Before she got into the Sebring, she turned to her friend and hugged his huge torso.

"Good luck," he whispered. "Stay safe and let's hear from you when ya can. You got my address, right?"

"I do and I will," she said. She slid under the wheel, waved to Dominic, and pulled out of the alley.

She'd been fighting high levels of adrenalin for the last hour. She was aware two FBI agents assigned to accompany her to St. Thomas were already inside her apartment garage, waiting. After leaving The Dugout, she texted them on the number Rizzo had provided that she was on the way. A third agent parked in a Lincoln at the curb would be on the lookout and alert the two agents in the garage when she arrived.

Thirty minutes later, the Sebring rolled down the ramp to the rising garage door. Nicole checked the rearview mirror as she reached to activate the remote to close it. She caught sight of a shadowed figure leap from the hedges at the corner of the building and dart under the descending door and into the garage.

* * *

Agent Dave Connors' radio jumped alive. "Alpha-three to Alpha-one. An apparent hostile entered the garage carrying a handgun. He slipped under the door before it came down."

The agents ducked between two large SUVs, drew their weapons, and waited. Nicole's Sebring passed by and continued to the rear of the garage, with the gunman jogging close behind. When he came abreast of the two agents, Connors, a six-three former Notre Dame linebacker, leaped out and drove his shoulder into the attacker's chest, pile driving him to the cement floor. The weapon flew out of the gunman's hand and bounced on the cement to one side. Lew Barrow arrived a moment later and dropped onto the man's chest, pinning his arms. Connors got to his feet, retrieved the fallen weapon with a handkerchief, and pocketed it. With his 9mm pointed at the man's head, he told him, "Don't move or you're a dead man."

Barrow slid off, got to his feet, and looked over at Connors. "We should let the locals take care of this."

Connors nodded with understanding and kept his Glock pointed at the attacker. Barrow walked off to a distance where the attacker couldn't overhear him and pulled out his iPhone. Before he placed the call, he caught Nicole's attention and signaled her to stay put.

Barrow tapped 911 on his keypad and told the responding operator, "This is FBI Agent Lewis Barrow. I'm at building number 204 of the Boulevard Gardens complex at Sixty-eighth Road and Austin Avenue in Forest Hills. My partner and I have apprehended a man who tried to assassinate a resident in the building's garage. We will need local NYPD assistance as soon as possible to take the man into custody." Barrow provided his official ID number, his FBI unit, and details about the attack without giving away too much information.

Within five minutes, two RMPs pulled up outside the garage entrance. The agent in the Lincoln called Connors to open the door. Nicole activated her remote and two uniforms from the Twelfth Precinct on Austin Avenue entered with weapons drawn. Barrow waved and met them halfway with his hands raised. He held out his ID for their examination.

"Listen, officers," he said in a low voice, "this guy is a *Mafia* soldier and belongs to the Gambino family. They sent him to whack the lady over there." He pointed to the Sebring at the rear and Nicole standing next to it. "We intercepted him before he could get to her. There's no need for him to know we're FBI for reasons of heavy security. If you would, in your interrogation, please don't refer to the Bureau in his presence."

Barrow waved to Nicole to come over. She produced identification for the officers and confirmed what happened in the garage. Five minutes later, two detectives from the Twelfth arrived. They introduced themselves as Detectives Cameron Fisk and Hal Cary. Agent Barrow explained the situation again, and Agent Connors turned over the weapon he'd taken from the gunman.

The agent introduced Nicole to the detectives as the object of the attempted assassination. Cameron Fisk studied her for a moment and broke into a smile. "Howdy, neighbor."

Nicole looked at him, puzzled. When the fog lifted, she smiled and said, "You're the gentleman in 7-H at the end of the hallway."

"That's me. What a way to get to know a neighbor, but it's nice to finally meet you."

The uniforms had cautioned Fisk about the need for secrecy, and he refrained from saying anything more. Fisk turned to Barrow and said, "Unless you prefer to do it in the morning, one of you guys needs to come down to the station house to complete the arrest statement. It won't take long."

"I'm afraid it has to be tonight," Barrow said. He looked at Connors. "Why don't you take Miss Adams and go on ahead as planned? I'll ride with the two detectives to the precinct and complete the report. When I'm done, I'll grab an Uber and meet you there."

"Sounds good," Connors said and turned to Nicole. "Lead the way," and they walked to the elevator.

Fisk approached the man still prone on the floor and helped him to his feet. "What's your name, pal?"

The man brushed the dirt from his black suit pants, took off his jacket, and straightened his white tie. Sweat marks had stained his black shirt.

"Vito Rossellini, and I wanna call my lawyer."

"You can call him from the precinct," the detective told him. "Let's go take a ride."

* * *

"There are soft drinks in the fridge. Make yourself comfortable. I promise not to be long," Nicole said as she disappeared into the bedroom to change and finish packing.

Connors walked into the kitchen and found two cans of Mountain Dew and one Diet Coke on the refrigerator door shelf. She had emptied the box of food. Smart move, he thought. Spoiled food can smell awful and destroy a refrigerator over a long period.

The agent took out a Mountain Dew and popped the tab. He returned to the living room, sat on the sofa, and looked around. He was struck by the pleasant, informal style of its decoration, the mark of a single woman living alone. How difficult would it be, he wondered, for her to leave this behind, however long it became necessary?

Nicole came out of the bedroom dressed in a navy cotton crew neck, lightweight but warm enough to handle the airplane's cooling system. She wore denim jeans and Sketcher's sneakers, with her hair tied back in a ponytail.

"I'm all packed," she told Connors. "We have time for a quick drink, don't we? After that garage experience, I could use something to lower my pulse rate."

"I'm afraid not. There's another agent downstairs waiting to drive us to the hotel at Kennedy. We can spend the time during the drive to review how we intend to handle those obligations you'll be leaving behind. That okay?"

"You're the boss. Let me get my bags and we can be on our way."

Connors waited on the sofa until she returned, pulling a sizeable roller with a carry-on bag mounted on top. She had a garment bag draped over her right arm. He jumped to his feet and rushed to her. "Here, let me take those from you." He grabbed the handle of the roller, but she held on to the garment bag.

"I hope I've packed enough," she said.

"It's a tropical climate, remember. Informal attire is the rule of dress in those places." He looked over and saw her smiling. "I read those travel brochures my wife gets all the time," he said with a grin.

"You mean I won't need my ski parka?"

"Not on this trip. All set?"

Her eyes panned the room like someone about to leave a revered place for the last time. "I'll need to sneak back here once in a while," she said aloud.

"Not a good idea if you want to stay safe. Before I forget, let me have your car key, apartment keys, and the key to your mailbox. We'll need access to those to ensure your life proceeds without problems."

Nicole opened her purse and took out the requested keys. "Here you go."

"I hope you've packed your checkbook and any other financial instruments you may need to pay the bills we forward to you. I wouldn't want to see you get thrown into debtor's prison."

Nicole smiled. "I have them."

Connors raised the radio to his mouth. "Alpha one to Alpha three, we're on the way down. We'll be exiting by the front entrance."

In the elevator, the agent told her, "When you get to your destination, be certain to change your cell phone provider and telephone number."

"Why do I need to change it?"

"So they can't track your phone's location."

"Good thinking," she said. "I'll do it as soon as I get there."

For a moment, the agent considered her status with the mob. She was guilty of crossing them, and he didn't expect the threat to her life would go away too soon. The mob had a long memory. But perhaps when those in top positions of the family die of natural causes or are helped by ambitious mob climbers, interest would wane. At least he hoped so.

* * *

West Side Manhattan – Sun. P.M. 6/21

"Yeah, they left JFK this morning on the nine-fifteen flight," Jack Fields said. "I was sure you'd like to know."

The call came in on Rizzo's cell phone while he was at the refrigerator reaching in for a can of Hires Root Beer. Flo sat on the sofa in the living room watching the yellow tennis ball whizz back and forth over the net; it was a hot rally between two Europeans with names she couldn't pronounce. Rizzo remained in the kitchen and listened to Fields describe Vito's attempt to whack Nicole in the garage.

"The two agents handled the interruption in the garage with finesse."

"They tell the cops who they were?"

Fields chuckled. "They couldn't very well keep it a secret. But they left the Guido in the dark. Lew Barrow, the agent who went to the precinct to sign off on the arrest, overheard the guy refer to them as 'them two bodyguards.' He got a big chuckle over the comment."

"Good. I'm eager to hear what Fusco's reaction is when he learns about her absence . . . why she suddenly vanished. I wonder if he'll suspect someone on the inside tipped her off."

"Not to worry. You're the tipster, and you're on the outside. How would he know?"

"Yeah, but my information came from someone on the inside. I worry about that."

"I guess you need to give him a heads-up."

Rizzo fell silent. He recalled how Fusco took Dom into his confidence about family matters. Dom would tell Vinnie, and Vinnie would—

"Damn! You're right," Rizzo said. "And I better do it soon."

"Okay, I'll let you go. Maybe we can meet for lunch this week. I'll give you a buzz."

"Bye," Rizzo said and ended the call.

Rizzo returned to the sofa, and Flo looked at him with the usual curiosity. "That was Jack Fields. He called to say Nicole got off okay this morning."

"To where?"

"I can't tell you. If I do, I'll have to kill you."

Her eyes opened wide. A smile broke out a second later. "Oh, funny guy. You mean it's top secret."

"Yes, but if you're nice to me tonight, I'll let you in on it."

"I'm always nice to you, aren't I?"

"One of the mob's goons tried to delay her departure for good," Rizzo said, and he dove into the story of the attack in the garage and the fast response of the two FBI agents. "But all's well that ends well."

"And they didn't hurt her?"

"The agents grabbed him before he reached her car."

"Lucky. He might have killed her."

Rizzo moved closer to her on the sofa and put his arm around her shoulders. "That was his intent, sweetheart. Orders from the boss, Sal Fusco." He nuzzled her ear and wet her cheek with a kiss.

She wiggled away. "So what happens to the man? He didn't kill her. Does he go free?"

"Not a chance. After the trial, I'm sure he'll end up in the slammer. They've got him on a Class C felony—assault with a deadly weapon. He'll get a minimum of three and a half years. Closer to seven, since he has priors. That's how that tune goes in New York."

"He's the one who followed you?"

"Same guy. Thinks he's Marlon Brando. He was one of the thugs tailing Nicole Adams on her days off."

"Well, she's gone now. I guess he's out of a job."

"In more ways than one, you might say."

Chapter Twenty-Two

Howard Beach Queens, NY Wed. P.M. 7/01

Carmine D'Angelo cocked his head to one side as he concentrated on the strumming mandolin music that filled *Il Cucina Sicilian*. The notes of "Come Back to Sorrento" wafted overhead from hidden speakers while his mind traveled back fifty years to his honeymoon week in that favorite Italian city.

He and Rose had spent seven romantic days checked into the decades-old Grand Hotel Excelsior Vittoria overlooking Naples Bay. The five years that followed were among the happiest of his life, despite his struggles to keep his trucking business afloat. An occasional delivery for a mob-connected associate helped, but around him, more substantial companies than his trucking operation were going under, victims of the '73-'74 Stock Market crash. The outbreak of the '73 oil crisis compounded the problem, and two years later, D'Angelo Trucking had no option but to take on the Gambinos as a partner.

To add to his torment, cervical cancer took Rose early, the one love of his life. It left him alone, childless, and bitter.

"Uncle, you okay?" Pete Barone said. "You look dazed."

D'Angelo turned to Barone and smiled. "I'm fine. This music . . . this song. It always reminds me of your Aunt Rose. Makes me sad until I remember the week we spent in Sorrento on our honeymoon."

"I'm sorry I never got to meet her. My mother used to say, of the three sisters, she was the one aptly named: a rose between two thorns."

"Oh, you met her, okay. But you were a baby when she died. You'd have loved her."

Enrico, the restaurant's owner and chef, appeared at the table. Attired in a chef's hat and a short-sleeve executive chef's coat that failed to hide his bulbous stomach, he greeted them with a confident smile. "*Amicu mio*, how was the Osso Bucco? Nice and tender?"

"*Delizioso*, Enrico. Always the best. *Mille grazie*."

"Your *vitello*?" he asked Barone.

"Perfect, thanks."

"Ready for freshly made *cannolis*?"

"And two *espressos*," D'Angelo said, smiling.

"What, no after-dinner drinks?"

"No, Enrico. Not tonight. *Grazie*."

The restaurateur moved off in the kitchen's direction, followed by their server. D'Angelo observed them until the two men disappeared through the double doors into the kitchen. He placed his elbows on the table, steepled his hands in front of his face, and closed his eyes. When he opened them, he said, "I'm worried, Pete. With all of this shit going down, I haven't heard a peep from Nunziata."

"Shouldn't you call him for a meeting?"

"I started to the other night, but I remembered he doesn't handle bad news well."

"But, uncle, you gotta talk to him sometime. I'm sure he's got the word by now."

"Yeah, you're right. I'll call him in the morning."

* * *

The door to *Il Cucina Sicilian* opened, and D'Angelo's two bodyguards exited onto the sidewalk. Frank, the taller of the two, looked up the street and motioned with a wave to the driver of the limo waiting at the curb. The car pulled up in front of the restaurant, and D'Angelo's driver, Mike, stepped out. His thumbnail flicked a stick match, and he put the flame to the cigarette hanging from his lips. He leaned an elbow on top of the limo, looked across to Frank, and asked, "How long?"

"They're finishing their *cannolis* now. Should be another ten minutes," Frank said.

"How's the family?" the driver asked. "They still down at the shore?"

"Yeah. It's been a quiet summer so far. That'll end in two weeks. She comes back and the kids get shipped off to camp for a month. Then the fuckin' demands start."

Mike snickered. "Hey, find a damn camp for her."

"That I could," Frank said.

"Frankie," the second bodyguard called to him, "I'm outa smokes. I got time to run across the street to the market, pick up a pack?"

"Yeah, sure, Bruno. Go ahead," he said and pulled at his button-down collar. The oppressive night's heat was such it made his shirt cling to his torso like a magnet.

The street was quiet, empty of traffic. In typical summer fashion for this neighborhood, people without air conditioning hung out open apartment windows, looking for relief.

Frank walked to the restaurant door, opened it, and saw D'Angelo and Barone get to their feet. He let it close and went to the front of the limo. Moments before the restaurant door opened, Frank hurried across the street. It appeared as though he intended to call back Bruno, the other bodyguard. Instead, he stopped and turned around.

D'Angelo and Barone stepped out of the restaurant, paused, and looked up and down for the two bodyguards. Mike hurried around the front of the vehicle to open the door for D'Angelo.

From out of the darkness, a black sedan careened up the street and screeched to a stop within a few yards behind the waiting limo. Two gunmen, attired in dark suits and wearing ski masks, stepped onto the sidewalk. Mike spotted them. He dove to the ground and rolled under the limo.

In tandem, the gunmen let loose a barrage of gunfire from their automatic weapons. D'Angelo and Barone took most of the bullets in their upper bodies. The impacts jerked them every which way. Both targets landed in a heap on the cement pavement. Their bodies lay perpendicular to each other. The two assassins dove through the opened rear door of their vehicle, slammed it shut, and their driver raced away from the horrific scene. The black sedan disappeared out of sight before the sound of gunfire ceased echoing.

Frank watched in disgust, not so much by the bloody scene, but more with the realization he had played a role to make it happen. He had no choice, he told himself, or Sal "The Hat" would have him whacked next.

* * *

FBI's Manhattan Office – Thurs. A.M. 7/02

Rachel's voice on the intercom interrupted his musing. "Jack, Lieutenant Machado on line one."

Fields smiled and turned from his window to face the speakerphone on his desk. He held the smile with no difficulty when he answered. "Bob, I heard a few of our friends celebrated the Fourth a few days early this year."

"Yeah," Machado said, "that's why I called. We missed the fireworks."

"Kind of expected, don't you think? The don couldn't be happy with D'Angelo as the family's underboss. I mean, his performance these days. Had to be an embarrassment. Of course, anyone on the inside can understand it wasn't entirely his doing. Most of the blame rests on the shoulders of his *capo*, Sal Fusco."

"Yeah. In that criminal society, when the *capo regio* runs amock, the underboss can get it in the neck. It stands to reason, when a soldier bungles an assignment, the *capo* shares in the blame."

"I would imagine Sal's days are numbered."

"I suspect you're right. By the way, how'd the transfer of our pearl of a girl go?" Machado asked.

"Perfect, I'm happy to report. The flight arrived on time. Her new host met them and escorted them around to inspect her private haven."

"I would say she deserves a medal, I mean for the way she helped us shut down the Gambino's money laundering."

"A brave lady," he told Machado. "She's entitled to every bit of protection we can provide."

"Boy! What a place for a safe house: year-round sunshine, warm blue water, soft breezes, white sandy beaches. I can't imagine what's not to like about it."

"I doubt there will be a problem," Fields said. "The two FBI agents returned the next day. From all they observed, she appeared delighted with her new environment."

"Before they left, they reviewed the procedures and protocols they expected her to follow."

"I hope she adheres to them. I wouldn't want her location compromised by an inadvertent disclosure—like sneaking back into the city."

"Might be prudent to have the person we appoint as liaison to remind her of it now and again."

"A thought hit me a few moments ago when you suggested Sal Fusco might be next."

"What's that?"

"The order for the hit on D'Angelo? It had to come from the don. Right?"

"Yeah, I agree. No one can take out an underboss without approval from the top."

"But the shooters were not from within the family. We know that because it's how they work. Bring in people from the outside to do the hit. That way, it can't be connected to the don."

"Right. So who did the don give the order to?"

"Had to be Sal Fusco."

Both men remained quiet for several moments. When Machado broke the silence, there was a sense of concern in his tone. "I'm worried. If he's been elevated to underboss, it will make him more dangerous."

* * *

Chelsea Area, Manhattan - Fri. P.M. 7/03

Rizzo had his keys in his hand and was prepared to march out the door when the office phone rang. "Damn! Why is it always when I want to get out of here?" he mumbled and returned to his desk. He reached for the phone and put it to his ear. "Lucas Rizzo Investigations, how may I help you?"

Several moments passed before the caller's low voice spoke. "This Luke Rizzo?"

"It is. What can I do for you?"

"This is Sal Fusco. You know who I am?"

Rizzo dropped into his desk chair and pulled the phone from his head. He squinted at the instrument. Was this a joke?

"Yeah, I know who Sal Fusco is," he said, "but I'm not sure that's who you are."

The voice laughed. "Why you surprised?"

"What reason does Sal Fusco have to call me?"

"What reason? My reason is this. We need to talk. I got questions, and you got answers. Simple as that."

"If you are Sal Fusco, and not some clown jerking me around, how can I be sure?"

"Okay then. Listen to these names. Nicole Adams, Mario Langella, and Angie Russo. They sound familiar to you?"

Rizzo hesitated. If he denied it, he would surely ring false. Fusco was aware of his role in the arrest of Langella outside of Ruby's. And he already suspected a connection between him and Nicole. "Okay, you're for real. What is it you want?"

"Like I said, I need answers to questions."

"I'm not sure I have those answers. Go ahead, ask."

"Not on the phone. But hey, how about I buy you dinner? We talk it over while we dine like business people. Okay? Any restaurant you prefer. You pick it. Out in the open so you don't feel like somebody gonna threaten you."

"Tonight?"

"Yeah, you got another date?"

Rizzo resisted the urge to chuckle. This was unexpected and ridiculous, but he was curious. There was no way he could turn down the invite without angering the man. "And what if I can't answer your questions? You stick me with the check?"

"That's funny. No, funny guy. I'm sure you can answer several of them. That'll be good enough."

"Yeah, okay," Rizzo said. "What time and where?"

"Say, nine o'clock. Anywhere you like."

"How about Italian? You like Italian food?"

"Well, duh. Is the pope Catholic?"

Rizzo grinned. A sense of humor. Maybe this won't be so bad. "You familiar with La Luna, in Little Italy?"

"Never been there."

"A great menu. I'll call down. Reserve a table for nine o'clock. It's on Mulberry."

"See you there," Fusco said and ended the call.

Rizzo pulled his iPhone from his pocket and punched in Bob Machado's fast dial office number.

"Hey, Luke. What's up?"

"Well, you're not gonna believe who called me."

"I'm listening to the smile in your voice. It's a good bet I'd be wrong with three guesses. So, tell me."

"Sal 'The Hat' Fusco."

"You gotta be kidding. What the hell did he want?"

"Wants to ask me a couple of questions. I'm sure I can predict what they are, but he wouldn't agree to handle them over the phone. Face to face only. He invited me to have dinner with him tonight."

"Alone? Just the two of you?"

"Yeah. Intimate, like a date. At least he didn't say anyone else would be there. Oh, he'll have a couple of his goons at another table to keep watch on him. That's for certain."

Machado paused before he asked, "You think it's wise? I mean, what the hell does he want to know he couldn't find out on his own?"

"And if I had any answers, why would I tell him?"

Another long pause. "How about, he's got an offer you can't refuse?"

"Like what?"

"Like holding one of your inside sources hostage."

"Holy shit!" Rizzo drew a breath. His mind raced. Could Fusco use Vinnie or even Dominic that way? "I'll go ape if he's gone that far."

"Yeah, holy shit," Machado repeated. "What are you gonna do if he hits you with a move like that?"

"Well, I can't say what I'd do until I hear him out. So I better not stand him up."

"Where are you supposed to meet and what time?"

Rizzo failed to respond, his concentration buried in worry. He wrestled with how to handle the threat if it came to that. What would he do?

"Luke?"

"Huh?"

"I asked where and what time. I have an idea."

"Nine o'clock. La Luna on Mulberry in Little Italy." Rizzo slammed a fist on his desk. "God damn son-of-a-bitch. Ah, sorry, Bob, but the damn hostage option has me scared shitless."

"So cool it. Don't get all worked up before you sit down with the guy. He might pull a Carlo Gambino on you."

Rizzo sat up. "What the hell is that?"

"I've read a lot about the man. There's one characteristic most historians agree on—besides his delight in using an ice pick. He took pride in his business acumen and his ability to negotiate."

"You mean I should look out for an ice pick while he massages my ego?"

"No, Fusco's not a brave man. If he wanted to take you out, he'd leave it to his crew. I don't understand how in hell he got his button. But what the hell. They say Frank Costello never made his bones with a hit either. As a businessman, yes, but no bones."

Rizzo's head throbbed. "What, then? Go armed?"

"That's the last thing you should do. Perhaps Fusco will try to negotiate with you for the information he wants. And whatever you do, don't bring up D'Angelo's name. Two nights ago, they whacked the underboss."

"No shit! Nunziata order the hit?"

"Who else?"

"Well, I'm not gonna find out what Fusco wants unless I meet with him."

"Listen. Here's what we'll do. I'll send two undercovers down there to have dinner in the place while you're with him. I've got a pair I've used a few times for situations like this. They come off like the perfect married couple. We'll make their reservation for nine-fifteen. They'll be there the entire time you are. You won't make them. They're that good."

"Thanks, Bob. I'll touch base with you in the morning if I can avoid the ice pick."

As soon as Rizzo rang off, he reached into the center drawer and pulled out a piece of paper. He had it tucked in the back corner. He stared at the numbers and his hand shook. By request of the owner of the numbers, Rizzo had never entered it into his address book. He punched in the seven digits and held the phone to his ear, listening to its steady pulse. After a dozen rings, he heard Vinnie's voice. "I'm not here. Leave a message." Rizzo slammed back in his chair and screamed, "Son-of-a-bitch!"

Chapter Twenty-Three

Lower Manhattan – Fri. P.M. 7/03

Rizzo stood in front of La Luna's doorway at the corner of Mulberry and Hester. He looked up and down both streets and failed to spot a black limousine parked within view that looked like it belonged to Fusco. Early by fifteen minutes, he was confident he had arrived first. Rizzo intended to secure a table on the side of the restaurant with the brick-lined wall. With the wall at his back, it would assure him no one could slip in behind him. Rizzo shared a penchant for caution, along with *Mafia* big shots.

Emilio stood at the podium to the left of the entrance as Rizzo came through the door. The host opened his arms and greeted Rizzo with the familiar warmth of an old friend. He glanced at the reservation book. "Mr. Rizzo, you are early. We'll have your table ready in about ten minutes."

"That's fine, Emilio. But if you can," he said and pointed, "I'd like one of those tables on that side against the wall."

"Oh, certainly, Mr. Rizzo. There's one about to be vacated. They're settling their check now. It'll be yours in a few minutes, as soon as we can clear and reset it."

"Perfect. My guest is a Mr. Sal Fusco."

Emilio's jaw dropped. Rizzo caught the change in expression. "You know him?"

"Oh, yes. Not from La Luna, but from . . . well, you understand how talk gets around among those of us who work in the same profession."

"I know what you're thinking, Emilio. You needn't worry. He invited me to dinner . . . for a business discussion, that's all. It'll be a quiet evening with plenty of *cibo delizioso e l'amicizia*."

Emilio touched his arm. "*Paesano, per favore*. I can guarantee the delicious food if you make certain of the friendships."

The couple leaving the table earmarked for Rizzo arrived at the podium. They shook the host's hand. "*Grazie*, Emilio, grazie. Everything was wonderful."

"So happy you enjoyed it. Come again soon."

"We will. Thanks. Good night."

Emilio nodded and turned to Rizzo. "Come. Your table is ready."

Seated, his back to the wall, Rizzo had a clear line to the front door. At ten past nine, Rizzo spotted Fusco, his hat a dead giveaway. The *capo* entered, stopped, and looked around.

"Good evening," Emilio said with his usual warm smile.

Rizzo watched as Fusco continued to scan the restaurant. Then Rizzo remembered they had never met. The *capo* ignored the host and kept searching the tables until he spotted Rizzo's raised arm.

"I'm meetin' Luke Rizzo," the *capo* told Emilio. Without waiting for Emilio to escort him, Fusco made straight for Rizzo's table.

Emilio trailed behind, and when they neared, Rizzo got to his feet and extended his hand.

"Mr. Fusco. Welcome."

"Yeah, nice to see you too, Rizzo."

Emilio had taken a position behind Fusco. The host's face locked in a frown; he made it clear he did not appreciate Sal's breach of etiquette. Rizzo had picked up on it. "Emilio," Rizzo said smiling, "this is Mr. Sal Fusco. Treat him well tonight. He may come back again."

The host's eyebrows jumped.

Fusco ignored the introduction and pulled out the chair to the left of Rizzo. The Borsalino remained on his head. When Emilio suggested he'd check it for him, Fusco declined. Instead, he took off the hat and put it on the chair next to him.

"Would you gentlemen like to start with something to drink?" He placed the menus and wine list on the table.

Rizzo trained his eyes on Fusco and waited for him to respond.

"Yeah, bring us a bottle of the most expensive Chianti Classico you have," Fusco said.

"Consider ordering it by the glass?" Rizzo said.

Fusco squinted, and he flashed a puzzled look at Rizzo.

Before the *capo* could speak, Rizzo said, "I don't drink, Sal. I'm AA."

"Well, shit. I ain't gonna finish a whole bottle by myself. Okay," he said and looked at Emilio, "make it a glass then."

Emilio asked Rizzo, "Anything for you?"

"Do you offer any of the non-alcoholic wines?"

The host nodded. "We do. A few labels. Not a lot. How about a nice St. Regis Cabernet?"

"Sold."

Emilio signaled to a server attired in black trousers and a maroon vest over a white dress shirt and gave him the order. He turned his attention back to the table and said, "Gianni will be your server. He'll take good care of you, I'm sure. Enjoy."

When the host was out of earshot, Fusco said, "What the hell's wrong with this place? Non-alcoholic wine? Shit!"

"Well, if you were AA, you'd get bored with Virgin Mary's. Non-alcoholic wine is a great option."

"How come you're AA?"

Rizzo smiled. He never expected a conversation with a *Mafia capo* would touch on the personal. But maybe it was a good sign.

"Because you asked, I'll tell you."

"Yeah, tell me."

"I drank much more than I should have when I was a cop. It did in my first marriage, along with my kidneys."

"What kind of cop?"

"Narcotics . . . undercover."

"Yeah?" A smile crept from his mouth like a child about to meet the Lone Ranger. "That musta been fun."

"It had its moments. No shortage of close calls. I like private work better."

"How much fun can that be? I mean, chasin' deadbeat husbands and cheatin' wives."

"I get little of that. More of the domestic crime variety, like investigating pilferage for large retail establishments, or finding a missing person now and then. Stuff like that."

It occurred to Rizzo the man behaved like a reader of mystery novels, romanticizing the role of a crime fighter. Perhaps Fusco once entertained a career as a cop before joining the *Cosa Nostra*. Nah, not a chance.

Gianni appeared at the table to deliver the two wines. He asked, "Would you like to hear tonight's specials?" Without waiting for a response, Gianni rolled out a detailed description of the four items not on the menu. Rizzo thought one sounded better than the next.

Fusco and Rizzo exchanged glances.

"No thanks," Rizzo said. "We'll order from the menu."

Fusco nodded in agreement, and asked Gianni, "You ever have beef braciola on the menu?"

"I'm afraid not, but the chef can make it for you. It would take a while."

"Ah, forget it. I'll order from the menu."

"*Va bene.* Take your time. I 'll be back to take your orders whenever you're ready."

"*Saluti,*" Rizzo said, picking up his wineglass.

Fusco raised his glass and motioned it toward Rizzo. "*Saluti.*" He sipped then set it down and turned his head. While the *capo's* eyes scanned the restaurant, Rizzo noticed the pause when they landed on two men at a table across the room. They had entered the restaurant about five minutes behind Fusco. The obligatory bodyguards, Rizzo decided.

As if seeing his boys reminded him, he looked at Rizzo and said, "You carryin'?"

It took Rizzo a few seconds to grasp the question. "Are you kidding? Of course not."

"Good. You carry, don't ya?"

"Not when I'm having dinner with a pal," he said as he pressed his right ankle against the .38 Colt Cobra in the ankle holster on his left.

Fusco's smile reappeared. "Good answer."

"Why don't we look, then order?" Rizzo said and picked up a menu.

After they studied the bill of fare, Rizzo flagged the waiter. Both men recited what they wanted, and Gianni listened with intensity.

"You gonna remember all that?" Fusco asked Gianni. His ability to remember their orders without writing them down on an order pad evidently impressed the *capo.*

Fusco chose the *Calamari Friti* (fried squid) as an appetizer, and *Vitello Alla Saltimbocca* (Veal Scaloppini sautéed in butter with spinach, prosciutto, mushroom and sherry wine sauce topped with provolone) as his main course. Rizzo went for the *Pollo Alla Griglia* (tender chicken breast, seasoned with lemon and herb spices) and no appetizer. Gianni delivered a second glass of wine with their meals and they ate in silence except for one moment.

"You Italian, no?" Fusco asked as if the thought had popped into his mind between sips.

Rizzo, caught with food in his mouth, swallowed and said, "That's right. Sicilian. The family came from a town southwest of Palermo. Partinico."

"I've been there. Close to Castellammare del Golfo."

"About eight miles," Rizzo said.

Fusco smiled as though he'd returned to a storage of fond memories. They resumed eating in silence.

The mention of Sicily's popular seaside resort town reminded Rizzo of the stories his great grandfather had spun for him as a child. Castellammare del Golfo had been the home of the two feuding *Mafiosi borgatas*, headed by Salvatore Maranzano and Joe Masseria. The two gangs came to New York in the early thirties and conducted a bloody mob war with each other until Lucky Luciano stepped in. Peace was restored after he had both bosses, Maranzano and Masseria, removed—*Mafia*-style. Rizzo wondered if Fusco might be related to one of them .

"*Parli Italiano?*" Fusco asked at one point when he looked up from his dinner.

'No. Much to my regret, my folks spoke Italian when they didn't want me to know what they were saying. I picked up a phrase or two, not enough to carry on an intelligent conversation."

"That's a shame. A beautiful language," Fusco said and resumed cutting into his veal.

When Gianni removed the main course plates, the items left on the table were two demitasse coffees, two *cannolis*, and a Sambuca for the *capo*. Fusco looked over at Rizzo and said, "You ready for questions?"

"Okay, but let me say this first. I'll be as honest as I can in my responses. If I tell you I don't know, it's because I have no information or awareness of what you're asking. So don't badger me. *Va bene?*"

"*Va bene.*" Fusco leaned back in his chair and took the napkin from his lap. When he reached out, he dropped the napkin on the table like the starter of a footrace. "What's your connection to the woman, Nicole Adams?"

"No prior connection until I was hired to find her."

"Why'd she disappear?"

"My client had no clue, but he saw her taken away in a limo against her will. That's when he came to my office and hired me to find her."

"How does he connect to her?"

"Oh, that's a long story, but I'll try to give you a synopsis version. Thirty-five years ago, she was a Playboy Bunny at the club in Manhattan."

"No shit?" Fusco exclaimed like the information was brand new to him.

"My client was an ad agency exec. He arrived at the club one afternoon for a business lunch with the promotion manager of *Playboy Magazine*. That was, in case you forgot, Roy Dickerson, the former manager of Time-out Enterprises."

"I remember, smartass."

"Nicole was their assigned Bunny at the lunch, and the advertising guy lost his marbles over her."

Fusco stared.

Rizzo continued the narration. "My client waited for her to get off work and took her to dinner at a restaurant in the Village. She turned out to be gay, and it was the last time they were together. Thirty-five years later, he was shopping in D'Agostino's on Third Avenue. That's when he saw her outside on the sidewalk talking with a man wearing a Borsalino."

Fusco grinned.

"He recognized her and his heart went pitty-pat again. When he raced out of the market to find what was going on, he called out her name. That's when the limo driver knocked him to the sidewalk. They whisked her off in the limo and he watched her disappear up Third Avenue."

The *capo* nodded as though he approved of the way Rizzo related the incident. "How'd you find her?"

"My client said before the driver closed the door, she shouted to him, 'Roy Dickerson, the Playboy Club'." The Playboy Club doesn't exist any longer. I called the magazine. They found him in their retired-employee records, but they wouldn't give me his number. Instead, they called him, and he called me. That's how I found she worked for Time-Out Enterprises. I told Dickerson what happened to her and he suggested I visit The Dugout bar."

"He knows why she disappeared?"

"If he did, he didn't let on."

"What'd you do when you found her?"

"My client insisted we go there. He wanted to see for himself she was okay. When we got there, she was reluctant to speak to us. I gave her my business card and asked her to call me."

"Did she?"

"Yes. We made a date to meet on the Staten Island Ferry so we could speak in private. We met on a Sunday. On the ride over, she explained how the owner of the business harassed her. She didn't know how to handle it. She said she was afraid of him."

"She say why she was afraid?"

"Because the shithead kept hitting on her."

"No other reason?"

"No. Look, Sal, there was no point in dancing around. I didn't fall off the turnip truck this morning. I put a few guesses together, but that wasn't my concern. I was hired to find her. She turned up okay. My responsibility was done. End of story."

"Not yet. There's the situation with you up in the Bronx. The time they arrested a guy I know."

"You mean the piece of shit, Langella?"

"You fingered him for the cops."

"Bullshit! They already had him fingered. The Suffolk cops asked me there to confirm his ID."

"How'd you come to know him?"

"The prick roughed me up some time ago. I showed up at his watering hole, Ruby's, in the South Bronx. I was looking for a guy for my client. Mario didn't like the questions I asked. He showed me the door. You don't think I'd forget his face, do you?"

"The cops knew you could ID him? How come?"

"I told them I'd met him before. Back when I first visited Ruby's. I went there for the Suffolk major crime unit. They were my client. A minor assignment they contracted out to me. Help them locate a guy they were after for dealing in sex trafficking. They had info he hung out at Ruby's bar."

"Langella?"

"No, damn it. Not him. Somebody named Cusack. He was a pal of Langella's. That's why he tossed me out of Ruby's."

Fusco remained silent for several moments. When he spoke, his face looked more relaxed, like he was satisfied with Rizzo's answers. In a soft voice, he said, "Okay, *paesano*, where's Nicole Adams?"

Rizzo stared at the *capo* with a confused expression. "I don't understand the question."

"She's gone missin' again. Any idea where she is?"

Rizzo shrugged. "Sal, this is the first I've heard about it. I don't have any damn information that could help you. The last time I saw her or spoke with her was on the ferry ride to Staten Island over a month ago."

Fusco became silent again. This time, he came out of it with a smile. "Let's finish our *cannolis* and call it a night. Before we go, lemme give you a bit of advice. In the future, make damn sure the contracts you take on don't conflict with certain parties. They may not be people as understandin' as me."

"I hear you, Sal."

Chapter Twenty-Four

Mid-Town Manhattan – Sat. A.M. 7/04

"Why this place?"

Rizzo grinned and looked through the glass and metal latticework of the 360-degree wall surrounding the observation deck—out to the massive jungle of skyscrapers. The morning was clear with few clouds, and the views from the Empire State Building were forever.

"Because the scenery is great, and who in the circle of your friends would ever come here?"

"You're right. If they did, it would be to push a whack-job over the ledge. But now, with this new barrier around the observation deck, the job is impossible. It's a shame. The only spot left is from the Brooklyn Bridge."

Rizzo found it difficult to hold back laughing at Vinnie's macabre sense of humor. "Man, you gotta stop hanging with those guys."

"It's funny," Vinnie went on, "I haven't been up here since I was a kid. And here I am with my kid friend at the top of the Empire State Building. After almost forty damn years."

Rizzo turned his head toward the Borough of Queens. "It's a great city, isn't it? Too bad there are so many shitheads out there on the dark side trying to destroy it."

"Are you referring to any particular shithead?"

"How's your coffee? Hot enough?"

"Yeah. Mickey Ds? Right? I can always tell. Which shithead?"

"Sal Fusco. I had dinner with him Friday night."

Vinnie's eyes jumped wide. "You what! How the fuck did that happen?"

Rizzo smiled at Vinnie's astonished expression. "He called me for a date. We met at La Luna."

"Holy shit! That's like dining with the devil. Nothing good comes of it. Take my word."

"Well, it was an invitation I couldn't refuse. He said he had lots of questions and I might have the answers."

"You shoulda told him to go fuck himself."

"I asked my guy at the OCU what he thought. He suggested it might be possible Fusco was holding my inside source hostage as a chip to get the information he wanted."

Vinnie's head whipped around, and he glared at Rizzo while a hellfire burned in his eyes. "You told him about—"

"No, goddamn it, no. Relax. What kind of asshole you think I am?"

"Well, what the fuck you tell him?" His anger was that of a thirteen-year-old Vinnie in the old neighborhood, ready to kick ass and take on the entire block of kids.

"I mentioned once I had a source inside the family that whispers things to me. No names."

"Bro, I hope not."

"Hey, they know I'd go to the mat before I'd give up anyone. The mob may have their vow of *Omertà*, but my principles are stronger."

"Well, why then is Fusco suspicious of Dom and me?"

"I didn't say he was. He's not, and nothing he said at La Luna would lead me to believe otherwise."

"He don't know about you and me, does he?"

"Hell, no. But Dom has been your source for inside shit going down. If old Sal ever got a smell of a leak somewhere, Dominic, his schmoozing buddy at The Dugout, could become a suspect."

"Yeah, and that happens, it'll be a big problem for me too. Fusco knows how Dominic and me connect. That we go back a ways in his crew."

The grim look on Vinnie's face told Rizzo the man understood his liability.

"That's why this meeting?"

"Yeah. I wanted to run by you the questions he asked. They left me with a sense he smells something about the second disappearance of Nicole Adams."

"Oh, shit!"

Rizzo covered the bases, giving Vinnie a quick review of the subjects Fusco asked about and the answers he provided. "I could be wrong. If my OSU guy hadn't tossed the idea of a hostage at me, I'd never have given it a second thought. We wouldn't be here. But I needed to give you a heads-up, anyway. Forewarned is forearmed. Isn't that the way the saying goes?"

"Okay. I'll give Dominic a holler."

"Yeah, and maybe we cool it with our meetings. At least for a while."

The two friends remained quiet for several seconds, Vinnie staring at the container of coffee in his hand, Rizzo gazing through the glass wall toward Queens until Rizzo reached out.

He took Vinnie by the back of his neck. "I love you, my brother. You know that."

"Yeah, bro. I do. Not to worry."

* * *

West Side Manhattan – Sat. P.M. 7/04

Rizzo put his iPhone to his ear after seeing the caller readout.

"Happy Fourth of July," Fields said. You out in the backyard having a barbeque?"

"You're kidding. Us city folk order in. We have no backyard. You called because you want to hear about last night. Right? Find out if I escaped getting skinned alive by Sal Fusco?"

"Yeah. How'd it go?"

Rizzo and Flo were on the sofa watching an early Wimbledon men's singles match from England. Flo leaned in and whispered, "Want me to leave?"

"No, no. Stay, sweetheart. I'll go in the kitchen." He got to his feet. "Hold on a sec, Jack," and he walked out of the room. "Okay, now."

"Still keeping secrets, eh?"

"Hey, this is a woman who gets frightened by Scooby-Do reruns."

Fields chuckled. "Well, I hope last night's dinner had nothing frightening on the menu."

"No, it went well. I answered everything; the harmless ones truthfully, the sensitive ones omitting key facts, and those that would cause self-incrimination—"

"You took the fifth."

"No. Better. I lied outright. It was one of my best performances. He saved the most troublesome one for last. He asked me, 'Where's Nicole Adams?'"

"And you said—?"

"I told him I didn't know she was missing. Haven't seen or talked with her since the ferry ride over a month ago."

"He buy it?"

"Seems so. Before leaving, he issued me a warning. Told me to be more circumspect in my selection of future clients. Make sure their needs don't conflict with certain people."

"That's what he said?"

"Yeah, but not as eloquently. Hold on a minute."

Rizzo walked to the kitchen door and looked out. Flo remained on the sofa, glued to the tennis match.

"It's okay. She's still involved with tennis on the TV. What occurred to me is this. As well as last night turned out, I don't believe Fusco has given up trying to find Nicole. Now that they've whacked D'Angelo, and he's out of Fusco's way, the man will become a loose cannon. Do you have any idea if the *Mafia* has tentacles that reach all the way to the Virgin Islands? Any mob activity going on down there?"

"I'm not aware of any, but that's a good question. Let me research it. I'll get back."

"Okay. Don't forget to watch the Macy's fireworks tonight. It's on TV."

"I know. Bye."

* * *

Chelsea Area, Manhattan - Monday, P.M. 7/06

"I'm not sure, Bob. He seemed satisfied with my answers," Rizzo said, "the best I could tell. But who can say for sure? The man won't let up until he finds Nicole Adams."

"Well, at least you survived the inquisition. It can go either way with The Hat. But thanks for the update. Oh, I forgot. That tag number you gave me? Registered to Time-Out Enterprises. No surprise."

"Wow! You work fast. It's been only three months."

"Well, shit, you already knew who it belonged to. Sorry about that. Must have forgotten to follow up. I owe you one."

"I'll make note of that."

"Stay out of trouble and we'll speak soon."

"Yeah, I'll try." Rizzo pressed the red button on his cell phone.

Pocketing the instrument, he prepared to close up for the night. He opened the desk drawer to take out his Glock 9mm when he heard the sound of someone trying the office door. Nelly's attempt to take him out had caused him to become extra wary. Now he locked the door whenever he was in the office. No one unexpected was going to walk in on him.

"Who is it?"

Silence.

"Can I help you?"

Silence.

Rizzo went on alert. He thought about the phone call he'd received a little over a month ago that produced no response to his greeting. He ended up with Vito, the Marlon Brando imitator, on his tail during his trip home. The warning he'd received from Vinnie right after that prompted him to consider with certainty that the person on the other side of the door was far more lethal than Vito.

Rizzo reached into the drawer and picked up the Glock. He racked the slide to chamber a round and got to his feet. A shoulder-high steel-framed file cabinet stood against the front wall to the far right of the door. Rizzo moved into the two feet of space between the cabinet and the side wall and squatted. The position put him out of range in the event his visitor unloaded a few rounds through the door.

If the visitor was a *Mafioso* and armed, Rizzo couldn't decide if he'd shoot to kill or just wound him, as he did with Nelly. The thought no sooner passed through his mind when several gunshots splintered the door frame around the lock. Two men crashed through. Their automatics sprayed fire across his desk and into the opened doorway to the supply closet.

Rizzo remained crouched between the corner wall and the cabinet. The question of killing or wounding was no longer an issue. He pushed up, took in air, and squeezed off two shots in rapid succession. One went wide and one hit the nearest man in the side of his head and sheared off part of his skull. The second man turned in Rizzo's direction with a surprised expression. Rizzo fired two more shots. Again, only one hit the man, but it was in the middle of his forehead. The shot blew brain matter out the back.

The office filled with the smell of cordite, while the sound of gunfire continued to resonate off the walls. Rizzo stood over the two attackers and looked for movement. None came. They were both very dead.

He kept his attention on the open office door, watching for a possible hidden backup in the corridor. A few minutes of complete silence helped to lower his soaring heartbeat. Rizzo drew in a deep breath, puffed his cheeks, and blew it out before he returned to his desk.

He'd been in the office later than usual this night. He hoped the personnel of the other three firms on the floor had departed the premises by now. It would spare them the circus-like atmosphere law enforcement would create once he made the 911 call.

Within ten minutes, two uniformed patrol officers from the Thirteenth Precinct responded. Rizzo identified himself and described what happened. A search of the floor found the three other companies had closed, their employees gone. The officers cordoned off Rizzo's office doorway, the exterior of the elevator door, and the fire door. They made notes in their logbook and put in a call for the CSU investigation team and the detectives on duty.

Two investigators from the Thirteenth's Detective Squad arrived. Rizzo knew Vince Christopher, a senior detective with street smarts and years of service. He gave Christopher his description of the attack and the way it went down, while the second detective recorded it on a hand-held device.

"I'm sure the shooters were from the Gambino family."

"Wow, Rizzo. This seems like old times," Christopher said with a broad smile. "What's with you and all these mutts always trying to blow you away?"

"I don't know, Vince. I'm popular. What can I say?"

"First, it was that Russian last year. Tried to take you out in the Flatiron's stairwell."

"Yeah, he never learned to go down the stairs properly."

"And now, a couple of *goombas* trying to whack you. Bro, you're in a dangerous career field."

The two uniforms gave copies of their notes to the detectives and departed the scene when the investigation team arrived. Rizzo watched the techs go through their routine. They made sketches, snapped photos, and took an inventory of the gunmen's weapons and the personal items found in their pockets. Detective Christopher removed wallets from the two dead bodies. He called in their identity to the desk officer at the Thirteenth and asked that the medical examiner come to do his thing. Four hours later, the technicians finished their work and removed the tape from the elevator door. The ME supervised the body bags' ride down to a transport vehicle.

As Christopher and the investigating team prepared to depart, he told Rizzo, "I'm sure you want to get the hell out of here and go home. We'll see you at the precinct in the morning. You can make your formal statement then. And by the way, they identified the two mutts as Gambino soldiers. Nice company you keep," he added with a chuckle.

Rizzo remained at his bullet-ridden desk and stared at the damaged front door. He thought about the expenses he faced to make his workplace right again. No chance his "Good neighbor, State Farm" would be there for this one.

To begin, he would need a new door. His shot-up desk and chair were beyond repair, but the fusillade of lead spared the new couch, side chairs, and coffee table. Bullet holes appeared on three walls and the side and back walls of the supply closet. Gunshots took out the windowpane behind his desk, where Mr. Coffee died an untimely death.

Then there was the cleanup. He knew the bloodstains on the wood floor would be a bitch to remove. *Why don't these guys wait until I'm outside to try to kill me?*

He remembered Flo's hysterical reaction to Nelly's attempt on his life. This latest episode, for certain, would push her closer to the edge. He considered calling her to say he'd be late, but he knew it would unleash questions about why. Long ago, he promised himself never to lie to her, and he didn't want to violate the vow. He would wait. He needed to be standing in front of her when she went ballistic.

Rizzo gathered up everything of value along with files he considered sensitive. He put them into the locked safe in the closet and hoped the crime scene tape would discourage the curious ones in the morning from entering.

While the elevator descended to the lobby, Rizzo patted the side of his jacket covering the holstered Glock. He remembered Vince Christopher's comment about being in a dangerous career field. He'd never doubted it. But now he'd become a preferred *Mafia* target, and the danger had intensified three-fold. For a while, he thought Sal Fusco had bought his answers. But he guessed wrong. He wondered if it wasn't too late to change career fields.

Chapter Twenty-Five

Chelsea Area, Manhattan – Tues. A.M. 7/07

Rizzo made the trip to the Thirteenth Precinct in the morning to complete the required formal statement on the mob's attack. Before he could reach the front door to leave, a couple of detectives he knew in the squad pressed him to retell the story. His marksmanship amazed them—those headshots that took down both *goombas*.

Back in his office, he dropped onto the sofa and panned the scene, appraising the damage. A shiver crept down his spine. He pushed back into the throw pillow and closed his eyes. The image of the gunmen, their automatics blazing, crawled across his mind like a movie re-run. Death had taken his measure again, and he'd survived.

Rizzo got to his feet after he sensed someone at the door. The building manager stood in the doorway, an incredulous look on his face.

"Seems you had some unruly visitors last evening."

"It was a hell of a party," Rizzo said, grinning. He waved at the destruction and said, "I'm sorry about all this. Fortunately, I wasn't hurt. Two bad guys tried their best to cancel me."

"What in the world happened?" the manager asked. His wide-eyed expression remained on his face.

For the fourth time, Rizzo related the events of the attack, but in this retelling, he left out the shooters' mob affiliation. The manager did not need to know.

"I'm aware the damages are my responsibility," Rizzo told him. "I'll pay for all the repairs. How soon can you arrange for the work to begin?"

"I'll call you when I get back to my office. The priority is to install a new door. I'm sure I can have it done in a day or two. Does this happen often in your business?"

"God, I hope not."

The manager remained staring until Rizzo's iPhone chimed with his ringtone, "Take Five."

"Excuse me a minute." Rizzo walked to the desk where he'd left the phone.

Before he picked it up, he heard the departing manager mumble, "Oh, my, the wife's not gonna believe this."

"Luke Rizzo," he said, while still chuckling at the manager's comment.

"Machado, here. I caught the report this morning. What the hell happened last night? You were on the way home after we got through talking."

"I was, but two guys, I didn't get their names, paid a visit to my office. They didn't bother to knock. Shot out the lock and stormed in."

"You're still here, so it's safe to say you got them?"

"Yeah. But they left my office in a mess. By the time the boys from the One-Three packed up, I didn't get home 'til after eleven. Missed dinner, damn it."

Machado laughed. "Rizzo, you're one of a kind."

"Tell that to my wife. She's convinced I'm trying to get myself killed."

"She may be on to something. Perhaps you should refill the moat and seed it with fresh alligators. Your dinner Friday night with the charming Fusco was not as it appeared. He still doesn't trust you and wants you dead."

"I got that message last night. And since he's about to climb the ladder a rung, he's become more dangerous."

"Yeah, the D'Angelo whack job came as a big surprise."

"To you, maybe. Almost two months ago, a little birdie whispered in my ear Fusco was angling the don for the hit."

"How come you said nothing? We could have—"

"You're kidding me. No way would I say anything about it and violate the trust of my source. Besides, it was a family matter, and nothing that affected public safety."

"You didn't know that. It could have involved collateral damage."

"Fortunately, it didn't. Well, except for a few holes in D'Angelo's limo. You should see the collateral damage they did to my office," Rizzo said as he looked around.

"Yeah, but nothing that affected public safety. See ya," Machado said with a chuckle.

"Hey, I'm the public," Rizzo shouted, but Machado had already hung up.

* * *

It's the best burger in town," Rizzo said, snapping open the cap of the Heinz Ketchup plastic squeeze bottle. He watched the drip of the condiment landing on his cheeseburger with sautéed onions and mushrooms. "I come here at least twice a week for lunch."

"And you have the same burger each time?" Fields said. "You're in a rut."

"No. Ask anybody who works in this neighborhood: where's the best place in Chelsea for a great burger? They'll tell you The Lantern Coffee Shop every time."

"Well, gee, Rizzo. I'm flattered you invited me here to lunch as your guest. It isn't often a member of the federal government gets to dine in such lavish surroundings. And with a menu of culinary offerings that would please James Beard." Fields smirked as he picked up half of his ham and cheese sandwich and took a bite.

"Do I detect a note of sarcasm?"

Fields grinned, and he reached for the tall glass of iced tea in front of him. "Not in the least. Unless you plan to stick me with the check."

"No, I said this was on me."

They ate in silence, surrounded by greasy smells, shouts of coded lunch orders, and the sounds of sizzling burger patties the cook tossed about on his hot plate.

"Okay," Fields said. "So, tell me, what's on your mind?"

Rizzo had raised the cheeseburger to his mouth and stopped. He lowered the burger and placed it back on the plate. "I'm not still on the clock with you guys, am I?"

"I believe it ended when Nicole boarded the flight on that Sunday morning. Unless you feel we should have continued it. If so, I'd be happy to listen to your reasoning."

"No. That's what I figured too. She's safe in your hands, which is where we wanted her. Out of danger? Yeah. For the time being, at least."

"What then?"

"Last night, in my office, two of my big fans paid me a visit." He paused to be sure he had Fields' complete attention. "I had just hung up the phone after a call from Bob Machado. I was getting ready to leave when someone rattled the doorknob."

Fields stopped chewing. He leaned into the table for a closer listen and wouldn't require Rizzo to speak louder.

"I called out, 'Who's there?' but got no answer. I made a guess: Fusco's enforcers, in a hurry."

"You didn't open the door, did you?"

"My mama didn't raise no fool. No. Of course not. I didn't need to. They simply shot out the lock and marched in—with guns a-blazing, as a novelist of western stories would write. I had taken cover behind a tall file cabinet to the side of the door. Clever me caught both men off guard. Two out of four headshots sent them to hell."

"Good lord! That's four *Mafiosi* in the past thirty days. If we give it more time, maybe we can get rid of the rest of them that way."

"Not on my dime. My wife wants me to give up this life of crime-fighting. Become a priest."

"Seriously, Rizzo," Fields said. "I believe you have a problem. We have a problem, I mean to say."

"You said it, Kemosabe. Masked man needs help from government man to avoid being killed by bad hombre, Fusco."

"Okay. I hear you. You're back on the clock. Let's put our heads together with Machado and the OSU. See what plan we can come up with."

"A simple one, I hope, like bringing the life of Sal Fusco to an end."

Fields conveyed an expression that rested on the statement's ambiguity, but he said nothing.

Rizzo finished the burger and remained silent while he watched Fields put the last bites to his ham and cheese sandwich. He sat with his fingers wrapped around a Hires Root Beer and stared as if waiting for the can's icy feeling to provide a wealth of otherworldly guidance. His thoughts bounced between his recent life-threatening episodes and the growing danger to Vinnie and Dominic.

The assignment from Harry Fox to find Nicole Adams resulted in constant peril for himself and a load of worry for

Flo. It can't continue, he thought. The roles Vinnie and Dominic played had put them at risk of exposure and placed their lives in jeopardy. Rizzo decided Fusco had to be removed—one way or another.

The server arrived at their table and dropped the check in front of Fields. Before Fields noticed, Rizzo reached over to snatch it away. He looked up and saw the agent's mouth form a grin.

"What's the status of the two Dickerson killers?" Rizzo said. "They arraigned yet?"

"Oh, yeah. A while ago. But the Suffolk County DA is still trying to work a deal with Langella. He wasn't the one who pulled the trigger. They've offered him a reduced sentence if he cooperates. He would need to testify it was Sal Fusco who gave the hit order."

Rizzo wasn't sure Mario Langella was a made man, bound by the vow of *Omertà*. Angie Russo was, although he had the weaker spine of the two assailants. Rizzo hoped the DA dangled the carrot in front of Russo as well.

"You ready?" Fields said, and he got to his feet.

The cashier at the checkout counter slid Rizzo's credit card back to him. He signed the receipt and reached into the large jar of cellophane-wrapped mints. Grabbing two, he put them into his pocket. He turned his head and asked Fields, "You want a mint?"

"I'll pass."

Fields stood at the curb looking for a taxi. In the next moment, he spun around to address Rizzo. "Did I read you right, in there?"

"You mean about Fusco? Yeah. If circumstances dictate, and I'm in danger, I'm gonna take the shot. And I won't miss. You have a problem with that?"

"No. Just be sure you're standing on the right side of the law. That's all."

* * *

West Side Manhattan – Wed. P.M. – 7/8

The following evening, Flo Rizzo rolled the company VW Jetta to a stop inside the Avis garage entrance and opened the door to step out. She swung her legs around in her seat and shot a fast look through the rear window to the other side of Fiftieth Street. He was there again, the same man present these past three evenings. He was tall and had no problem seeing over the roofline of the parked car. She had her first glimpse of him Monday evening as she left the garage for home. She thought nothing of it except to notice the way he rested with his elbows on the roof of the sedan he leaned against. He stared with intensity in her direction; his direction appeared to be focused on the garage opening. Then he showed up again on Tuesday, a bit earlier that evening. And again, this evening, in the same position, waiting, the same fixed stare across the street.

If asked to describe him, she couldn't give a complete one. He had his entire body, save for his arms and head, hidden behind the vehicle. During the past three days, his black, curly hair, his height, and ever-present sunglasses were all she remembered.

Ernie, the attendant on duty, came over to her. "Hi ya, Flo. How's it goin'?"

Flo hesitated before she stepped out of the Jetta. "Ernie, don't turn around now, but have you noticed the man on the other side of the street? The one leaning on the roof of the green Camry . . . dark hair, sunglasses." Flo got to her feet and stood facing Ernie so he could see over her shoulder without being obvious.

"Oh, yeah. I see him. What about him?"

"Well, I've noticed him there three days in a row. I can't imagine what that's about."

"Is he following you?"

Flo recalled the recent threats on Rizzo's life but was reluctant to share them with the employee. "I don't know, Ernie, but I'm scared."

"Shit, I'd walk you home, but I'm alone here on duty tonight."

"That's all right, Ernie. It's still light out. I'll be okay."

"Tell you what. Don't walk back to Eighth Avenue to go home. Go through the back of the garage here. The gate to Forty-ninth is open. Then cut through the service alley of the restaurant on the south side to Forty-eighth. Luke does it a lot when he returns a vehicle."

Flo thought about it. "No, Ernie, I'll be safer on the street than cutting through alleys."

"Yeah, I guess you're right."

"I'll be fine, Ernie, thanks," she said and started walking east on Fiftieth.

She focused her eyes straight ahead during the trip, not daring to glance behind or to her left. At the corner of Eighth Avenue, she made a right and released the gulp of air she'd been holding in. With only two blocks more to Forty-eighth, she'd make the turn west and be a hundred yards from home.

* * *

West Side Manhattan – Thurs. A.M. 7/8

The next morning, Rizzo visited the Midtown North Precinct on Fifty-fourth Street and spoke with the duty officer. He explained to him about Flo's experience with the stalker outside the Avis garage. Dave Hammond and Anthony Valez were the two detectives assigned to look into the problem. Both were acquainted with Rizzo and happy to assist.

* * *

West Side Manhattan – Thurs. P.M. 7/8

The detectives arrived at the garage at five-fifteen. Tony Valez parked their unmarked vehicle twenty yards east of the garage, on the opposite side of Fiftieth Street. From their position, they could see Rizzo seated in the glass-enclosed Avis office chatting with Marie, the cashier.

Rizzo had provided them with Flo's limited description of the stalker: tall, black curly hair and dark aviator glasses. He told them Flo's usual arrival from her Avis office at LaGuardia Airport was around six-fifteen. Following Hammond's suggestion, they got there well before her ETA. In the event the stalker made an earlier appearance, they would have time to spot the man and observe his behavior. If he showed the customary earmarks of a person waiting for someone, they'd be assured of having the right man.

Valez focused his surveillance up to the corner of Ninth Avenue on both sides of the street. Hammond had his eyes glued to his side-view mirror on the approaching foot traffic coming from Eighth Avenue.

At ten of six, Hammond's phone sounded once. Rizzo's signal. He'd spotted a tall man with the description Flo had provided. Valez's eyes jumped to his rearview mirror. He saw the man cross the street from the downtown side and slip through two parked cars. When he stepped onto the sidewalk, he walked west until he reached the side of a white Nissan Altima twenty yards ahead.

The detectives remained in their vehicle and studied the man. He would lean his back against the Nissan and push off to look around. At one point, he lit a cigarette and tossed it before he finished. Now and then he'd glance at the Avis garage.

After fifteen minutes of taking in the man's behavior, Tony Valez said, "It's time to go." He opened the car door, slid out of his seat, and fast-stepped across to the other side, dodging an oncoming car. He slowed up, walked west to the corner of Ninth Avenue, and turned left out of sight. When the light changed in his favor, he strolled back across and paused at the north corner.

Dave Hammond remained in the vehicle, watching his partner for a few moments. With Valez in place, Hammond gripped the door handle and pushed it open. He got out and glanced up the street to the waiting Valez. His partner nodded and started toward the man. Hammond got there first and stood to the man's side.

The stranger gave him a quick look. "This your car?"

Hammond didn't answer.

Valez came up from the other side and said, "You waiting for someone?"

The man turned his head and looked at Valez. "Nah. Killing time, that's all." He stepped back and said, "Sorry. Didn't mean to block you from—"

"Friend, wadda ya doing here?" Valez said.

Rizzo had exited the Avis office and came across the street. He circled Valez and Hammond and stood facing them with his back to the building. The stalker became aware they had him pinned on three sides.

The man jerked his head from Valez to Hammond to Rizzo. His eyes flared. "Fuck you guys doin'?"

Valez pulled out a wallet from his inside pocket and flipped it open. He held it up long enough for the man to see his badge. "Now, I asked you, wadda ya doing here?"

The stalker stared into Valez's face. "So, I'm waitin' for somebody. That a crime?"

Valez shook his head and wrinkled his nose. "That's bullshit, my friend. How come you're standing here in this same spot four nights in a row? You arrive about the same time and stare across at the Avis garage."

"Yeah? So what?"

"So, one of three things is what. You're either stalking someone, or casing the garage for a planned robbery, or you're a vagrant waiting to be pulled in for vagrancy. Which is it?"

"You guys crazy? I'll leave if that's what you want."

Valez turned to Rizzo and nodded.

Rizzo came forward and stood facing the man. "*Paesano*, I vote for the stalking charge. And the person you're stalking is my wife."

"You shittin' me? I don't know your wife from a hole in the ground. I ain't never—"

"Save the righteous indignation for Sal Fusco when you tell him how you blew this assignment." The Guido's surprised expression told Rizzo all he needed.

"You gonna arrest me, or what?"

"I'm not, but if these two detectives here are inclined to, they might."

Valez snickered. "No, my friend. But we find you hanging around here in the future, we will. So beat it."

Before the man could leave, Rizzo moved up close to the stalker's face. "Tell Sal Fusco, when you see him, Luke Rizzo blew away the two shooters he sent to whack me the other night. All it took were two headshots. Tell Sal to keep the hat on. His head might be next."

The man was halfway to Ninth Avenue before Valez and Hammond stopped laughing.

Rizzo shook hands. "Thanks, guys. I owe you one at the Palm Steak House. I'll be in touch. We'll set up a date."

"You need a ride home?" Hammond asked.

"No, thanks. I told my wife I would wait here for her. After this experience, she's gonna need a bit of comfort food."

Chapter Twenty-Six

West Side, Manhattan – Sun. A.M. 7/12

He'd gotten the call right after breakfast and repeated the news to Flo as they sat on the sofa. Carla told him the main entrance was on York Avenue, facing the East River. The address was 1275. He promised they'd be there by eleven.

When he disconnected, he could hardly speak. Flo looked at him with moist eyes. "When was he admitted?"

"Friday night after EMS picked him up off the floor of their apartment in Yorkville and took him to the hospital emergency room." Rizzo got up and walked into the bathroom for Kleenex. He blew his nose twice and returned to the living room sofa.

Flo studied his face. He was fighting tears. She wrapped an arm around him and put her head against his shoulder. "Oh, it's so sad. I guess there's little they can do at this stage."

"They ran him through a bunch of tests and found his condition had worsened beyond any chance. He's not expected to survive past the next few days." Rizzo shrugged and turned his palms up. "Memorial Sloan Kettering is the best cancer hospital in New York City. If they're throwing in the towel, I guess I gotta believe them."

"Oh, poor Carla," Flo said. "She has to be devastated. Even though they both expected it would happen soon."

They sat in silence for several minutes until Flo's worry reached the surface. "I hate being guilty of practical thoughts at a time like this, but . . . I mean, Carla is struggling with her career right now. Will she manage to—"

"Yeah, she'll be okay. Vinnie did well with the union's compensation package, and thank God, he's covered by their medical insurance plan. His medical bills have to be through the roof. He discussed it with me the night we were having drinks at the bar in Joe Allen's. That's when he first told me he had lung cancer. I didn't mention it to you because Vinnie asked me not to. But don't worry. Carla will be all right."

Flo took her head from his shoulder and stood. "Let me go shower and dress now if we're going to be at the hospital by eleven."

* * *

East Side, Manhattan

The taxi pulled off York Avenue and into the curving drive in front of the main entrance of Memorial Sloan Kettering. They exited, and once inside, Flo took Rizzo's hand. As they approached the reception counter, she said, "You okay?"

"I'm fine." He pushed out a smile when he realized Flo had assumed the role of emotional supporter. That's my responsibility, he thought, but I'm gonna need help to get through this.

They reached the neatly attired young lady behind the counter, and Rizzo gave his name. "The patient is Vincent Alcamo," he said.

She looked down at the computer screen and typed in Vinnie's name. The young lady raised her chin and smiled. "That's room 405A. You can use the bank of elevators over there," she said, pointing.

They entered a waiting elevator and rode it to the fourth floor. During the elevator's ascent, Rizzo kept thinking, My God, I'm about to lose my oldest friend.

Rizzo had no siblings, but he and Vinnie always viewed their relationship as a brotherhood. He felt Flo gripping his arm like she expected him to collapse at any moment. Her sense of concern was genuine, and he loved her for it.

The floor nurse directed them to the room. "He has two visitors in there now, but I imagine two more won't matter," she told them.

The door was ajar when they arrived. Rizzo peeked in to be sure they had the right room and saw Carla and Dominic seated in chairs on each side of the bed. Carla saw them first and came forward to greet them with warm hugs. Dom got to his feet and reached out to shake Rizzo's hand.

"Dom, this is my wife Flo," Rizzo said in a whisper.

"You don't have to whisper," a weak voice from the bed said. "I ain't dead yet." Vinnie let out a faint chuckle and called out to Rizzo. "*Paesano, veni ca.*"

It was a semi-private room, but the second bed was unoccupied. The view outside the double window provided a glimpse of the East River and Roosevelt Island. Rizzo panned around the room and noticed it was void of any signs of aggressive treatment: no IV and no ventilator. An oxygen resuscitator on four wheels was tucked away in one corner, in standby mode.

With his buttocks balanced on the edge of the bed, Rizzo heard Vinnie whisper, "Come closer."

He adjusted his position, bending at the waist, and put his cheek to the side of Vinnie's face. His right hand lay flat on the bed for balance.

"Bro, wanna ask you something."

"What?"

"A favor."

"Anything."

"They're gonna move me to a hospice place for the rest of my time."

"Yeah, I already guessed that."

Vinnie took in several deep breaths, turned his head away from Rizzo, and coughed twice. "Will ya watch out for Carla for me after I go?"

"Of course, I will. Both of us will. You don't need to ask. We're there."

"She's not gonna sell the condo on Eighty-Seventh—"

"That's good."

"But when she comes up against somethin' she can't handle alone." He took in a deep breath. "Like when she doesn't understand somethin'. Will you help her out?"

"In a flash. Don't worry about things like that. We'll be right there for her."

Vinnie closed his eyelids. His lips trembled, attempting to hold back tears. After a silent moment, he opened his eyes and turned his head to face Rizzo.

"Most important, bro . . . yeah, important." He paused again to catch his breath. "You need to stay alive. Watch out for Fusco. Talk to Dominic."

It was clear Vinnie didn't know Fusco had already unleashed his dogs. He wasn't aware of the two Guidos' attempt to whack him in his office. Rizzo decided not to mention the attack.

Vinnie slipped his hand out from beneath the sheet and covered Rizzo's right hand with it. It felt cold. Rizzo twisted around and planted his left on top. "My brother, you are the best."

Flo's grip on his shoulder made him look up. "You're monopolizing him. I want a hug." Rizzo jumped to his feet and stepped away to allow Flo to sit in his spot. She gently laid her head down on Vinnie's chest. "My sweet friend," she whispered. "I'm so glad I got to know you."

"That Luke, he's a lucky guy," Vinnie said to the top of her head. He tried to smile.

Rizzo watched and choked up.

It was twelve-thirty when Luke, Flo, and Dominic entered the elevator to ride it down to the lobby. Carla remained in the room. She wanted to stay with Vinnie for another three hours. The hospital planned to move him to hospice in the morning.

Outside of the hospital entrance, Rizzo took Dom's arm. "You scheduled to work today?"

"Uh-uh. I traded days with another bartender so I could come here."

"You got time to go somewhere and talk?"

Dominic lowered his eyes and nodded. "Yeah. Maybe we should."

Rizzo turned to Flo. "Sweetheart, we're gonna walk you to First Avenue, where I'll get a cab to take you home. I need private time with Dominic to chat about a few things. I'll be home later, okay?"

"Want me to wait for you to make lunch?"

"No. Dom and I will grab something out," he shouted over his shoulder as he dashed off the curb to flag down a cruising taxi heading north. Flo got in and Rizzo gave their address to the driver. He watched the taxi take off as the light changed. It sped to the opposite side of the avenue and turned left at Sixty-ninth Street.

"Lemme ask you," Rizzo said to Dominic with a smile. "You worried about someone seeing you with me?"

"Nah, we're friends from The Dugout. Who's gonna think any different?"

"Sal Fusco might, but I doubt he ventures this far north of Little Italy. How 'bout we hit this great Italian bistro I know, three blocks south of us. It's open for lunch and they have a great light menu. My treat."

"I'm game."

They strolled south and reached the restaurant in minutes. Felice 64, tucked into the southeast corner of Sixty-fourth and First, had a double-wide front entrance. It was early enough to secure a table far enough away from other diners to allow for privacy.

They were shown to a table against one wall. Rizzo sat on the banquet facing out, enabling him to see through to the front door. Dom took the outside chair. Above Rizzo's head, several levels of continuous shelving lined the wall, front to back. The shelves were filled with an impressive assortment of wine bottles.

"Wow! This place is amazing," Dominic said after he looked around. "The décor is out of sight."

"The times I've been here, the menu was outstanding. I'm sure you're gonna like it."

Rizzo ordered a lunch-size salad of chilled prosciutto slices, buffalo mozzarella, Kumato tomatoes, and fresh organic basil with extra virgin olive oil. Dominic opted for a medium-size bowl of mussels, white wine, cherry tomatoes, garlic, parsley, and toasted bread. Rizzo had iced tea and Dom a glass of white wine.

When they finished and the server cleared the dishes, Rizzo sat back and took notice of the occupied tables around them. None were close enough to allow someone to eavesdrop. "I've got a proposition for you," he said to Dominic.

Dom set his wineglass to one side and studied Rizzo's face with curiosity. "Is this where the music builds and the suspense increases?"

"I wish it were that inconsequential. But first, let me go on the record with something. It's the same as I told Vinnie. I would go to the mat before I gave up my sources of information as it relates to Nicole Adams." Rizzo lowered his voice at this point. "The mob may have their vow of *Omertà*, but my principles are stronger."

"Vinnie told me that. He trusted you. I do too."

"Okay. You have my word from here on out. I will protect anything I learn from you with the same level of confidentiality."

"I believe you."

"Good. Now let me continue by citing a statement of the obvious." Again, he lowered his voice. "I would like to see Fusco neutralized. That's because he's bent on having me whacked, and he's an all-around bad guy. Other concerned parties I work with would like to see him go away long term. I confess I'm not sure how you view him."

Dominic stayed silent, signaling he was not ready to commit himself.

Rizzo leaned into the table and brought his hands up to cover his mouth. He felt like a baseball catcher conferring on the mound with his pitcher. "There's no question he's gunning for the underboss spot now that D'Angelo is out of the way."

Dominic gave an unconscious nod as though he was listening to a news broadcast. It was obvious to Rizzo that Dom and Vinnie had talked about that possibility before.

"We both know the way it works within any family operation. The order for a whack job like D'Angelo's has to come from the top."

Again, Dominic nodded without changing his expression.

"But Nunziata has deniability. It was Fusco who gave the contract to the two out-of-town shooters. And here lies the opportunity to make Fusco disappear."

"You mean, without whacking him?"

Rizzo laughed. "Now you're seeing the picture."

Chapter Twenty-Seven

Chelsea Area, Manhattan – Mon. A.M. 7/13

Rizzo stood to the side of the desk, his iPhone to his ear, and gazed at the framed blowup of his son over the sofa. The weight of silence at the other end of the call was worrisome. Would Jack Fields go for it? The sound of the agent's breathing was all he heard until Fields spoke into his intercom.

"Rachel, ask Ralph to come to my office, then get me Bob Machado."

"Yes, sir," the agent's long-time secretary replied.

"Luke, you gonna be there for the next hour?"

"I'll be here, Jack."

"Good. I'll get back to you then. Bye," he said and clicked off.

Rizzo remained standing for a moment admiring his new, commercial 18-gauge steel door, retrofitted to the opening and faced with a panel of faux wood. They made the door an inch and a half thick at Rizzo's request. And they added the lever lock and latch guard. Another feature he asked for was the small one-way window inserted at eye level. The building management had selected the door manufacturer, and even at three times what a normal door replacement would have been, Rizzo was happy to pay for it. It took a little longer than the building manager's estimate, but it was worth the wait.

Rizzo crossed the floor to the front of the office and stopped at the five-drawer metal filing cabinet in the corner. He patted it with fondness, remembering how it had protected him during the Guidos' attack.

He opened the top drawer and withdrew a folder from a file tabbed as Financial. The folder, labeled Office Expenses, contained receipts and bills relating to his operating expenditures during the first half of this fiscal year. Rizzo carried the folder to his desk and opened it.

During the next half hour, he reviewed all the expenditures incurred by normal day-to-day operating purchases, making special note of those expenses for which he had the Gambino mob to thank. Rizzo wondered if the IRS would allow him to carry Sal Fusco as a business expense.

Rizzo always ran his investigation business with prudence. Staying within his budget was never an issue. He kept his operating expenses well within his annual income. And these past few years of working contracts for the FBI provided him the cushion he needed to make up for the leaner times. He looked up at his new office door and smiled. Now, this was a worthwhile investment, he thought.

Dave Brubeck's "Take Five" interrupted his musing. The caller readout showed it was Jack Fields. "That was fast."

"Yeah, and how fast can you get over here?"

"I'll put on my Superman cape and fly."

* * *

FBI's Manhattan Office - Mon. A.M. 7/13

"We're waiting on Bob Machado before we start, Fields announced. "Anyone for coffee?"

Rizzo raised his hand. No one else did.

Fields pressed the intercom button and said, "Rachel, coffee for Mr. Rizzo, please. Black, I believe."

"You're correct," she replied.

He looked over at Rizzo seated on the sofa, his finger still on the button, and said, *sotto voce*, "You want to take her with you when you leave?"

"I heard that, Jack."

A minute later, Rachel entered, carrying the coffee mug, and placed it on the end of the coffee table in front of Rizzo. She looked down at him and winked. He smiled back.

Carter Brooke, the head of the New York office, opted to sit in. He sat in one of the side chairs while Ralph Brancuso and Rizzo occupied the sofa. Fields rolled his desk chair around to face the sofa head-on.

"How've you been?" Carter Brooke asked Rizzo after several seconds of awkward silence. "Haven't seen you since the San Juan assignment."

"Busy dodging bullets on this one, Mr. Brooke. But I feel we can get close to the finish line with any luck if you and Jack sign off on the plan."

Rachel's voice broke in over the intercom to announce Machado's arrival. "Send him in," Fields said.

Machado entered holding a coffee mug and took the vacant chair.

Fields nodded to Rizzo. "Okay, Luke, let's have what you got."

"I need to open with a caveat. My source knows of this gathering, but not who's involved. I told him I would first speak with the interested parties to see if what I had in mind was workable. He would remain anonymous until we agreed to explore the plan with him."

"And he'd be receptive to helping execute the plan?" Fields said.

Rizzo grinned. "Well, he's not on board to whacking Sal Fusco, as I'd suggested, but removing him by legal means is something he could agree to. The truth is he's not a big fan of the *capo*."

"Continue," Fields said.

"Okay, here's how I see we could set it up. The source, while not a made man, is in a position where Fusco occasionally engages him in family matters of utmost secrecy. Fusco, for reasons I will not explain, often takes him into his confidence."

"And he'd rat out Fusco?" Brancuso asked with a note of incredulity in his tone.

"Don't get ahead of me, Ralph. Let me remind you of all our recent success with Nicole Adams and the roving bug."

A knowing expression crawled across everyone's faces.

"That's right," Rizzo said, nodding. "My source would have his cell phone in his pocket or nearby when these chit-chats take place. We'd have the same van parked on a street recording as we did with Peter Barone."

Carter Brooke raised a hand. "Luke, why would your source be willing to cooperate this way, put his neck on the line? Is he already in a vulnerable position with the Gambinos?"

"No, sir. Not right now. But he sure as hell will be if he goes along with the plan."

"How so?"

"As soon as you arrest Fusco and he is made aware of the incriminating recording, my source's life expectancy will be that of a second lieutenant leading a charge in battle. That brings me to the one condition he will no doubt ask for."

"Immediate protection and safe passage?" Brooke said.

"Yes, sir."

"What do you figure Fusco could say to incriminate himself?" Machado said.

Rizzo turned to the OCU lieutenant. "Bob, have the Suffolk prosecutors made any headway getting one of the two Dickerson killers to cooperate? You know, fingering Fusco as the one who gave the order?"

"Not yet. Not that I'm aware."

"Well, because Fusco tended to speak freely in the company of my source, there's a possibility it could produce a conversation where the *capo* misspeaks. Where he says something that amounts to admitting to that role."

Fields jumped to his feet. "Wow! How soon can you meet with your guy?"

Rizzo grinned. He'd never witnessed such an enthusiastic reaction from the agent. "Can I offer him protection and safe passage, like Mr. Brooke mentioned?"

"You can offer anything he wants, within reason, of course," Brooke said.

"That's the one guarantee," Fields said. "We will protect him."

"Okay, I'll call him tonight. Maybe meet with him somewhere after he gets off work. It'll be another of those late nights, so will you please write a note to my wife, that she should excuse me for staying out late?"

"I'll have Rachel prepare one," Fields said.

* * *

Chelsea's West Side – Tues. A.M. 7/14

Rizzo sat at a table in the rear with a Coke when Dominic came through the front door of the Landmark Tavern. It was close to one-thirty. He set down his soft drink and waved to him, then realized the place was empty except for three regulars at the bar. The man couldn't miss seeing him.

Dominic walked to the back to the table and sat down. His eyes did a quick scan of the three customers sitting at the bar.

"Don't worry; this place hasn't seen a *goomba* from anyone's crew in fifty years."

Clancy, the rotund bartender, came hustling over. Dominic smiled up at him and said, "Hey, bro, how are ya?"

"Pretty fine, boyo. What can I getcha?"

"Let me have a Michelob, no glass."

"Got it," Clancy said, and he was off.

"How long have you been here?"

"Ten minutes. I didn't figure you'd make it before one-fifteen. What time you close up?"

"One o'clock." He looked up at Clancy, who'd arrived with his Michelob. "Thanks, man."

Rizzo waited until Dom took a couple of swigs before touching off the conversation. "You thought any more about jumping into the deep end?"

"Yeah, I guess so. If the risk isn't gonna drown me."

"Are you willing to sit down with my interested parties and listen to their pitch?"

"Do they know who I am?"

"Dominic, what did I tell you on Sunday at lunch?"

"Yeah. Sorry, but you can't blame me for worrying."

"And until you commit, they won't have your identity and you won't have theirs."

Dominic held the bottom of the bottle with both hands and stared. Rizzo could almost hear him thinking. Dom brought the bottle to his mouth with an unsteady hand, took another pull, and then set it down again.

Rizzo studied him, trying to imagine the large man in his former role as the enforcer for the mob. It didn't quite compute with the charismatic, gentle giant Rizzo had come to respect. A serious question remained as to whether Dominic would accept the challenge he was about to put out there.

"Nobody's gonna take out Sal . . . whack him?"

"That's what I said."

"Then how they gonna remove him? That's what I don't understand."

"Well, I'll tell you this much. The plan is to set him up to incriminate himself with no help from anyone. The way Barone was set up."

"You mean, bug his phone . . . his office?"

"Not quite. Neither device was used to nail Barone, but keep that thought in mind."

Dominic squeezed his eyes as though trying to understand what Rizzo had said. Several seconds passed before he opened them and said, "Okay, I'm in. I'll talk with your guys. But if I don't like the deal, I walk. Right?"

"Of course. It's not the *Mafia*. Keep in mind, though, they'd expect you to sign a commitment of non-disclosure. Think it would be a problem?"

Dom raised the bottle again and took several swallows. No," he said, bringing down the Michelob and wiping his mouth with the paper coaster. "They play fair, I'll play fair."

"That's the way they work. When's your next day off? I'll need to schedule a meeting."

"A week from tomorrow. I already traded this coming Wednesday with another bartender. That way, I could have Sunday off to see Vinnie. Remember?"

"Okay. I'll arrange a time for a week from tomorrow." Rizzo noticed the grim look on Dom's face. "Hey, what's with the troubled expression? You're doing the right thing."

"I hope so, bro. I hope so."

* * *

Upper East Side, Manhattan – Fri. P.M. 7/17

The Dawn Greene Hospice was an easy trip for Vinnie, not that he was aware of the location's convenience or cared about it. Like Sloan Kettering, the hospice was on York Avenue, but four blocks north, between Seventy-first and Seventy-second Streets. Rizzo hoped the facility would provide his friend with a level of care and attention that would make his last hours on earth as comfortable as possible.

Rizzo held Flo's arm as they entered the room. Carla had her chair pulled to the side of the bed, and she had Vinnie's hand cradled in hers.

"Don't get up," Flo said as she walked up behind her, took her by the shoulders, and kissed the top of her head.

Rizzo went to the opposite side of the bed and stood there in silence. He gazed down at Vinnie and noticed his eyes were closed and his breathing almost non-existent. He sensed a shock of pain in his upper chest. "Is he—?"

Carla looked up through misty eyes and said, "No, he's heavily sedated and can't feel or hear anything. The nurse doesn't believe the end is far off."

"Oh, God," Flo exclaimed.

Rizzo grabbed for the chair and sat, certain the sudden weakness in his legs would cause him to topple over. He rested his elbows on his knees, and in his bent-over position, he supported his head with his hands.

His mind raced with thoughts of the occasions he'd witnessed death outside of his immediate family, deaths he delivered, or the deaths at the hands of someone else. Those deaths, he realized, were in most part the detached experiences of a law officer. Not since his mother's passing had he known the heavy impact brought on by the loss of a person he loved. Vinnie's death, for certain, would be one of those.

Chapter Twenty-Eight

FBI's Manhattan Office - Wed. A.M. 7/22

It was close to ten o'clock when Fields emptied his second mug of coffee. He had arrived in the office at eight in a heightened state of anticipation. "Are the two surveillance vans we used for the Barone recording ready?" Fields said into the speakerphone.

"They are, Jack," Brancuso said, "but aren't we getting ahead of ourselves? Rizzo and the guy are not due here for another hour. We don't know yet if he's gonna cooperate."

Rachel entered, and picked up the mug, and exited.

"Well, Rizzo told me he's close to a hundred percent the man will work with us. We need to satisfy the concerns he has. I don't see it being a problem unless he goes stupid on us with his demands."

"That's unlikely," Brancuso said. "He's more apt to turn us down outright if he feels the risk is too great. The burning question in my mind is what's his motivation for hanging Fusco out to dry."

"That can be an area for you to probe. Why don't you plan on coming here around ten-thirty? We can go over a few things before they arrive. I'm eager to get this operation up and running as soon as possible."

"Will do," Brancuso said, and rang off.

* * *

Rizzo noticed him hesitate when the elevator doors opened and he spotted the framed FBI shield hanging on the wall facing them. Dominic had been unaware of their destination until they stepped off the elevator into the reception area.

"Holy shit! The Feds?"

"Not to worry. These guys will play fair. Grab a seat," Rizzo told him and waved to the receptionist behind the glass-enclosed cubicle.

"Good morning, Mr. Rizzo. I'll tell Agent Fields you're here."

Rizzo nodded and sat in a chair opposite Dominic.

The big man wore the expression of a four-year-old waiting in the barbershop to get his first haircut. Rizzo could empathize with Dom's wariness. They were about to ask him to do something the mob—and most anyone with a sense of loyalty—would consider betrayal. The term, Rizzo was certain, didn't exist in Dom's vocabulary—until now.

Brancuso came through the door into the reception area and, holding it open, motioned to Rizzo. "Luke, you guys ready?"

Rizzo got to his feet and looked down at Dominic. "All set?"

Dominic rose to his full six-five and Rizzo introduced him to Brancuso. The agent examined his size with surprise, and Rizzo caught the look. He thought about making a joke like saying to the agent, "Don't screw with him or he'll break you in half," but he didn't.

They followed Brancuso down the corridor to Fields' office, where Rachel looked up from her desk. "Coffee?"

"Not for me, thanks. Dom?"

"No, thank you."

Rizzo made the introductions and everyone took a seat.

"Mr. Biondo," Fields began, "thank you for coming in today to listen to our proposal. The four of us can assure you we understand the weight of concern you have about placing yourself in our trust."

Dominic had locked his attention on the agent's face as he spoke. When he heard the word trust, Rizzo saw him flash a questioning expression at him.

Fields continued. "If you choose to take part in our plan, you have our complete assurance we will not ask you to be anything more than a hands-off conduit of information."

Rizzo noticed the lost expression on Dom's face. He jumped in. "Jack, maybe you can explain to Dominic what you mean by a conduit of information."

"Oh? Yes. Sorry, Mr. Biondo. What I meant is your role would require you to carry your cell phone in your pocket as you do normally. Nothing more. You would not be involved beyond that. I'll expand on that in a minute."

"You clear on that, Dom?" Rizzo said.

"Yeah, but I don't understand. Why would you need me for that? Everybody carries a cell phone these days."

Bob Machado spoke up. "Jack, why not spell out the plan now for Mr. Biondo? Explain what we're doing and how his cell phone comes into play. He has to know what's involved before he can make an informed decision about coming on board."

Silence fell over the room while Fields weighed the soundness of Machado's suggestion. All eyes turned to the agent as they waited for him to speak.

"Mr. Biondo," Fields said, "I understand it's difficult to commit to something like this without knowing all the details. For that reason, I'm happy to lay our cards on the table so you have the full picture before you decide. But you'll need to sign a confidentiality agreement in the event you opt-out."

"That's the thing I mentioned to you the other day," Rizzo said.

Dominic nodded.

"This agreement," Fields continued, "would bind you to keep silent about our plan and the identity of those of us in this room. If you breach this agreement, you could alert Sal Fusco, and make it impossible for us to devise another plan in the future. But, more important, you would put yourself and Luke Rizzo here in great jeopardy with the Gambino family. I'd like you to remember, if you break the agreement, you will face a penalty. Do you understand those terms?"

"Yes, sir. I do. I'll sign it."

Rizzo's gaze carried to Dominic's face. He appeared relieved.

Fields and Machado spent the next two hours detailing for Dominic how the roving bug worked, how his cell service provider programmed it, and how they expected him to act when he was at work.

Rizzo was glad to see Dominic was comfortable with his role. The plan required nothing of him other than to behave as he normally would when Fusco visited The Dugout. He would simply schmooze with him as he always did.

The Bureau had already drafted a service contract for him to sign, detailing the generous compensation package he would receive and a guarantee of FBI protection. After the completed operation, if he felt the need to disappear, the Bureau would provide safe passage to anywhere he chose under his new identity.

Before leaving, Dom gave his iPhone to Bob Machado with the promise he would get it back in the morning.

"How about we grab lunch," Rizzo said during the elevator ride to the lobby. "You gotta have a few questions they didn't address up there."

"Okay. I'm in."

* * *

Chelsea Area, Manhattan

The taxi dropped them off at the entrance to the Lantern Coffee Shop, where they found an empty booth along the window side of the restaurant.

"It's a good menu," Rizzo told him, "but their burgers are outstanding."

Dom ordered a Rueben sandwich and a chocolate egg cream. Rizzo had the usual cheeseburger with mushrooms and sautéed onions, with a can of Hires Root Beer.

Rizzo popped the tab on the soft drink can and looked over at Dom. "Here's something odd. I've been coming here for lunch since I opened my office. I never knew they made chocolate egg creams. Man, that's a throwback to when I was a kid hanging out at the local candy store."

"Yeah, we had them too, in Bay Ridge, where I grew up."

"Bay Ridge, Brooklyn. Irish and Italian, right?"

"And many Jewish families. They owned most of the local retail stores."

"Ah, New York," Rizzo said. "It's the true melting pot."

Their lunch orders arrived, and they ate in silence. When they finished, Rizzo asked, "How was the Rueben?"

"The Dugout's is better. Hey, I got a question."

"Shoot."

"Was the cell phone trick how they got to Barone, him talkin' on it with his banker?"

"Yeah, he was using his cell phone, but they didn't bug it. You should be able to figure out the rest."

Dominic wrinkled his brow for a second. Then he broke into laughter.

"What?"

"Barone. He was so goddamned sure they bugged his cell phone. Then, it had to be the office they bugged. Oh, that's funny."

"I'm certain he had no clue," Rizzo said.

Dominic's eyes squinted. "So whose phone was it?"

"If I tell you, I'll have to kill you."

Dom smiled. "Nicole's. It had to be hers. I'm gonna ask her."

It was Rizzo's turn to squint. "How the hell you gonna do that?"

"I got her P.O. box number. She wrote to me last week."

"Not smart, man. She's supposed to be off the radar screen. Don't let the Feds find out. Or Fusco. He hasn't forgotten about her, you know."

"Why do ya think I'm gonna do this for the Feds? The sooner we get the son-of-a-bitch out of the way, the sooner we can all relax."

"I guess I don't have to remind you she's gay."

"So what? That don't mean a damn thing. She's a good friend and a good person. That's all this is about."

"I believe you. Still, be careful with her location. She say how she likes it there?"

"She loves it. One problem though."

"Uh oh."

Dominic leaned into the table. "The owner of the place is sellin' it."

"So the Feds will find her another place."

"Shit, I hope so."

"Before we leave, was there anything else they didn't clarify for you?"

"Yeah. Can I still use the phone like always? To make calls or get 'em?"

"Yes. Make them or receive them, even if you're standing in front of Fusco. But watch what you say. Your conversations are being recorded, same as his. Don't give away any secrets you don't want the listeners to have."

"You mean, like which waitress in The Dugout gives the best—"

"No, you jerk. You know what I mean. Any more questions?"

"How about if I hear Sal say somethin' that's sounds incriminating? Should I call you?"

"Hell, no. Don't do a damn thing. You let the conversation flow naturally. And for God's sake, don't try to steer it. Fusco is no dummy. If he senses you're trying to trap him into saying something, you're gonna end up dead."

* * *

West Side, Manhattan – Thurs. A.M. 7/23

The landline telephone on the bedside table woke them. Rizzo lifted his head to see the digital readout on the clock. He waited for a second to allow the numbers to come into focus. It was six-thirty.

"Hello."

"Luke," a sobbing voice spoke. "He's gone. He passed away a few minutes after midnight. I'm sorry to wake you this early, but I was sure you'd want to know right away."

"No, no, Carla. That's all right. I'm sorry. Were you able to say goodbye to him while he was still conscious?"

Flo rose to a sitting position and listened. Tears rolled down her cheeks.

"At the end. He opened his eyes and looked at me. He couldn't speak, but he didn't need to. "God, I loved him so much."

"As he did you, Carla. You thought about what you want to do about, well, about the burial?"

"He wanted to be cremated. I'd arranged for that in advance . . . a funeral home nearby . . . Thomas Cooke. I asked them for a brief memorial service this Saturday evening. That's all he wanted."

"I'll call Dominic Biondo now. Get him to make a few calls to some guys who were friends with Vinnie."

"That would be sweet of you. I'm sorry his brother, the priest, isn't still alive."

Flo leaned in and asked, "Are you okay, Carla. Do you want me to come over?"

"I'll be fine, Flo. The cremation is later today. I'll be busy with that."

"Okay, but why don't we pick you up tonight for dinner, if you haven't made plans." Flo looked at Rizzo with a quizzical expression. He nodded his assent.

"That would be wonderful."

"Great. You shouldn't be alone. We'll come by for you around seven-thirty. Be in the lobby. Watch for the cab."

"I'll be ready."

Flo left the apartment for work at eight-thirty. While Rizzo cleared the breakfast dishes, he remembered the slip of paper with Dom's telephone number. It was in the shirt pocket he wore yesterday. He retrieved it, sat at the kitchen table, and punched in the number.

"Dom, it's Luke. Didn't wake you, did I?"

"Hell, no. I was just gettin' out of the shower. What's up?"

Rizzo's throat went dry. "Vinnie passed last night."

Dominic let several seconds go by before he replied. "Well, shit. It ain't like we didn't know it was coming."

"You're right. Carla phoned us earlier."

"Is there gonna be a funeral service?"

"No. He's gonna be cremated. She's arranged for a brief memorial service on Saturday evening at the Cooke Funeral Home. On Eighty-sixth and Lexington. I told her you'd call a few guys Vinnie considered his friends."

"Yeah, the guy in the IBEW union he reported to. They had a good relationship. I don't have his number, but I'll call the union headquarters. A couple of guys in our old crew were friendly with him too. Maybe I can get word to them."

"Good. I'd hate for the guest book to go empty of names except for ours."

"I'll get on the calls before I leave for work."

When Dom mentioned work, Rizzo's mind jumped. "Hey, if Fusco drops in The Dugout between now and Saturday, don't, for the love of God, mention Vinnie's dying. That's all I need is for him to show up at the funeral home and see me."

"I won't say a word. But it might be fun to watch how you'd handle it."

"Don't even think about it. I'd shoot you first before I shot him."

Dominic chuckled and said, "Bye."

Chapter Twenty-Nine

West Side, Manhattan – Thurs. P.M. 7/23

The group of women standing in front of Joe Allen's was chattering away at the entrance. Rizzo climbed out of the taxi and approached. "Excuse us, ladies. If going to the theater, you're gonna be late for your eight o'clock curtain." Like the Red Sea, they parted to allow them passage into the restaurant.

Inside, Rizzo spoke to the host at the podium and he led Rizzo, Flo, and Carla to a table in the main dining area. The brick wall at their back was lined with framed posters of Broadway shows, all flops by the critics' standards. This was the tongue-in-cheek humor of the restaurant owner, which Rizzo was certain most out-of-towners missed.

Once seated, Carla looked around and said, "I can see why you like this restaurant. "It has such an appealing ambiance."

"This is where Luke used to hang out when he was single," Flo said. "He liked to ogle the Broadway chorus girls that came in after the shows ended. Then he met me." Flo smirked, Carla laughed, and Rizzo frowned.

"She's not wrong," Rizzo said, "but the true reason is, besides having a great menu, I know the owner. We were in high school together."

"You never told me that," Flo said.

"Oh, there's lots I've never told you."

Seth, the server, interrupted before Flo could respond. "Hi, people. It's always nice to see you." He dropped three menus on the table and asked, "What can I start you off with?" His eyes landed on Flo. "A Big Jack for the lady?"

"Hey, Seth, cut it out," Rizzo said. "We gotta stop coming here. You're getting to know us too well."

"My favorite couple," the server replied with a sing-song in his voice.

"Yeah, a Big Jack," Rizzo said. "Carla, what would you like?"

"White wine spritzer would be fine."

"Virgin Mary, no celery, thanks."

Seth moved off toward the bar and Rizzo turned to Carla. "He has the hots for Flo. I'd be worried if he wasn't a Broadway show gypsy."

"Oh, you're being silly," Flo said.

"Yes, I am."

Seth returned with their drinks, set them down, and said, "Whenever you're ready to order, give me a wave."

When he walked away, Flo turned to Rizzo. "And why didn't you tell me the owner was your friend?"

"Because then I'd need to admit I might not have graduated from high school if it wasn't for Joe."

Flo's astonished expression demanded he continue.

"Math was my weakness, but algebra was complete Greek to me. If I wasn't sitting next to Joe during tests, I'd have never passed the course."

"You mean you cheated?"

"Shush, lower your voice. You're embarrassing me."

Carla was shaking with the giggles when Rizzo shot a side glance at Flo. They both smiled, pleased they had Carla relaxed.

After several sips of the wine spritzer, Carla's expression turned serious. "I guess we all have things in our lives we'd like to keep private. Vinnie did."

Rizzo tried to hide his surprise. Was she referring to his *Mafia* involvement? Did she know? Rizzo waited for her to continue.

She looked at Rizzo and, unashamed, said, "I'm sure you're aware of his brother's association with the gangsters in Florida and how he died."

Rizzo couldn't tell if she'd posed it as a question, but he answered it as one. "Oh, yeah. A long time ago."

"It surprised me when he told me about Richie, but I guess he thought I should know. Right after that, we got married. And then he told me about his other brother, Frank, the priest in the family. Like he needed to balance the scales."

"He had an interesting family."

The conversation lulled for several moments until Rizzo suggested they look at the menu. "If you like calf's liver, it's the best here."

Carla wrinkled her nose.

Rizzo shook his head. "Am I the only one in this universe who loves calf's liver? Try the grilled sea scallops instead."

"Now, that sounds good," Carla said. "What about you, Flo?"

"I'm a meat and potatoes girl. I'll go with the New York strip steak."

"Okay, then," Rizzo said, "are we ready to order?"

Both women nodded. Rizzo flagged down Seth, and after taking their orders, he asked, "How are we on drinks?"

Rizzo looked around at the glasses. "Fine, for now."

Those patrons not going to the theater occupied the restaurant section, but the Allen regulars filled the stools at the bar. Until Rizzo took the oath of sobriety at AA several years ago, he numbered himself among them on a semi-regular basis.

"By the way," Rizzo began, "I spoke with Dominic this morning and he promised to get in touch with Vinnie's boss at the union. He also said he'd try to reach two of the guys Vinnie used to work with."

Carla looked up and her eyes pinched. "If you mean who I think you mean, I hope they leave their guns at home. They're from a phase of Vinnie's life, a life he tried to put behind him."

Rizzo hesitated. Her words showed she knew about Vinnie's role in the mob. She looked at him with a shade of guilt on her face.

"I'm sorry, Luke. I guess I should have told you. Vinnie hid nothing from me. That's why I found him so loving."

"I can understand," Rizzo said. "But you need to understand something else. In that rough underworld of people, they can form real friendships. Take Vinnie and Dominic, for example. I sensed, in the little time I've known him, Dominic would give his life for Vinnie if faced with the choice. Those guys Dom said he would contact might fall into that category, friends of Vinnie's. If they show up at the service, it would prove their friendship. If they don't, no great loss."

Carla stared, absorbing Rizzo's words. After a moment, she nodded. "You're right, Luke. I hope they come."

* * *

Howard Beach, Queens, NY – Thurs. P.M. 7/23

The man dressed in black stood in the darkened entrance of a pet store across the street, down twenty yards from the mob's Howard Beach storefront clubhouse. He had exited his vehicle earlier and left the commonplace black car at the curb instead of watching from within. In this neighborhood, he was certain anyone sitting behind the wheel of a parked automobile would appear conspicuous and easy to spot.

His target had left moments ago, but he needn't follow. The man was going home. He noted the time in the small spiral memo book he carried in his inside jacket pocket.

He'd been shadowing the man for the past two weeks and learned enough about his daily routine to feel he was getting close. Soon, he thought, it would be time to pull the lever on this assignment.

One important characteristic he spotted early was the consistency of Sal Fusco's habits. He wore his Borsalino fedora every day, everywhere. Another was the ever-present limo driver. Most nights, the driver would drop off Fusco at the front entrance to his Long Beach, Queens apartment house no later than eleven o'clock—like this night. In the morning, the driver would pick him up at ten.

Last Friday, the bartender at The Red Zone sports bar on Atlantic Avenue in Brooklyn had tipped him off to another of Fusco's constant habits. He'd posed the question sounding like he was curious. "Hey, who's the guy in the stupid Borsalino? Does he ever take it off?"

The reply from the bartender appeared innocent enough, but also protective.

"A local guy. He eats here most Friday nights. His grandson is the restaurant's chef."

That information went into the assassin's memo book with several check marks.

* * *

Upper East Side, Manhattan – Sat. P.M. 7/25

The chapel was an open area situated to the right as you entered the Thomas Cooke Funeral Home. The Reverend Michael Orson, from Carla's local parish, stood at the podium, flipping through the pages of his prayer book. Carla, Flo, and Dominic sat in the front row.

Dom turned to Flo and whispered, "Where did Luke go?"

She pointed to a doorway at the front corner of the chapel. "Men's room."

Mel Bracken, a vice-president in Vinnie's union, sat two rows behind them. The remaining rows were empty until three men came through the front door, stopped to sign the guest book, and entered the chapel. Dominic turned his head to see who they were. He froze. Accompanying the two members of Vinnie's old crew he had contacted on Thursday, was Sal Fusco. The two friends filed into a middle row of chairs. Fusco, still wearing his Borsalino, spotted Mel Bracken and came forward.

Dominic jumped to his feet and moved toward the *capo*. "Hey, Sal, glad you could make it. Be right back." He wrinkled his nose and said, "Gotta take a piss," and he sped off toward the corner doorway. Dominic went through it and walked down a long, carpeted corridor lined with several viewing rooms. Midway, he found the door to the men's room and pushed through. Rizzo was at the washbasin, running his hands under the faucet.

"Luke, you gotta get outta here. Fusco just walked in with the two guys I called about the service. They musta mentioned it to Sal, and he came with them."

"Damn, I had a feeling this would happen. And I left my nine at home."

"There's a few empty viewing rooms outside," Dom said, motioning to the door. "Pop into one of them and hide there until Sal leaves. I'm thinkin' he ain't stayin' long because his driver, Gino, didn't come in with him."

Rizzo backed into the toilet and closed the door halfway. "Okay. Check if the coast is clear."

Dominic opened the men's room door and peeked out. "It's clear," he whispered. "Go to the room at the end. I'll come get you when Fusco leaves."

Dom returned to the chapel and found Fusco still in conversation with the IBEW executive. He approached the *capo* and stood next to him.

"Excuse me a moment, Mel," Fusco said. He turned to Dominic. Lowering his voice, he said, "Which of those two women is Vinnie's wife?"

"The one on the left," Dom said, pointing.

Fusco turned back to the union man. "Please excuse me, Mel. I gotta go pay my respects. Then, I have to leave for a meeting. But it's been nice seeing you." He removed the Borsalino and said to Dominic, "C'mon, introduce me."

They walked to the front row and stood before the two women. "Carla, this is Sal Fusco. Sal, Vinnie's wife, Carla Alcamo. And this is Mrs. Cooper, her neighbor."

Fusco reached down and took both of Carla's hands into his. "Mrs. Alcamo, my deepest condolences for your loss. Vinnie was a respected man with lots of friends. We're gonna miss him."

"Thank you for coming, Mr. Fusco."

"I'm sorry I can't stay for the service, but I wanted to come by to meet you and pay my respects."

"That's quite all right, I understand. Thank you again for being here." Carla raised her eyes toward the ceiling and said, "I'm sure Vinnie appreciates it."

Fusco nodded and turned to Dominic. "The lady has any problems with the funeral arrangements, you get in touch with me. Okay?"

"Right, Sal."

The *capo* shook Carla's hand again, smiled at Flo, and headed for the exit.

After Reverend Orson's homily, Carla said goodbye to Vinnie's two friends and Mel Bracken, thanking them for attending the service.

* * *

Rizzo thought of revisiting the restaurant where he and Dominic had lunch, Felice 64, but it was too far to walk. Besides, no one wanted anything more than a cup of coffee. The Starbucks on Eighty-Seventh and Lexington was a short walk from the funeral home. Carla had suggested it.

They carried their four coffee concoctions to the table, then waited until Rizzo returned from the men's room with a wet paper towel to wipe down the sticky tabletop.

"That was such a sweet homily the Reverend Orson gave," Flo said. "Did he know Vinnie?"

"Not well," Carla said. "Vinnie started coming to church with me after he received the fatal diagnosis. He wasn't religious."

"No surprise," Rizzo said. "Vinnie's terminal cancer was his motivation to rediscover church-going. That kind of reaction is not unique," Rizzo smiled. "I'm reminded of something Lenny Bruce, the off-beat comedian of the '60s, once said. I can't recall the exact wording, but it went something like, 'People stay away from the church until God calls.' Not verbatim, but close enough."

Dominic snickered. "You're old enough to remember Lenny Bruce?"

"Yeah. Of course. He died before I was born, but someone gave me two of his albums when I was in my teens. The quote I just butchered was from one of them."

Carla tapped Dominic's arm. "I just remembered something I wanted to ask you. The man you brought up to me to express his condolences. Mr. Fusco. Who is he? I never heard Vinnie mention him."

Dominic shot a look at Rizzo. "Sal Fusco's somebody who knew Vinnie before he worked with the union. The guy always thought Vinnie had a lot of smarts and recommended him to Mel Bracken for the position with the union."

"Well, it was nice of him to come. What did he mean by his comment about the funeral arrangements?"

"Nothing specific," Dom said. "He's somebody who carries a lot of weight with many unions. That's all."

Rizzo tried to change the subject, but before he could, Carla asked Dom the inevitable question.

"By the way, why did you introduce Flo as Mrs. Cooper, my neighbor?"

Rizzo quickly grasped the significance of Dom's identity diversion. "That was because of me."

Carla looked at Rizzo and waited for him to explain.

He grinned. "He's not fond of me. Dom didn't want him to know I was there." Rizzo caught Flo rolling her eyes.

"And that's why you disappeared into the men's room?"

The grin became a broad smile. "Well, no. Nature called. Dominic came back to warn me Sal Fusco had arrived. No one expected him. I found a comfortable viewing room in the back and stayed until the man left."

"Well, I suppose you'd rather not go into details. I'll drop the subject."

"Thanks," Rizzo said. "That would be best."

Chapter Thirty

Jamaica Avenue, Queens - Mon. A.M. 7/27

"I understand this guy, Sal Fusco, doesn't show up every day," Detective Artie Franks said. He had finished his run-through, double-checking the monitors and recording equipment, and reached for his headphones. "Not like the Barone guy, but of course, he worked here. Fusco doesn't."

Detective Dave Dowd looked up from the folder on his lap. "Machado said he was one of Gambino's *capos*. His gig was the money-laundering operation run out of this place and the four other sports bars. He's also the one who gave the order for the hit on Lieutenant Dickerson's brother. That's what we're trying to nail him on."

Dowd glanced down at the folder and pulled out the briefing sheet from their meeting with Machado. "We go on alert any time we hear the mention of Sal or Fusco. When he comes in, his usual routine is to sit at the bar and jawbone with the barman, Dominic Biondo. He's the one with the roving bug on his cell."

"What time of the day or night? Machado say?"

"Mostly nights," Dowd said.

Franks held up the earphones and waved them for emphasis. "Then why in the hell do we need to be monitoring the place starting at nine in the morning?"

"You know something, Artie? You're getting to be a regular pain in the ass. It's because we gotta be prepared in case he shows up during the day. With Barone and the general manager no longer around, Fusco is responsible for the legitimate operation of the bars. At least until the Feds get around to closing them down."

"By himself? What the hell does he know about running a sports bar?"

"He's got a manager at each one, but he likes to pull surprise visits."

Franks put on the earphones and tested sound levels. This was the first day of surveillance, and the technicians were working on the final setup of the second van. The routine they would follow was the same as the first assignment two months before.

Each day, they alternated vans as well as the van's position on the avenue. It could be fifty yards south of The Dugout one day, then thirty-five yards north of it the next. The important thing was not to become conspicuous. The second pair of detectives used a midnight black vehicle. Every third day, they swapped vans, the black one used during the day, the gray one at night.

"Hey, Artie, I hope you didn't forget your service weapon."

Franks removed the earphones and looked at Dowd. "What?"

"I said I hope you remembered your nine. This guy is a real *Mafioso*, not like Barone. He was only an associate."

"So?"

"Well, if we're made, he ain't comin' a-knockin' on the door to ask us to leave."

Franks hung the headphones around his neck and shook his head. "Dave, you like playing the voice of doom, don't you?"

"Could happen, you know."

"Yeah, like the Mets could win the World Series."

Dowd guffawed.

* * *

FBI's Manhattan Office - Tues. A.M. 7/28

Jack Fields looked up as Brancuso hurried into the office. "I got the call. Grab a seat. I'll fill you in," Fields said, motioning to the chair at the side of his desk. He was smiling like a lottery winner. "The Suffolk DA and the Bureau believe Angie Russo is ready to turn against the Gambino family and cooperate with us. The Bureau will give him immunity from prosecution and offer him the WITSEC Program if he cooperates."

Brancuso asked, "Does it include naming Sal Fusco as the one who gave the order to kill Roy Dickerson?"

"Of course it does. They're faxing me all the details. We can review them later today."

"I guess we won't need the surveillance at The Dugout. They're already set up. Shall I ask Machado to pull them?"

Fields shook his head. "No, we should keep them in place for a while longer. It's always possible Russo could change his mind, and we'd have to start over."

"Yeah. Or somebody gets to Russo before he can talk. It's what happens if they don't isolate the person, not give him proper protection."

"If we can nail Fusco by his indicting himself on tape while conversing with Dom Biondo, we'd have him on RICO. That's better than hearing it from Russo. Fusco can always deny it and then it's his word against Russo's."

Brancuso got to his feet. "Call when you get the fax."

* * *

Jamaica Avenue, Queens - Fri. P.M. 7/31

Friday night, around ten o'clock, Dominic reached into the refrigerator box to grab a couple of bottles of Heineken. He hadn't noticed Sal Fusco as he neared the bar. He'd come in through the back door after his driver had parked in the alley. Gino trailed Fusco and, like always, dropped into the two-seater near the kitchen order station to wait.

Dom lifted his head in time to see the *capo* slip onto the stool at his end of the bar.

"Hey, Sal. Be right with you," he said. He uncapped the Dutch beers and delivered them to a couple of women on the opposite side.

"How's the crowd tonight?" Fusco asked after Dominic came back. "The Red Zone was mobbed while I was having dinner."

"A little light for a Friday. We had them backed up at the bar during the twofer hours, but it started thinnin' out around eight-thirty. Wanna order some dessert?"

"Nah, just coffee. Got a fresh brew in the pot?"

"Comin' up." Dom reached for the carafe on the burner. He picked up a mug from the small stack and filled it. Looking back to Fusco, he asked, "Sure you don't want something to eat?"

Fusco shook his head.

Dominic set the mug in front of him and moved off to respond to a customer. He refilled the man's glass from the Michelob tap and returned to Fusco.

"Shame about Vinnie," the *capo* said as if it had been on his mind for a while. "He was a good man."

"Yeah, the best."

"Lung cancer, huh? Funny, I never saw Vinnie smoking."

"Oh, yeah. Like a chimney. Three packs a day."

Fusco picked up the mug of coffee and brought it to his mouth. He stayed silent for several seconds as his eyes panned the restaurant across the top of the mug.

Dominic sensed Sal was in a pensive mood. It was during these times he realized it was best not to intrude with idle chatter. He kept his distance, staying busy with customers around his end of the bar. Once, he walked back to the kitchen to check on an order that was taking too long.

Fusco set the emptied coffee mug on the bar, and Dominic reached for the canister to pour him a refill. "You sure I can't get you something from the kitchen?"

The *capo* screwed up his brow. "You think they got any cheesecake left?"

"Lemme call back, find out." A minute later he told him, "Yeah, they're sending a slice to you now."

Fusco devoured the cake like it was the first food he'd eaten all day. Dominic watched and suspected the *capo* was stewing over something big. It was a matter of time before it would spill out. Fusco could not hold in anger or frustration for long.

Fusco pushed the cake plate away and took a sip of coffee. Dominic resisted asking why he seemed upset. He remembered Rizzo had cautioned him not to lead the conversation.

"Vinnie's wife is a looker," Fusco said.

The comment came from left field, surprising Dom. It wasn't what he guessed was on the *capo*'s mind.

"She sure is. I'll bet you didn't know she's an actress."

"No kiddin'. Movies?"

"Broadway musicals. She has a part in one that opened a few weeks ago."

"She's nice," he said. "A classy lady."

Dominic moved off to another customer. When he returned to his spot in front of Fusco, the *capo* motioned to him to come closer.

"You know something? You and Vinnie were the best team I ever had in any of my crews. The guys I have now? All of them, *stunade*."

"They're not all that bad, are they, Sal?"

"You don't think so? Listen to this," he said and leaned closer and lowered his voice. "I sent some guys to whack someone out on Long Island. One of the *gavones* leaves his hat on the deck of the beach house."

"Holy shit!"

"Yeah, and they get him on his DNA. Now he's toast. I can't figure out how the fuck he got to be a made man."

Again, the *capo* motioned to Dom to come closer. Dom kept his face expressionless as he listened.

"Now, I get info leaked the other day from the Suffolk County DA's office. The prick is about to cooperate with the Feds."

"That doesn't sound good."

"It's a fuckin' disaster. I gotta send somebody out there to shut him up."

A chill ran down Dominic's spine as he came back into an erect position. Was Fusco going to ask him to take on a contract?

Fusco raised his arm to look at his wristwatch. "I gotta go," he said and dropped from the stool. "See you in a couple of days."

Dominic saw Gino get to his feet when he spotted his boss walking toward him. The driver was never far away. Together, like Frick and Frack, they disappeared out the rear door and into the night.

He wondered if the Feds got the whole conversation recorded. He fingered the cell phone in his back pocket and thought, if they didn't, they'll never get another chance like tonight.

* * *

FBI Headquarters, Manhattan – Sat. A.M. 8/1

Machado called Fields the moment the detectives in the van played the tape for him.

"That's right," Fields said. "Most nights, he's at the clubhouse in Howard Beach until around ten-thirty. Wednesday night should be no different. Two of my agents will be in their vehicle on the street, waiting to make the arrest. Can you have your detectives there at the same time as backup? I don't expect he'll give us trouble, but you never know."

"No problem," Machado said. "Unless you object, I'm going to ride along with my guys. I'd like to see his expression when he sees he's being arrested by federal agents and realizes that means RICO."

"I'm glad we waited to catch him on a recording. The shooter, Angie Russo, ended up doing a one-eighty on cooperating. This recording is much better anyway."

"I'm curious. Why Russo's sudden change of mind?"

"Easy," Fields said. "The leaker in the Suffolk DA's office delivered a counteroffer from the mob. 'Keep your mouth shut or you die.' Hard to ignore."

"You buy that? Could it be something else?"

"Nah. He got the message. He knows the mob can always get to him."

"That reminds me, Jack. As soon as you guys play the recording for Sal Fusco, he's gonna believe Dom Biondo was wearing a wire during that conversation. It's gonna get hotter than hell for the man. Have you contacted him to plan for his protection?"

"Rizzo called him last night. They'll be here early Monday morning. Dominic is due to be at work at eleven, but we'll have time to explore what he wants to do."

"The man wears a target on his back until he goes underground. Be nice if the judge refused Fusco bail."

"Probably not."

"Yeah, I know. Besides, he still has his shooters to do the job."

* * *

FBI Headquarters, Manhattan - Mon. A.M. 8/3

Jack Fields sat at his desk, reflecting on the direction the case had taken. In all his years with the Bureau, he couldn't remember ever achieving the same level of success taking down a mob activity. His team brought an end to the Gambino family's money-laundering operation, along with its key people. And they did it in less than four months. He thought about all those cases in the past that consumed years to reach fruition. None came with the ease and satisfaction of this one.

He acknowledged the large debt the Bureau owed to Nicole Adams and Dominic Biondo for their roles in making it happen. As the Bureau had done for Nicole, Fields would offer the same package to Dominic. His disappearance, like Nicole's, had to be handled with care and with dispatch.

He glanced at the digital readout on the clock and pressed the intercom. "Rachel, I was expecting Luke Rizzo and Dominic Biondo at eight-fifteen. It's now eight-thirty. Have you heard anything from them?"

"No, Jack. Want me to try Mr. Rizzo's cell number?"

"Wait another ten minutes, then call. It's not like Rizzo to be late for meetings. And Mr. Biondo has to leave for work by ten-thirty."

Five minutes later, Rachel announced their arrival. "Thanks, Rach," he said. "I'll get them."

"Sorry to be late, Jack," Rizzo said, following the agent into his office. "I had to get rid of a tail before meeting Dom at the entrance downstairs. Fusco doesn't seem to give up too easy."

"You sure you lost him?"

"Yeah."

Fields scanned Dominic's face as Rizzo and the man took seats on the sofa. Fields dropped into a chair facing them.

"How you feeling, Dom?"

Dominic raised his chin and stared at the ceiling as if looking for an appropriate answer. "Okay, I guess."

"Well, maybe by the time you leave here today, we can lower your anxiety level."

Dominic forced a smile.

"Let me say again before we start, the Bureau values and appreciates your cooperation in this matter. It's beyond anything I can express in words. We acknowledge the risk you took and the risks you might face in the future. Our promise to you is to mitigate those risks to the point of making them non-existent. I hope you understand that."

Dom nodded without looking at Fields.

Fields wondered where to begin. He decided on the WITSEC Program. If Dominic had something else in mind, he'd stop and give him a chance to express his thoughts.

"I guess a good place to start is with the Witness Protection Program. I'm sure you've heard of it," Fields said. "We've already received approval from the Attorney General's office to offer it to you."

Fields noticed Rizzo was about to speak, but he thought better of it when the agent glared at him.

"WITSEC affords protection," Fields continued, "by providing witnesses and their family members with new identities. It provides documentation, housing, and help with basic living expenses such as medical care and—"

Dominic raised his hand to signal the agent to stop. "I know all about WITSEC," Dom said. "I have an uncle and his family in the program. It's been great for them, but I don't think I wanna get into it."

This didn't surprise Fields. Dominic was a single guy with no family restrictions. He assumed Dom would prefer to chance it on his own.

"Okay, that's your choice. Do you have something in mind? Are you ready to share it with us?"

Dominic leaned forward and rested his elbows on his knees. He lifted his head as he spoke. "I want a new identity: passport, driver's license, social security number, that sort of thing. I need your protection from being tracked down by legitimate means. You gotta know the Gambinos have lined the pockets of people from every official agency in the country."

"We can arrange that," Fields said. "It may take a little time, but in the interim, we can provide you with a living arrangement somewhere safe. How about expenses?"

A grin appeared. "I could use a little help there. At the start. Not forever. I got a small nest egg stashed, but it might take a while to get to it."

Fields looked over at Rizzo and found him smiling. "Okay, then. Do you have any idea where you want to disappear? We'll provide all transportation and travel expenses."

"Yeah, I do. But I'd rather not say. I'll make my own travel arrangements. If you give me enough now to cover my get-out-of-town expenses, I'll be happy."

"That won't be a problem," Fields said. "Meantime, we'll set up a safe house for you to use. We're not arresting Fusco until Wednesday night. You should be okay on your own for the next few days. It's when Fusco hears the recording that things will explode for you. That won't be for at least a week. By that time, everything should be in order and you'll be on your way."

"The Lord willing," Rizzo announced.

Chapter Thirty-One

Chelsea Area, Manhattan – Wed. P.M. 8/05

It was nine-thirty Wednesday evening when Rizzo slid the two folders into the file and closed the metal cabinet drawer. He had called Flo earlier to tell her he would be late; he needed the time to update the monthly bookkeeping he'd neglected for the past two months.

Rizzo retrieved the Glock 17 and belly holster from his desk. Once he had it belted around his waist, he pulled down on his sweatshirt to cover the weapon. His left ankle holster carried the Cobra 38mm, always in place except for those times he met with Fields at his office. There, he couldn't have a weapon.

Before switching off the light, Rizzo glanced through the small one-way window in the door. He saw no one lurking on the other side.

Rizzo moved out into the hallway, shot a look toward the fire exit, and inserted his key to double-lock the door. Sensing someone had stepped off the elevator, he turned to look over his shoulder. A figure had come up behind him.

The stranger stood there in ominous silence. A thick-set man with staunch shoulders, he wore a Members Only waist-high jacket and, underneath it, a black-collared shirt. Rizzo would have taken him for a potential client except for the 9mm Beretta hanging at his side.

Rizzo completed locking the door and faced the stranger. He eyeballed the weapon in the man's hand. "My guess is you're not looking to hire someone to catch your cheating wife."

"Turn around, funny guy, and put your hands on the wall."

Rizzo ignored the demand until he felt the barrel of the man's weapon jab his ribs."

"Do it, funny guy, or you won't live to hear what Sal Fusco has to say."

"Oh, why didn't you tell me I was going to a meeting? I thought this was just another Big Apple mugging." With reluctance, Rizzo lifted his hands over his head and placed them on the wall.

The thug pinned his weapon to Rizzo's side and reached around. He yanked up Rizzo's sweatshirt and removed the Glock from the holster. When he had it in his waistband, he pulled down on his jacket to cover it.

"Okay, now we can take a ride down to the car and say hello to Mr. Fusco. Move," he said, gesturing with his Beretta toward the elevator.

They stepped out into the empty lobby and exited onto Fifth Avenue. Fusco's black limo waited at the curb. Rizzo scanned the avenue, hoping for anything that might offer help, like a parked police RMP. No luck.

The gunman shoved him toward the vehicle. Rizzo considered running but dismissed the idea. He realized if the man were to fire at him, it would put innocent pedestrians on the street in danger.

Fusco stepped out of the vehicle and came toward his driver. "Here, take this," Gino said and handed him Rizzo's Glock.

Fusco took it, opened the rear door of the limo, and slid onto the back seat.

"Get in," Gino said, "or I'll drop you right here." He pushed him toward the open door. Rizzo stumbled against the vehicle, regained his balance, and got in. He turned and stared at the barrel of his Glock in Fusco's hand, aimed at his head.

* * *

Howard Beach, Queens, NY - Wed. P.M. 8/05

A Lincoln Town Car with Jack Fields and three FBI agents pulled to the curb opposite the doorway of the mob's storefront clubhouse in Howard Beach. Behind them, a Crown Victoria with Bob Machado and two detectives came to a halt. The seven lawmen alighted from the two vehicles at the same time.

A few men in their thirties, casually dressed, idled on the sidewalk outside the clubhouse. They stopped smoking and talking to stare at the newly arrived vehicles and their passengers.

Jack Fields approached the nearest man and said, "Is the door locked?"

The man he spoke to gawked at him like he didn't understand the question. He shrugged. The others moved closer to the curb, trying to increase their distance from Fields.

The agent paused, looked back at his team, nodded, and went to the door. He pushed down on the handle and it swung open with ease.

Four members of Fusco's crew, seated at a round felt-covered table, were playing cards. Their heads jerked up in unison when Fields and Brancuso came through the door. Two more men at the small bar on one side of the large open room turned on their stools. A large trestle table, positioned against the wall on the opposite side of the room, was unoccupied.

The agent scanned the men in the room. Fusco was not among them. He motioned to Brancuso. "Check back there," and pointed to the door at the rear.

A man at the card table stood. "Who ya lookin' for?" he asked Fields.

The agent waited until Brancuso came out of the backroom and shook his head.

"Sal Fusco. Has he been here tonight?"

"Not tonight," the crew member said. "I seen him earlier today, but not since around three o'clock."

Nothing in the man's voice led Fields to believe he was covering up for Fusco. "You expect he'll be back tonight?"

"Jeez, I doubt it," the man said and dropped back down into his seat at the table.

Machado came through the door and said to Fields, "Jack, one man out here said he saw Fusco leave the club around three-thirty. He left alone with his driver."

"Well, it seems we picked the wrong night. Damn! The one time he broke with his pattern and didn't hang around."

"You suppose he got wise to us?"

"I don't. But now, sure as hell, he is. He's going to force us to hunt for him."

* * *

Long Island City, NY – Wed. P.M. 8/05

Fusco kept Rizzo's Glock leveled at him as they weaved through streets and avenues across Manhattan. During the drive, Rizzo shifted in his seat and felt his iPhone pressed against his right thigh. Until this moment, he hadn't realized they'd forgotten to take it. He waited until Fusco turned his head to speak to Gino and slipped his hand into his pocket. He fingered the right button to silence the instrument. With no calls to alert them, he might get lucky and keep it.

They entered the Queens Midtown Tunnel, and with light traffic, completed the crossing in little time. After the limo exited the tunnel on the Queens side, Rizzo caught a glimpse of the 108th Precinct building on the north flank of the tunnel's toll booths. He sighed in frustration.

The limo turned off Borden Avenue at Second Street and headed east. Rizzo thought about pushing open the door and pitching himself out as they slowed at a stop sign. But he realized the futility of the idea. He'd no doubt take a bullet in his back before he could get to his feet and out of range. Instead, he made mental notes of their direction and of what was visible as they passed under streetlamps. He might need the information later on.

They slowed at the intersection of Second Street and Fifty-fourth Avenue and stopped in front of a one-story warehouse that occupied the southeast corner. It was a long, rectangular, cement building, windowless and dark. The streetlamp in front spilled enough light for Rizzo to see the transom over the front door. He could make out the lettering above it: Paglia Hotel and Restaurant Linen Supply.

The area was commercial, but the building did not appear to be in use. A high chain-link fence to one side contained the empty parking lot. Two wide roll-up doors on the parking lot side had padlocks securing them.

Fusco's driver turned through the open gate and drove to the rear. He exited the limo and walked around the front of the vehicle to the door at the corner of the building. Rizzo watched him reach into his pocket and take out a key. When he had the door unlocked, he motioned to Fusco and returned to the limo. He pulled open the rear door, raised his weapon, and said to Rizzo, "Out. This is where the tour ends."

Rizzo exited and stood looking at the building. Fusco slid across the rear seat, rose to his feet, and jabbed Rizzo's Glock into his back.

"Let's move. Open the door, Gino."

Rizzo remained still except to make note of his surroundings. He turned his head and said over his shoulder, "You wanna tell me what's going on?"

"You'll find out once we get inside. Now, move!" Fusco punctuated his command with another jab in the back with Rizzo's Glock.

Gino held the door while Rizzo passed through. Fusco followed him. The interior was pitched in blackness until Gino found the light board. He flipped one switch and the overhead fluorescent tubes flickered to life on the front half of the cavernous warehouse.

Ahead, toward the middle of the warehouse, Rizzo saw rows of palettes stacked with large plastic-wrapped bales. Linen products, abandoned along with the building. Was this where Fusco intended to leave him to die?

* * *

FBI Headquarters, Manhattan Thurs. A.M. 8/06

Jack Fields returned to the office to make out a report on the Howard Beach fiasco for Carter Brooke. He approached Rachel's desk in the anteroom and stopped when he noticed the blinking light on her telephone console. The digital clock readout showed it was twelve minutes after midnight. Someone was leaving a message.

He pressed the speakerphone button and leaned over the desk. "This is Jack Fields," he said, cutting off the caller's message.

"Agent Fields, it's Flo Rizzo again," she said, her voice filled with frustration and fear. "I've been calling for the last hour, leaving messages. Luke hasn't come home, and he hasn't called me or answered his phone. He said he'd be at the office working late, but not this late."

"You tried his cell?"

"Yes, of course. I thought he might be involved in something with you."

"No. I haven't seen him since Monday morning. We had a meeting in my office, but he's not doing anything for us at the moment."

"I'm frantic. What should I do? Should I call the police and report him missing?"

"Don't do that. It's still too early. They'll tell you to give it more time." Fields thought about Dominic. Maybe he knew something. "Mrs. Rizzo, give me 'til mid-morning. I'll make a few calls. "I'm sure there's a good explanation. Meantime, stay calm."

"Agent Fields, that will not be easy."

"I'll get back to you."

* * *

Long Island City

"Over there," Gino said, pointing ahead to the front row of linen bales. "Move!"

Fusco slipped Rizzo's Glock into his waistband and led the way. Rizzo followed while his thoughts raced to figure a way out of the situation. The 38mm Colt Cobra, still in his ankle holster, would give him that option, but he would need the right opportunity to get to it.

He reached the front row of bales, turned the corner, and came to an abrupt stop. The sight of Dominic, in a chair that had toppled over on its side, rocked him with a hopeless feeling. Dominic lay on the polished cement floor, his body still in the chair, his wrists lashed to the arms of the chair, and his ankles tied with rope to the two front chair legs. Rizzo rushed to him and put his finger to his carotid artery. He was alive but not conscious.

The *capo* and his driver stood back watching Rizzo as he worked the big man and the chair upright. After several tries, Rizzo got it righted and steadied Dom in it. The multiple bruises and cuts on Dom's cheeks and around his swollen eyes revealed he'd received a brutal beating issued by Fusco and Gino. Both eyelids were closed, his forehead bloodied.

Rizzo was sure Dominic had been ambushed. That's how they got him under control and to this warehouse. A large clot of blood appeared in Dom's hair on the back of his head—no doubt the blow that initially rendered him unconscious.

Rizzo glared at Fusco. "Lucky you knocked him out first. He would've destroyed you two lightweights if you hadn't."

"Maybe," Gino said, "but you're not that tough, are you? So we don't need to worry."

"Why don't you sit your ass down in that other chair," Fusco said. "Let's see if your answers to my questions are the same as what Dom told us."

Rizzo sat in the second chair and looked at Dominic slumped over. He stared off into the lighted front end of the warehouse; his thoughts were coming fast.

What the hell were the questions? It wasn't about the recording made by Dom's cell phone. At this point, the *capo* wouldn't know about it.

Something flashed across his mind: The tail on him yesterday morning. He'd been positive he lost him. Was he wrong? Did the guy follow them into the FBI building?

If that was it, what were the answers Dom would have given? They'd brutally worked him over, so Rizzo suspected he'd answered truthfully. Told them he hadn't known he was going into the FBI's Manhattan office until he arrived there. Lying would have brought certain death, and Dom was still alive. Yeah, but for how long? How long did he have?

* * *

FBI Headquarters

Fields called Rizzo's cell phone number, but the instrument was turned off. He punched in Dominic's cell number and got no response. Coincidence? Something ominous about that, he thought. His next call went to the Bureau's tech group on the floor below.

"Anderson," the voice answered.

"Hey Phil, Jack Fields. Glad you caught the duty tonight because I need help that's right in your wheelhouse."

"Sure, Jack. What do ya need?"

"Can you trace the locations of two cell phones, different cell numbers?"

"Easy."

"One of the phones turned off."

"No difference. What are the numbers?"

When Anderson called back, Fields learned both phones showed the same location. No surprise.

"In a building at the corner of Second Street and Fifty-fourth Avenue, Long Island City," Anderson told him.

"Phil, you're the best. Thanks." He disconnected and dialed another number.

"Operations, Agent Esasky."

"Ryan, Jack Fields. Who's on duty tonight?"

"Gomez, Littlefield, Spencer, and Stein."

"Ask them to meet me down in the garage in fifteen minutes. Come armed. There's a good chance we might meet up with a few bad guys."

"Will do, Jack."

* * *

Long Island City

"You ready to answer a few questions, tough guy?" Gino stood a few yards out in front of the two chairs, his 9mm in his hand. Fusco leaned against the pile of linen bales at the far end of the row, fingering the grip of Rizzo's Glock still stuck in his waistband.

"What could you ask me you don't already know?" Rizzo said, nodding his head toward Dominic. "Whatever he told you is what happened."

"I want your version, wise guy. What were you and Dominic doing in the FBI's building? You got an answer?"

"No."

A bullet whizzed past Rizzo's ear and lodged in the linen bale midway from the top. The deafening sound of the gunshot resounded off the warehouse walls and ceiling.

Gino waited until the ringing noise level eased. "Another no answer like that, the next one won't miss. And we'll dump your body in the river," motioning with his head toward the East River, two blocks away. "You'll come up somewhere in New Jersey."

Rizzo hesitated until he saw Gino raise the weapon again. "We had a date to see one of the Bureau's agents."

"What about?"

After pausing again, Rizzo swallowed. "They wanted Dominic to wear a wire while he worked behind the bar."

"To listen to who?"

Rizzo looked over at Dominic and shook his head.

Another shot rang out and a second bullet pierced the bale to Rizzo's left. Before the last reverberations of sound disappeared, a stranger's voice came out of the darkness behind the front end of the row.

"Toss down the gun. I'm here for Fusco, no one else."

Gino spun around to face the intruder. "Who the fuck are you? How'd you get in here?" Gino raised his Beretta to fire, but before he could, two rounds from the assassin's gun hit him in the chest and flipped him to the floor.

The man in black rounded the corner of the front row and looked down the line to Fusco. "That one was a bonus, Mr. Fusco. You're the one I'm gettin' paid to do."

Rizzo bent over at the waist, looking like he wanted to get out of the man's line of fire. He had his .38 out of his ankle holster in a flash and came up firing two shots at the gunman. One hit him in the chest and the second, a tad higher, entered his throat and out the back of his skull. The man wheeled from the impact and thudded to the warehouse floor in a heap.

Fusco froze in place by the suddenness of the gunplay. He couldn't speak. Rizzo rushed to him and reached for his Glock still tucked in the *capo*'s waistband.

"This is your lucky day, Sal. I guess the don hired an assassin to do you. He missed his mark. Too bad. Maybe I should use his gun and finish the job."

Fusco's knees wobbled, gave out, and the *capo* fell to the floor in a faint. The Borsalino hat lay beside him. Rizzo went back to the chair, sat for several minutes, and kept his eyes planted on the inert Fusco. He reactivated his iPhone and called the private number of Jack Fields.

"Rizzo, good God, are you all right? We're on the way. We got your location off your phone's GPS."

"Don't hurry. I got the situation handled."

"What's happened? Are you with Dominic?"

"Yeah, he's here. We're sitting having a friendly conversation with Sal Fusco. Tell you all about it when you arrive. By the way, maybe you'd like to alert the boys in the One-Oh-Eight precinct. They'll want to be here. Tell them they're gonna need a couple of buses."

Chapter Thirty-Two

East Side, Manhattan – Sat. P.M. 8/08

Dominic leaned his buttocks against the hospital bed as he bent to tie his Reeboks. The stretch of his torso toward the floor caused his face to fill with pain.

Rizzo jumped from the chair. "Here, shit. Lemme help."

"That's okay. I got it." He looked up at Rizzo. "Thanks. That bastard Gino, he musta kicked me in the ribs a dozen times while I was on the ground. I got lucky. X-rays showed nothin' broken, but everything is sore as hell. The gash in my head took six stitches."

"What did they hit you with, a two-by-four?"

Dominic grimaced. "I don't know what it was. I never saw them in the dark. I'd locked up The Dugout and came out the back door to go to my car. When I turned around to check on the door, make sure it had locked, my head exploded. The Fourth of July again. It was worse than when that cop's bullet creased my skull. I was sitting in that chair, tied to it when I came to.

"Well, Gino ain't kicking anybody anymore. That assassin guy was using a cannon, judging by the size of the holes he left in Gino's chest."

"Without you, we all coulda ended up looking like a punchboard."

Rizzo returned to the chair. "The don hired the guy to whack Fusco. I don't think he intended to kill you or me. Probably, not even Gino, except the fool drew on him."

The change of clothes Rizzo had purchased for Dominic at a Marshall's outlet was a perfect fit. Dom told the nurse to burn the clothing he wore when they brought him into New York Hospital on Thursday morning. He didn't need reminders of the devastating ordeal he'd suffered at the hands of Gino and Sal.

Dom pulled the new sweatshirt over his head and struggled to get it past his bandaged face. Rizzo watched him.

"You're a good pal," he said as his head popped through the sweatshirt opening. He smiled "You saved my ass, but you're also a good personal shopper."

"Well, shit, we can't let you leave this place looking like a homeless person. Which reminds me, you decide yet where you're gonna go?"

"You mean, into hiding?"

"Yeah, for at least a year. They'll lose interest in you after that."

"Hope so. I got a few options but haven't decided yet."

They went silent when an orderly pushed a wheelchair into the room. "You ready to roll?" the man asked.

Dom screwed up his face. "I need that thing?"

"Until I get you outside."

"Oh, okay."

They stood at the curb to wait for the Uber to show. Rizzo asked, "You settle up accounts with Jack Fields about your new identity credentials? And the walking-around money they owe you?"

"Yeah. They'll have everything ready in a week."

"Where are you staying until then?"

"At my apartment. I'll be all right there."

"You can bunk in at my place. You'd be a lot safer there. I don't think my wife would mind."

"Nah, but thanks anyway. I'll be fine."

A 2019 Ford Taurus pulled to the curb in front of them. "Biondo?" the driver asked through the open passenger side window.

Dominic acknowledged him and prepared to climb in when Rizzo told him, "Okay, but you get even a sniff of trouble, you call me. You hear? I thought Fields had offered you a safe house until you were ready to leave?"

The big man slid onto the rear seat and rolled down the window. "He did, but when I said I wanted a female agent for protection, he laughed and said they'd rush the new documents."

* * *

Chelsea Area, Manhattan – Fri. P.M. 8/14

Angelo's, at the north end of Madison Square Park on Broadway, was busier than the last time he joined Fields there for lunch. This time, the maître d' greeted Rizzo with a smile and pointed to the table where the agent waited.

Rizzo laced his way through the occupied tables to the one on the back, left side. Fields sipped his iced tea, looked down at the menu, and didn't notice Rizzo approaching.

Rizzo came up from behind and put his hands on the agent's shoulders. "Jack, are you new to this *Mafia* game? Always have your back to the wall and your face to the door. You don't want to let them take you by surprise."

Fields looked up. "Ah-ha, the mob's worst nightmare has arrived. Grab a seat."

The server came to the table to take Rizzo's drink order. Before speaking to him, Rizzo turned to Fields. "You know, if I were back in my alcoholic days, I'd use this euphoric feeling as an excuse to get blotto. Instead," he said, looking up at the server, "I'll celebrate with a Virgin Mary. Thanks."

The man nodded and was off to the bar.

"You deserve to be happy," Fields said. "Look at all you helped accomplish."

"Yeah, but it sure got dicey in that warehouse."

Fields folded his arms across his chest, leaned back, and grinned. "Hey, you and Nicole played major roles in getting rid of the Gambino underboss and his nephew."

"Yeah, with an assist from a few *goombas* from the Chicago mob, of course."

"We shut down his money-laundering operation, didn't we? And don't forget, you found the Mets cap with the DNA. It got Suffolk PD the two killers of Roy Dickerson."

"Actually, it was his brother who found it."

"C'mon Rizzo, you're being modest. Weren't you the one who insisted on going back out there to check with the neighbors?"

"Because I knew how sloppy Suffolk's investigators could be."

"And your latest bit of heroics. It delivered us Sal Fusco. He's in custody and ready to punch Carl Nunziata's ticket."

"You think he will?"

"Oh, yeah. He's pissed beyond belief. And when he does talk to us, we'll hit the don with RICO. Now, I'd say that represents a damn good day's work. Getting rid of those nasty *Mafiosi*, I mean."

The server arrived with Rizzo's Virgin Mary. "Be back in a minute for your order," the server said and moved off.

Rizzo removed the celery stalk. "Love celery, just not in my drink." He took a large bite out of the stalk and picked up the glass. "And I love Sicilians. Just not those in the mob."

* * *

Charlotte Amalie, V.I. – Three months later

Their connecting Delta flight from Atlanta touched down on the runway with the smoothest landing Rizzo could recall in recent years of travel. No sooner had the plane's nose wheel settled on the concrete runway when the pilot slowed the Boeing 757 and brought it to a stop well before the end of the runway. The plane made a left and taxied back to their gate at the Charlotte Amalie Cyril E. King Airport.

Flo opened her eyes and removed the earbuds. "I don't mind takeoffs. It's landings that get to me."

Rizzo chuckled. "And to think I met you for the first time when I landed at an airport in Pittsburgh."

"That was a good landing. Oh, I brought lots of sunscreen. Remember how burned you got in San Juan?"

"I won't fall asleep on the beach again, that's for sure."

Rizzo gazed out the window, watching the activity at the various gates they passed. The travel book he'd purchased last week made mention that Charlotte Amalie's airport was the busiest in the US Virgin Islands .

"Is Nicole supposed to meet us?" Flo asked.

"No. She said it's a short taxi ride, and all the drivers know the Galleon House."

"After these last couple of months of your *Mafia* fun and games, I'm looking forward to these next ten days."

They deplaned and followed the other passengers to the baggage claim area. The busy terminal was small and easy to get around. Their bags arrived, and they loaded into a colorful mini-SUV taxi for the drive to the guest house.

The sky was cloudless. A soft wind blew through the driver's open window, keeping them cool during the ride.

"It surprised me when we got the letter from Nicole inviting us down to be her guest," Rizzo said. "More surprised to read she'd bought the place."

"How could she manage that with just the money from the sale of her apartment?"

"Didn't you read the part where she said she formed a partnership with Harry Fox?"

"You mean he's living here too?"

"No, but he comes down often. He's still bat shit over her, but he's content to remain as friends."

"And business partner. Now, that's a happy ending."

The taxi delivered them to the Galleon House in the heart of Charlotte Amalie. At the top of a hill, the SUV had to negotiate a narrow circular driveway to reach the front of the one-story rambling structure.

Flo stood at the foot of the steps leading up to the guest-house entrance. "Oh, my, Luke. Look at that sight. This place is so charming."

He took in the view that overlooked the town's post office building and beyond. Through the overhanging tree limbs, he could see out to beautiful Charlotte Harbor in the distance.

Before he could turn back, he heard a familiar voice from above. "Hey, let me help you guys with the bags." The large frame of Dominic Biondo bouncing down the eight stone steps came into focus. He was wearing tennis sneakers, a pair of white, billowy, cotton trousers, and a loose-fitting collarless shirt that was covered with a colorful design of flowers and birds. His spread of long arms was prepared to wrap Rizzo in them."

"What the hell," Rizzo shouted. "So this is where you landed? How long have you been here?"

"About a month and a half. I came down right after Nicole bought the place. She offered me a job as a bartender and assistant manager." He squeezed Rizzo in his arms and said, "Son-of-a-bitch, *paesano*, I'm glad to see you again."

Rizzo pushed out of his grip. "Easy, bro, you gonna break a rib." He gestured to Flo. "You remember my smarter wife, Flo?"

"Oh, yeah," and he opened his arms.

Flo raised her hands. "Dom, let's just shake. Leave it at that."

Dominic's happy roar of laughter filtered up through the warm tropical air. He gathered most of their bags, turned to climb the steps, and said, "C'mon, Nicole is bustin' to show you guys around."

Acknowledgments

I need to thank my good friend and reliable alpha reader, Linda Renick for her always on-target input. Additionally, I have two law enforcement contacts to thank for their valuable feedback: Retired Florida police sergeant Richard Vincent and retired NYPD undercover narcotics detective Robert Machado. Their vetting of my police and FBI scenes made my writing authentic. Lastly, my appreciation goes to Carole Greene, my agent and editor, and Joe Clark of BluewaterPress LLC, for their continued support and belief in me as a writer.

We hope you have enjoyed Howard Giordano's latest tale, *The Dark Side of the City.* If you did and would like to read more of Luke Rizzo's exploits cleaning up crime, please go online to www.bluewaterpress.com to peruse Howard Giordano's other titles, *Tracking Terror, The Second Target,* and *Crossing Into Darkness.*

Don't forget to investigate the other interesting titles offered by BluewaterPress LLC.